T0062940

Peace Stories:

Radiant Without, Radiant Within

An Anthology
edited by

Patricia Rife
and
Loretta A. Scott

Order this book online at www.trafford.com
or email orders@trafford.com

Most Trafford titles are also available at major online book retailers.

© Copyright 2009 Patricia Rife.
All rights reserved. No part of this publication may be reproduced, stored in a retrieval system, or transmitted, in any form or by
any means, electronic, mechanical, photocopying, recording, or otherwise, without the written prior permission of the author.

Anthology edited by Patricia Rife and Loretta Scott.

Permission granted to republish the Foreword "Writing Gandhi's Story" from Uma Majmudar, Gandhi's Pilgrimage of Faith:

From Darkness to Light , SUNY Press, © 2005 by the State University of New York Press (all rights reserved).

"Non-Violent Communication: A Nigerian Story" from When Students Love to Learn and Teachers Love to Teach ©2003

Marshall Rosenberg, reprinted with permission of PuddleDancer Press.

"Note to the Reader" by Mark Siegel from Benazir Bhutto, Reconcilliation, NY: HarperCollins Books ©2008

Permission granted to republish "A South African University Becomes Real" by Gayatri Erlandson and Louisa A. Dyer, editors,

Spirit in the Smokies Magazine, January 2006 issue, pp.26-27.

Print information available on the last page.

ISBN: 978-1-4251-7774-4 (sc)

Because of the dynamic nature of the Internet, any web addresses or links contained in this book may have changed
since publication and may no longer be valid. The views expressed in this work are solely those of the author and do
not necessarily reflect the views of the publisher, and the publisher hereby disclaims any responsibility for them.

Any people depicted in stock imagery provided by Thinkstock are models,
and such images are being used for illustrative purposes only.
Certain stock imagery © Thinkstock.

Trafford rev. 02/03/2016

www.trafford.com

North America & international
toll-free: 1 888 232 4444 (USA & Canada)
fax: 812 355 4082

Our Dedication: To all those whose lives are focused upon service to others in peace

Man will never accept peace as a normal mode of living until he has been thoroughly and repeatedly convinced that peace is best for his material welfare, and until society has wisely provided peaceful substitutes for the gratification of that inherent tendency to periodically let loose a collective drive designed to liberate those ever-accumulating emotions and energies belonging to the self-preservation reactions of the human species. . . . To discover [modern] leaders, society must now turn to the conquest of peace.

The Urantia Book

This anthology, which will grow as other stories are told and added, is dedicated to all those who "walk the talk" of peace: via the path of inner peace, the process of conflict resolution, and dedication to action in the world.

"Let there be
Peace on Earth
And let it begin
with me..."
~The Peace Song~

Peace Stories:
Radiant Within, Radiant Without

****

Editors

Dr. Patricia Rife is an Assoc. Professor in the Graduate School of Management and Technology, University of Maryland University College (UMUC), and was a Professor in the Matsunaga Institute for Peace, University of Hawaii system for 5 peaceful, busy years. She develops courses on topics ranging from "Sources of Conflict: An Ethical Approach" to "Biographies of Peace Leaders" and her latest "Conflict Resolution and Negotiation Skills for Managers" as a skilled instructional designer.

Dr.Rife has conducted historical research at the Max-Planck-Institute in Berlin; the Nobel Prize archives in Stockholm; the University of California-Berkeley History of Science program; Princeton and Harvard University archives. She has delivered public lectures on peace and the Nuclear Age at the Carter Center, Atlanta; Goethe Institute, San Francisco; Technion University, Israel; Boston University's Physics Department and the American University of Cairo. Dr.Rife is a specialist in online instructional design, women's empowerment programs, media analysis and e-marketing, the role of the Internet in changing global communications, and science & ethics themes. Her biography of the Jewish woman physicist who interpreted the process of nuclear fission in 1939 has been reviewed worldwide: see <u>Lise Meitner and the Dawn of the Nuclear Age</u> (Boston: Birkhauser/Springer Verlag 1999) and <u>Lise Meitner: Ein Leben fuer die Wissenschaft</u> (Frankfurt: Claassen Verlag, 1991). Dr. Rife's lifelong focus has been global dialogue projects and the fostering of educational communities. She empower groups and individuals to create *constructive social change* and *creative modes of action* as a global catalyst for action relating to peace.

* *

Loretta Scott, M.A. in Education, is a certified Life Coach (specializing in business and career advancement coaching) and an English as a Second Language (ESL) instructor. Ms. Scott has trained groups in consciousness-raising concerning the paradigm shifts from military to environmental concerns worldwide, from Brazil (Earth Summit Eco'92) to China (Fourth World Women's Conference'95).

Her life has been devoted to fostering ideas and elevating everyday language by empowering others. She has worked at grassroots levels to bring about self-empowerment and civic participation.

Her background includes building peace coalitions throughout southern California. She has worked with Robert Muller (former Secretary General of the U.N. and current President of the Peace University in Costa Rica) and Barbara Marx Hubbard's groups. She excels in working with language used in everyday communication to elevate cultural values. Loretta enjoys peace in Greeley, Colorado and sees poetry in Nature.

FOREWORD:
Stories Which Inspire!
An Introduction to our Anthology

by Patricia Rife, Ph.D.

****

Speaking our truth, between the rainbows of joy and teardrops of sorrow, releases a powerful sense of "peaceful presence". It has been said that "***grace is the state of being present in the Presence.***" Hence, our greatest grace may be illuminated via the lessons painted fresh, like fresco, through our actual lives – being <u>present</u> to our own stories! As a historian as well as biographer, I would also add that in reflecting and "becoming conscious" of cultural themes weaving in and out of our lives, crescendos and patterns emerge which deeply reflect the lives of others as well. As a historian, I collected these many "stories of peace" as representative voices from around the world; interpreting and giving meaning to the messages of the stories is up to you.

The ironic term 'world peace' has become almost abstract in our post-modern era. The Romans were steeped in the stories illuminating their own cultural contradictions and heroes, and often re-told the vivid moral myths of their predecessors. Plutarch was a great master in the gift of "life story" telling: living amidst cultural change and ferment from 46AD-119AD, he was a wise and thoughtful social interpreter. Plutarch's volume called <u>Lives</u> was read over again and again, and like ancient Aesop and countless sensitive playwrights and authors since then, his anthology was meant to illustrate moral and ethical *themes* in the weaving of tales about heroes and ordinary people.

Others since that period, however, caution us <u>not</u> to draw 'morals of from the story' of biography, but to hear the person speaking within the historical <u>context</u> in which they lived and struggled. Lives such as Madame Curie, whose discovery of radium changed the health of the world, or Mahatmas Gandhi, whose allegiance to the principles of simplicity and truth toppled the British rule in India, demonstrate 'peace' amidst the ever-shifting landscapes and ruckus of their professions and national political scene. Who can watch film "The Sound of Music" and not reflect upon the rise of Nazism, or hear the story of a visionary such as Hildegard of Bingen and not reflect upon the conflicting times as a nun who was "liberated" even within the Medieval confines and convents in which she lived?   As the wise 20th century philosopher Hannah Arendt once stated (who survived the concentration camps in France by eating grass and became one of the most seminal thinkers of our time), "Humans are 'conditioned beings' because everything they come in contact with turns immediately into a condition of their existence."   And she thoughtfully concluded in her seminal work <u>The Human Condition</u> that it was the *vitae activia*, a life lived in <u>interaction</u> with others in the <u>public</u> milieu, that gives the public realm its vitality – and our lives, a sense of meaning and purpose.   To follow this train of Western philosophic thought, if the public realm disintegrates, we too lose an invaluable sense of 'who we are'. Hence, biographical stories may illustrate ways of 'being' peace. Peace, yes, is an inner state but peace can also be "lived into the world"!

Many cultures do not share the Western view of public responsibility or participation, or identify with a "life well lived and service ethically given".   When I resided with Arabic-speaking families, the center of action seemed to focus around the living room or café', not the body politic.   Peace may be defined differently by a Buddhist or a Polynesian than by an American; peace may be a state reached after tensions for a Third World activist or media artist. Our modern era has expanded globally through technology so that cyber-communities can share a great deal across borders, races, ages – and link common interests together in a new 'global village' via the Internet, which has spawned important new 'peace movements'.   So much of this focus, however, has rested upon shared transactions, not the sharing of higher ideals or values, particularly relating to peace!   And hence, the purpose and reason behind this book – to initiate shared dialogue, to <u>hear</u> voices from different cultures and value perspectives, faiths and professions, and most importantly, weave together a volume in which diverse visions, definitions, and practices of peace are illustrated via *personal* stories. At the end of this humble volume, there is a creative 'workbook' section for you to write your <u>*own*</u> peace story – or at least begin! And we will also expand this volume, by publishing new expanded editions, for teens as well. Do you think they need role models? We do, and are dedicated to identifying new stories.

We live in a rapidly-shrinking global village, yet the concept of peace remains elusive. Lives illuminate the struggles that the 'dynamics' of peace require -- more vividly and dynamic than theories or concepts ever will. Christ taught in parables, and agree-upon ethics remain a vital link forging diverse groups together in their efforts to end violence and oppression around the world.   Whether we are focused upon the higher states of consciousness and stilling practices that lead us to inner peace (and the importance of maintaining such in the turmoil of everyday life) or the communication skills necessary to 'negotiate understandings' and reach peaceful solutions to potentially volatile situations or violent contexts, "peace work" requires discipline, practice and focus.   But the results are worth the effort! Tranquility seems a blessed state: 'peacetime' and 'wartime' are now recognized even by historians to be chronicled in vastly different ways, since the results are hard to measure.   Peace stories require interpretation, cultivation, and continued healthy interactions around the globe to bring forth the message that "peace is worth the effort", so we hope you enjoy the diversity of voices represented here.

Our solid and grieving Mother Earth also asks on many levels for healing and peaceful energies to resolve the major environmental upheavals we will face if the human population continues its exploitation, greed and misuse of resources. To give voice to this peace with our own environment, we must heal our own environmental interactions, weave new communities, learn to barter and trade, and open to new forms of higher consciousness, prayer, affirmations and ways of living on the Earth to 'give birth' to the new.   Biographers see the 'dark night of the Soul' as the release or shedding of old forms so that new can blossom, and many of our authors will bear witness to these 'rites of passage', including the mourning for wounding our Earth. But often it requires the fires of deep and even painful cleansing to make way for a more peaceful existence, to work toward coming "into balance" when so much is out of balance in our world.

The many essayists in this humble book speak volumes about peace work and peace manifestation in our world. I have encouraged them to write and spread their wings about their own chosen life-vignettes and themes. Hence, enjoy the lively diversity of style, with practical resources and references scattered for our diverse readers around the world!

~Patricia Rife~

Washington, D.C., Summer 2008

Non-Violent Communication: A Nigeria Story

by Marshall Rosenberg

Director, Center for Non-Violent Communication
La Cresenta, California

****

A colleague had asked me to mediate between a Christian and a Moslem tribe in northern Nigeria. I was nervous but also hopeful, because there had been enormous violence between the tribes – over a hundred people killed in the past year – and I was confident that I could help them resolve the conflict.

I would not have felt as confident if I had known then what my colleague did not tell me until we were walking into the session. "Be prepared for tension, Marshall," he whispered to me. "Three of the people in this room know that the person who killed their child is in the room too."

Well, then I was nervous! But I felt grateful for my colleague's persistence and goodwill. He had worked many months to bring these people together in this room. With him at my side to translate, I was reconnected to our purpose in gathering: to speak honestly from the heart so that everyone's needs could be met peacefully. I said to both sides, "I'd like whoever would lie to speak first, to say what your needs are in this situation. And after we get everybody understanding everybody's needs, then we'll move to finding some ways of meeting everybody's needs."

"X," the chief from one of the villages, was the first to answer. Instead of responding to my question, Chief X looked across the table and said, "You people are murderers." And someone from the other side responded, "Well, you have been trying to dominate us and we're not going to tolerate it any more."

Now there was even more tension than when we began.

I might have been worried, but I have come to expect this difficulty in conflict situations because usually people don't know how to express their needs. They only know how to tell what's wrong with the other side. So I took a deep breath and again reminded myself of our purpose in gathering. My job was to help everybody sense the needs behind whatever was being expressed.

I turned to X, who had just said, "You people are murderers!" and considered the need he was expressing with those words. I asked him, "Do you have a need for safety, and you need to be sure that whatever conflicts are going on will be resolved by some means other than violence?" Chief X immediately said to me, "Of course, of course that's what I'm saying!" Well, of course he didn't say that. He said that the other person was a murderer. He made a judgment rather than express his needs. But with my help, we had his <u>needs</u> out on the table.

Still, that doesn't mean that the other party heard it. So I turned to a chief from the other side and said, "Chief Y, would you please reflect back what X said his needs were?"

Instead of repeating back as I had suggested, a member of the second tribe screamed, "Then why did you kill my child?"

That started an uproar between the two groups. Again I admired my colleague, who worked patiently and lovingly to bring the room to silence. I knew that he cared deeply for his friends on both sides of the table. I knew his heart was as heavy with grief as anybody's in the room. I regarded him quietly, and thought about how scared he was feeling, and how deeply he yearned for harmony among his friends and peace in his community. Then I regarded the father who had lost his child, and felt his yearning as well, the same yearning for harmony, healing and peace.

I said to him, "We'll deal with your reaction to X's needs later, but at the moment I suggest that you hear his needs. Could you tell me back what Chief X said his needs are? Of course he couldn't do it. He was so emotionally involved in making intellectual judgments of the other side that he wasn't able to hear the feelings and needs that I had helped articulate. So I repeated the needs as I heard them. I said, "Chief Y, I heard X saying that he has a need for safety, and he has a need to feel secure that no matter what conflicts are present, they'll be resolved in some way other than by violence. So could you just reflect back what that need is, so that I'm sure everybody's communicating."

Chief Y was in so much pain, that it took a long time before he could do it. He needed empathy and acknowledgement for the grief he was suffering, and for his rage. He had to try several times, and I had to repeat the message at least two or three times before he could finally hear the other person's needs.

And then I reversed the process. I said to the second chief, "Y, I thank you for hearing that X has this need for security. Now I'd like to hear what your needs are in this." And Y repeated the judgment he had made earlier. "They have been trying to dominate us. They are a dominating group of people. They think they're better than everybody, and we're not going to tolerate it any more." Once again, this started a fight with the other side. I had to interrupt and say, "Excuse me, excuse me." And I went back to trying to sense the needs behind his statement that the other side was dominating.

I said, "Chief Y, are you angry because you're needing equality? You really need to feel that you're being treated equally in this community?" And he said, "Yes, of course!"

Now again, my job was to get the chief on the other side to hear that, which wasn't easy. But I knew we were halfway there. I looked at my colleague and saw that he knew it too. The tension had left his shoulders and the strain had left his face. I felt grateful to be a part of this tumultuous process, this beautiful though often painful process of unfolding peace. And I turned to the other tribe and said, "Could you repeat that so I'm sure that we're communicating." It took three or four repetitions before I could get a chief on the other side just to see the need that this human being was expressing. Finally one of X's companions was able to hear the other chief saying he ha a need for equality.

After we spent this much time getting both sides to express their needs, and to hear each other's needs, (this took over two hours as I recall), another chief who hadn't spoken jumped to his feet, looked at me and said something very intensely. I didn't speak his language, so I was very curious what he was trying to express to me with such intensity. As I waited for the translation I was wondering whether I had said or done something that he took offense at. But I was very touched by what my colleague translated. "The chief says, 'We cannot learn this way of communicating in one day.' And he says, 'If we know how to communicate this way, we don't have to kill each other.'"

This particular conflict had been about the number and placement of each tribe's booths in the marketplace. When everyone's needs were understood, we found that everyone shared the same objectives. Everyone wanted the market place to foster security, equality, dignity, and peace, as well as profit. When these shared needs were clear, the "conflict" almost resolved itself. The tribes were able to create schemes for sharing and rotating the booth spaces, and this "resolution" took only a few minutes. The real work had been to understand each other's needs.

I asked my colleague to tell the chiefs I feel grateful that they see what can happen when we hear each other's needs. He smiled at me, and I could see that already he was enjoying the fruits of the mending and healing in his community. As we left the room I saw a twinkle in his eye. We had talked with the chief who said, "We cannot learn this in a day, but if we know how to communicate this way we don't have to kill each other." We had talked, and already my colleague was organizing the trainings that would help the chiefs to learn this way of communicating, so that the chiefs themselves could pass the training on to others...

He's a busy man, my colleague, and I am grateful to know him.

©2003 Marshall Rosenberg, Reprinted with permission of PuddleDancer Press.

****

Marshall Rosenberg is founder and Director of the non-profit Center for Non-Violent Communication www.cnvc.org Humanistic psychotherapist Carl Rogers, creator of "client-centered" therapy, was an early influence on Rosenberg's theories, and he worked with Carl Rogers for several years before setting off to teach others how to interact in non-aggressive ways. His method became known as Nonviolent Communication. He is the author of When Students Love to Learn and Teachers Love to Teach *(PuddleDancer Press, 2003) as well as the classic* Non-Violent Communication: A Language of Life *(PuddleDancer Press, 2nd edition, 2001). To order, see www.puddledancer.com Dr. Rosenberg founded the Center for Non-Violent Communication in 1984, and since then the organization has grown to 200 trainers globally, providing training in 40 countries in North and South America, Europe, Asia, the Middle East and Africa, and offer workshops for educators, counselors, clergy, parents, police, health care providers, mediators, business professionals, prison inmates, government officials and military personnel. Funded by UNESCO, a CNVC team in former Yugoslavia has trained tens of thousand students and teachers. See www.nonviolentcommunication.org*

The Power of Affirmation

by Reverend John Strickland

Senior Minister, Atlanta Unity Church

Atlanta, Georgia

****

The world is familiar with the power of the spoken word. The spoken word is a simple and powerful way to transform lives. I don't believe that it was "a face" that launched a thousand ships, but the word spoken with power and authority.

Thirty years ago I began a serious study of consciousness. I recall a gathering in which a woman spoke of her young adult son. She was new to the idea of the power of the spoken word and was trying to convey the idea to her son. By all appearances she was only irritating her son. He was rebellious (what young adult in the United States in the 1960s and 70s was not?). The son set out on a backpacking/hitchhiking adventure around the country. At one point, he found himself in New York, in a dangerous neighborhood. Suddenly he was surrounded by a gang, wielding knives. Hs mother's words came to him. He did the only thing he could do: he used the power of the spoken word. He addressed the gang leader and said, "There is no need to attack me. Here, take my backpack and take anything you want." The leader softened and told the man, "This is not a neighborhood that you should be in. Keep your backpack and money. We will escort you to safety."

There is power in the spoken word. The above example is true. The man's peaceful attitude along with the spoken word saved his money and his life!

How does the spoken word work? A person becomes what he or she thinks about (the inaudible word) and what he or she speaks often. Our thoughts and words find their way to our sub-conscious mind. And what is in our sub-conscious mind finds a way into expression. This is a most important point. If we have had an unhappy experience with a person of the opposite sex we may over-generalize and say, "All men are no good," or "All women are this way." We may have several similar experiences and so we think and say many times that a certain type of person is this way. We might generalize to people in authority, people of different races, people from the "wrong" side of the tracks. We might say that everyone in my family is this way (bad at math, good at sports, etc.). The point is: some people may be that way and others may not. Everyone is unique. Maybe everyone else in your family is bad at math problems, but you may be gifted in working them.

My fifth grade teacher told me I was not a good singer. She spoke the word and I believed it. I spoke the same word again and again and convinced my sub-conscious that she was right. When I attempted to sing, others around me confirmed the spoken word about my singing. Many years later a patient, competent and loving voice teacher taught me to sing! What we think and speak repeatedly gets firmly entrenched into our sub-conscious and our sub-conscious finds a way to express it.

Many people in this world think and speak violent words about people they don't like. Sometimes they speak these words about people they don't even know. But they have heard the spoken word from parents, brothers, sisters, clergy, presidents, etc. So the spoken word alienates them from an entire class of people or of an entire nation or religion. The more the words are spoken, the more the speaker is convinced that he or she is correct. If all our lives we heard from learned people that the earth is flat we would repeat it and believe it. Then what would happen when someone discovered the earth is round? We would not believe him and we would call him a heretic. We might say that he is a danger to society, especially to young people. We might even try to kill him.

Let me share another example of the power of the spoken word. A friend of mine, as a young man, went to a very fine boarding school. He loved it there. He was happy with the teachers, the location, the activities. Over the winter holiday he went skiing and broke a leg. When he came back to school, he was moved to a first floor room in his dormitory. On this floor he was surrounded by malcontents. They hated school. They hated life in general. And they were smart and sarcastic. By the end of the spring semester my friend hated the school and life in general. He had been subjected to a constant barrage of negativity in the form of the spoken word. In time, without a conscious effort, the words that he had heard repeatedly, found their way into his subconscious and expressed themselves in his life. It took him many years to overcome that negativity and live a happy and full life.

I have a concern that we too often overlook the power of the spoken word. The words we speak and the words we hear have a powerful effect in our lives. If we watch television, read the newspapers, listen to the radio or just have casual conversations around the water cooler we are probably being bombarded by negative words. If we are not conscious the words sink in. One author wrote, "There is a saying from the East: we cannot keep the birds from flying through our hair, but we can keep them from making a nest there." And so it is with the words we hear. We must be conscious and vigilant. We cannot control the words we hear, but we can silently say, "No," to them if we are not in agreement with them. Sometimes I will talk back to the television set. I do not choose to accept negative, inflammatory words in my consciousness. I do not want them to make a nest in my soul. I have to be careful if I am at a movie theater or someone else's house! It can be embarrassing to blurt out, "No," to a motion picture screen!

I believe it is vitally important that we <u>teach</u> the young people of our world the power of affirmations (positive spoken words). Their words are helping to determine the rest of their lives. I believe it is important that we teach older people the power of affirmations. Their words may convince a youngster that he cannot sing when, in truth, he can sing. They may talk someone out of a career because they believe he is not smart enough or wealthy enough. They may teach someone to be prejudiced against a gender, a race, a nation or a religion. There is power in the spoken word.

The spoken word can teach us to be peaceful and non-violent. They can teach us to share and to love and to not be afraid of those who are different. The younger people are going to follow the behavior that is modeled by the older people. All of us are teachers, preachers, mentors and healers. We have an awesome responsibility to affirm those who look up to us. We have the opportunity to transform our planet through the spoken word. If we will not affirm peace, hope and love, then who will? Now is the time to affirm peace, hope and love for ourselves, for our children and their children and for the world.

*Reverend John Strickland, Senior Minister of Atlanta Unity Church, former Chairman of the Board of the Association of Unity Churches, and former Director of Silent Unity, a worldwide prayer ministry. He can be reached in Atlanta a*t john@atlantaunity.org

Heaven, Earth and the Phang Nga Province

by Le Ly Hayslip

Founder, East Meets West Foundation and
The Global Village Foundation to Help Rebuild Vietnam

Escondido, California

****

Phang Nga Bay has been featured in international movies, from James Bond's "The Man with the Golden Gun" to "Heaven and Earth" directed by Oliver Stone. It is part of the devastated region which was struck by the tsunami in Dec. 2004.

But life moves on, and Mother Nature still stands strong to show off her beauty that only can be appreciated by individuals through their own eyes. We don't understand how beautiful life can be if we don't seek out our own "perfect place" to find peace! In my life I have traveled to many places. My favorite place is peaceful and quiet, where I can experience those moments where life seems to be perfect. The mountains and land are covered with green. There are caves, blue seas and the bay scattered with over 100 uninhabited towers of limestone which are over 7 million year old. This beauty surrounds me when I am at Phang Nga Bay.

In 1992/1993, I lived in Phang Nga Province, Thailand for 6 months (together with more than 100 cast and crew members) during the filming of my life story "Heaven and Earth" by director Oliver Stone. When it came time to depart, I felt great sadness at having to leave this supernatural, soulfully-powerful spot. It brought us inner peace, helping our souls embrace the land, mountains, seas and friendly villagers. Since then, I had longed to return and visit this powerful place which holds such a very special place in both my heart and soul. It was here that the story of my life unfolded, acted out from a little girl as a rice farmer in a tiny village in central Vietnam onto the big screen of Hollywood.

In 2005, I had the opportunity to come back and help serve the victims of the tsunami waves in this Thai province. I fell in love with it all over again. I returned again in Feb. 2006 so that I could re-visit the "Heaven and Earth" movie set. Once again I was able to soak up the supernatural and tranquil surroundings that lay between Father in the sky and Mother earth. It is here that they merge together, at any time of the day, and they empower me to continue with my humanitarian works, doing my part to help make the world a better place for us all.

On my visit to the old "Heaven and Earth" filming location, there awaited a big surprise for me! A new spa resort, the "Bor Saen Villa", had come into being. It was like being in a dream or meditative state. It is here that I am truly being in heaven on earth! It is a place where ravaged souls can be healed. For me, a traveler to many parts of the world, nothing can match the beauty of Phang Nga Bay. After a hectic life in the U.S., and a heart intent on my relief work throughout Vietnam, I need this paradise. It is a perfect place to recap my lost soul, find rest for my weary body, and recharge my inner peace and tranquility. Only then do I have the energy and clear mind to continue working for the betterment of a part of our world that holds a special place in many people's hearts, my motherland of Vietnam.

In September 2007, I moved to Thailand to be Oliver Stone's technical advisor and consultant on his movie "Pinkville" about the My Lai Massacre during the US war in Vietnam. The writer's strike in Los Angeles caused "Pinkville" to be put on hold; it was then that I decided to give up my beautiful home in city of Carlsbad, San Diego, USA to live at "Bor Saen Villa". I invited our families and friends from around the world to come and enjoy life for the month of December and January in Thailand! In many parts of the world it is still winter with its snow, rain and cold temperatures, but not here in Phang Nga Province! Here, from "Bor Saen Villa", we went fishing every day on the dock in our own yard. We swam in our own pool. We spent time reading, writing or going to Phuket Island and out on the boats at the Phuket Boat Lodge. On the weekends, after a full day of snorkeling in the coral reefs off the most beautiful beaches, we could go to Krabi town where we could shop, eat a Big Mac at Burger King or even order Pizza with Swensen Ice cream for dessert. An international diet but local village!

Here in Asia, flowers blossom year round. Just as the birds in flight are enhanced by the aroma, or as the bees depend on the blossoms in their labors, so too do humans depend on these things in our quest for love. As humans, we consume the spices and harvests of autumn. The Creator granted humans these beautiful things while we live here on earth to go along with our courage, confidence, ambition, and intelligence so that we could master our vision of perfect life. Many of these visions are here: the flowers with their sweet aromas, the beautiful colors, and the morning drew draws the peaceful moments into our lives.

I am not writing this simply to promote "Bor Saen Villa" or Phang Nga Bay. I genuinely care for the "caring of" the human spirit!   In Vietnamese there is a saying: *"Tam bat an, hanh dong bat chanh."* If our spirit is not happy and peaceful to enjoy life here and now, then we will act out disharmony with others: we will <u>be</u> unhappy and not be calm. That will bring our world into "chaos." Please, take some time off and come to Phang Nga Province. Perhaps we can have a cup of Vietnamese coffee and I can serve you a bowl of Pho to go with it. You don't know what it is like until you experience true inner peace and calmness.

Life on earth is like school. We come to learn, and the only way to find ourselves is to reach out for knowledge and wisdom so we can grow and to progress. We cannot find the oneness without living in harmony with Mother Nature and Father Sky, and not without having trillions of stars to talk to. We cannot take anything with us but life's knowledge and peacefulness when we go. Good luck and enjoy the beauty of your being. Thank you, with Love and Peace.

****

Le Ly Hayslip is the author of <u>When Heaven and Earth Changed Places</u> (NY: Penguin Books, 1983, 2003) and <u>Child of War, Woman of Peace</u> NY: Doubleday, 1993. As Le Ly recalls: " It is said that in war, heaven and earth change places not once but many times". Le Ly (Lay Lee)'s biography is the haunting memoir of a girl on the verge of womanhood in a world turned upside down. The youngest of six children in a closely knit Buddhist family, Le Ly was twelve years old when U.S. helicopters landed in Ky La, her tiny village in central Vietnam.

As the government and Viet Cong troops fought in and around Ky La, both sides recruited children as spies and saboteurs. Le Ly was one of those children. Before the age of 16, Le Ly had suffered near-starvation, imprisonment, torture, rape, and the deaths of beloved family members. Miraculously, she held fast to her faith in humanity.

The Global Village Foundation was established in 1999 by Le Ly Hayslip, who grew up in a poor village in central Vietnam during the Vietnam War, to serve children and adults in the spirit of world peace. Hayslip's best-selling books are currently in use as curriculum at numerous universities across the country for Asian studies, literature, Women's Studies, and Vietnam conflict courses. They been published in 17 different languages throughout the world. In 1994, Le Ly's books about her life growing up in war torn Vietnam were adapted for by Academy Award winning director Oliver Stone (director of "Platoon" and other Hollywood films) for scripting, and were produced into the award-winning film "Heaven and Earth", available in paperback as well as on DVD via Amazon.com

You may read about her ongoing literacy and outreach Foundation work in Vietnam at
www.globalvillagefoundation.org

BOSNIA: Ten Years After War

Article originally published April 2, 2002 in the <u>Bosnia Daily</u>

Ibro Bajrovic is rebuilding his house to look just like it did before the Serb artillery shells destroyed it a decade ago. But Bajrovic, a 67-year-old Muslim, may as well build it smaller, because his son says he's never coming home, Associated Press writes. "Explain to me what changed since the war started," said his son, Mirsad Bajrovic, age 38, who now lives in Florida. Ten years after Bosnia's bloodbath began, a nation <u>and</u> its families remain divided. Some have hope, others despair. Some have returned; others are happy to stay away. Some are working to build a future; others are stilly trying to get over the past.

Hope for many Bosnian's died on April 6, 1992, along with the first victims of a war that would stretch over 3 years, kill 200,000 people, uproot 1.8 million people, and bring genocide, mass graves, and concentration camps back to Europe. Yugoslavia was falling apart, and Bosnia's ethnic groups (Muslims, Croats, and Serbs) began to wonder where their republic was headed. Muslims and Croats pressed for independence, while Serbs wanted Bosnia to stay in the Serb-dominated Yugoslav federation. Forty-thousand peace demonstrators massed in Sarajevo that April 6th, the same day the European Union's predecessor recognized Bosnia's independence.

But ethnic Serbs, armed and backed by Yugoslavia's president, Slobodan Milosevic, weren't prepared to let Bosnia go. Serb snipers fired on the rally, killing five people. By nightfall, the first artillery shells had slammed into the Bosnian capital. The siege of Sarajevo had begun. Mirsad Bajrovic was among the anguished demonstrators that day. By summer, his family's home was rubble. So were his dreams.

As a nurse, he treated hundreds of sniper and shrapnel victims, all the while hatching ways to escape the hell that had engulfed the city. In 1994, he managed to flee with his fiancé to Germany, where they married, and they eventually emigrated to the United States. Tens of thousands of young Bosnians have done the same, and more are following. Long lines of Bosnians in their 20s and 30s snake in front of Western embassies waiting to apply for visas. Sixty-two percent of young Bosnians see no future and want to emigrate, according to a recent survey by the United Nations Development Program. "Their parents made terrible historical errors," said Jacques Klein, head of the United Nations mission to Bosnia. "They almost destroyed their own future, and mortgaged their children's very heavily." NATO troops intervened in 1995, and a U.S.-brokered peace pact sign in Dayton, Ohio, ended the war, but not before Serb troops slaughtered 8,000 Muslims men and boys at Srebrenica in Europe's worst massacre since World War II.

Although the Dayton Accord reaffirmed Bosnia's independence, it froze the front lines and divided the country into a Bosnian-Serb republic and a Muslim-Croat mini-state. The ethnic frictions that tore the nation apart linger. International mediators "thought if they stopped the violence, it would end the war. But the war never ended," Klein said. Tens of thousands of NATO-led peacekeepers, including 3,100 American soldiers, remain in a land still strewn with more than a million land mines. Thousands of foreign diplomats, police officers, advisers, mediators, and administrators are trying to keep the nation going. Because of incessant bickering among Bosnia's ethnic groups, the international community has had to significantly broaden the powers of the top Western administrator to impose law and order and fire obstructionist politicians. The flag, the anthem, the currency all were imposed on Bosnia.

Yet some progress has been made towards peace. The United Nations says refugees are returning in record numbers. But many people seem exhausted by years of fighting, 40% joblessness, and an almost non-existent economy. Rare enthusiasts like Zlatko Lagumdzija, Bosnia's moderate foreign minister, insist there can be a compromise, full democracy, and eventually integration into Europe. "They cannot prevent us from getting there. They can only slow down the speed," he said.

*The journalist who wrote this article remains anonymous. The **Art Reach Foundation** sends teams of professionals to countries that have experienced severe natural disasters or military violence, to work with teachers and public health professionals. The teams organize, develop and provide resources for programs offering creative problem-solving and expressive arts activities for children who have been emotionally traumatized. Their award-winning work with children in Bosnia has gained the attention of peace leaders internationally. See their web site*
www.artreachfoundation.org

An Indigenous People's Peaceful Protest: The Flowery Wars of Chiapas

by Subcoyote Alberto Ruz Buenfil

Traveling with the Rainbow Peace Caravan, Chiapas, México and Medellín, Colombia

****

More than ten years have passed since that first day of January, 1994 when a handful of Maya Indians, wearing face masks and armed in many cases with just a stick, wooden rifles and their daily working tools, took by surprise-assault the six main cities in the southern state of Chiapas, deep into the green, humid Lacandon Rainforest of the Mexican southwest.

What at first looked like a simple suicidal act of protest against the imminent Mexican joining of the modern era through the NAFTA agreements turned out, in just a few days, to be an open challenge to the Federal government and its all-powerful state party (the PRI) and the Mexican military establishment. The national and international mass media began almost immediately to let the whole world know about the words, images and declarations issued by the enigmatic spokesperson for the emerging insurgent group, known as the *Ejercito Zapatista de Liberacion Nacional* (Zapatista Army of National Liberation). We'll use EZLN for its Spanish acronym. The leader of this protest? He was a *mestizo* man of unknown age, his face covered with a ski mask, a brown beret with a golden star on his head, a perpetual burning pipe in his mouth, a penetrating look in his eyes, two bullet holders criss-crossing his chest, dressed in battle uniform and muddy combat boots. His war name was Subcomandante Marcos.

The fighting lasted only nine days with a relatively small number of human casualties -- in spite of the violent response by the Mexican military, the bombing of Indian villages by air and land, and the advance of the largest army ever deployed in any one region of the large, diverse country of Mexico. The Maya Indians retreated almost immediately to the security of the thick jungles and high mountains of Chiapas, and public opinion in Mexico reacted with unexpected and unanimous decision, pressing the then-government of president Carlos Salinas de Gortari for a speedy and peaceful resolution to the conflict. The president saw no other choice than to declare a lateral "cease fire" and begin negotiations with the rebel Mayan Indian army.

Up to that point, everything seemed to reaffirm the common thesis that this was a desperate act committed by a historically forgotten and marginalized sector of society, not just in Mexico, but in all of Latin America in general. It looked like one more uprising of "the Indians" which had been condemned, like dozens of others before, to the extermination of its leaders, the massacres of its communities, and to becoming one more tragic anecdote --- to be archived in some dusty documents and file cabinets of a history generally unknown to the rest of the world.

However, to everyone's surprise, the "uprising" did not end like this. During mid-January 1994, the rebels in Chiapas initiated a previously unseen form of attack with very particular characteristics. Contrary to traditional actions seen in guerrilla wars throughout the last half of the 20th century, especially in Latin America, they took a new path, and political analysts, reporters and commentators rushed to try to interpret, compare and identify it with some of historical precedent – but even for native Indians, this movement was unique.

With each surprising move of the new Indian guerrilla, these many interpretations of "strategy" started to contradict each other and crumble. The constant kidnappings of politicians and financiers which were almost unanimously resorted to by revolutionary guerrilla groups of socialist and communist ideologies (whether Maoists, Stalinists, Trotskyites, *Castristas*, Sandinistas, or Guevaristas in Mexico), the gruesome kidnappings in Guatemala, El Salvador, Nicaragua, Peru, Bolivia, Argentina, or even the more recent ones by the FARC and ELN of Colombia, in Chiapas were reduced to one single non-violent kidnapping: that of an ex-Governor of that state. What was going on?

And even he was released unharmed shortly after, and having been tried by a "people's tribunal" was returned to his city of residency condemned to living out the rest of his life with the stigma of having been found to be an unjust, repressive, corrupt and racist governor! In other words, he was "unmasked" before public opinion and the mass media. That was his only punishment.

What were once "fundamental practices" of surprise and indiscriminate assaults, of constant and destructive guerrilla attacks on barracks, police stations, municipal offices, airports, roads, bridges and the general population (with great tragic losses of civilians and military personnel) – or the more dramatic blowing up of power stations and energy pipelines, taken from traditional manuals on "Guerrilla War" became, in the hands of the Zapatistas, reduced to *maintaining a passive resistance* inside the communities. Meanwhile, the Mexican government was fighting back, during a growing military siege carried out by land, air and water along the stretch of the Usumacinta River on the Guatemala border in south Mexico.

The Mayan Indian EZLN resistance was coupled with the intensive use of the Internet and a constant bombardment on the media about their cause (newspapers, radio and TV on the national and international level) along with the creation of several *Aguascalientes* (territories under Zapatista government) which were declared "Peace Camps" and settlements. In addition to the call to millions of people around the world to come and <u>witness</u> the efforts carried out in those areas to improve the lives of its inhabitants, the movement gained many sympathizers. And in several cases, the Peace Camps became the hosts of large international gatherings such as the "National Democratic Convention" (1994) and the "Galactic Gathering for Humanity" (1996).

Traditional organizational structures of guerrilla armies are often run by male leadership of a highly-politicized median background following some variation or reinterpretation of Marxist-Leninist ideologies: that is to say, a pyramidal hierarchy based on the principals of "Democratic Centralism" where orders and decisions are taken in a vertical descending fashion without the least input or discussion by the base constituents. But surprisingly, in the case of the EZLN, the organizational interactions took on a rustic and concentric, spiral-like growth from inside out, much like the movement of the universe. Indigenous populations and communities involved make decisions by <u>consensus</u> after much consultation. In the case of the EZLN, they then pass these decisions to their commandants, who in turn passed on these democratically-made decisions to another level of command made up by men and women called the CCRI

(*Comite Clandestino Revolucionario Indigena*) which, in turn, was expected to give instructions to the next level of command, thus following the principals of "Leading by Obeying." The main spokesperson of the Zapatista Army, Marcos, the only non-indigenous *mestizo* of that collective command, was only recognized as a "Sub-Commander", thus highlighting who is really making the important decisions in the organization: the people.

The main objective of guerrilla movements inspired by Marxist ideologies is political, economic and military destabilization of the state. In case of victory, they are expected to take over the government, re-establish the military and put in place a "revolutionary" political regime (following the models of the now-dissolved Soviet Union, Eastern European countries, China, Vietnam or Cuba).   However, in the case of the EZLN, the goals from the first moment of their appearance on the national and international scene have been and continue to be to strengthen civil organizations (NGOs); be an example of a just and libertarian social movement; recognize basic human rights for all, not just for indigenous people (and especially for those who never had a voice or a face in society); to dissolve their own army; and to defend autonomous communities and municipalities. In other words, these grassroots goals are to achieve empowerment of the individuals and communities, and to struggle for peace with justice and dignity for all under the principle of "EVERYTHING FOR EVERYONE". This movement never wanted anything to do with a presumed "power takeover" – they often told me: "Nothing is for us!"

While for many of the guerrilla groups of this last century, the ends have justified all their means (for which they currently employ alliances and strategies which are in total opposition to the principles that nourish them and give them a reason to exist), most become an armed group of the "opposition" political parties.   In places like the Basque region of Spain (ETA), Palestine (Fatah Movement) or Peru (*Sendero Luminoso*), at present the guerilla movements' situations have deteriorated, as these armed groups become increasingly protective and beneficiaries of the multimillion dollar business of cultivation, processing and distribution of illegal drugs, money laundering, kidnapping, indiscriminate massacres of civilians, generalized terror and violence -- and of the systematic recruitment of minors and mercenaries who kill and die for a miserable salary. From within the Rainforest of Chiapas, the EZLN offers a living example of a return to ethical principles when people DO choose to revolt in a peaceful manner, and reminds us that the use of violent means leads likewise to irremediably corrupted, dirty, illegal and vice-ridden ends. These are <u>not</u> in the common people's best interest in nations around the world.

After having lived 10 years in the rainforest before 1994, plus more than 10 years of passive resistance -- and at times surrounded by over 50,000 members of the Mexican military -- the Mayan Indians are a brave part of Mexico. Harassed constantly by paramilitary near coffee plantations, cattle ranches, and by very corrupted politicians and landlords, the EZLN has managed to remain to this date clean and unrelated to foreign forces and interests -- or to those contrary to their own ideals in their way of financing, recruiting, political autonomy and direct action. They continue to carry out their struggle with admirable impeccability in the name of those whose rights have been denied for centuries, being forced to die of hunger, curable diseases and sadness.

The ideologies which have nourished the guerrilla movements in Latin America, especially since the 1950s, are derived primarily from an Eurocentric line of thought, based on an analysis and criticism of history viewed from a colonial and imperialist Europe of the 16th and 17th century, a projection of the European industrial/capitalist development of the second half of the 19th century. It is also characterized by a nearly absolute ignorance of the history of the people of the ill-named third world countries (Africa, Asia and the Americas), and especially by the undervaluing of processes that, for centuries and millennia, maintained the delicate balance between indigenous cultures -- the first inhabitants of the planet -- and the natural elements, planetary and cosmic cycles which sustained them.

The EZLN is the first contemporary indigenous social movement which not only regained possession of its territorial, cultural, language, organizational and self-governing rights, but also its spiritual, artistic and educational rights. It does so according to its own original ways of thinking, its myths, legends, stories, gods, and magical metaphors like the insect character Durito and the wise old Indian hunter, Antonio. It especially does so utilizing the traditional poetry and images of the cosmology and wisdom of the Maya people.

The legendary commanders Ramona, Tacho, Moises, German and Esther, the actress Ofelia Medina, Bishop Samuel Ortiz, Subcommander Marcos and the rest of the 23 commanders who traveled in the "Caravan for Dignity" to Mexico City in the year 2001, like many others, have been and continue to be the main characters of a true cosmic-soap opera. The historic "Maya Flowery Wars" currently being waged for peace were conceived and historically carried out, from time to time, by their ancestors as well. Hence, resistance has a thread in indigenous culture. The "Flowery Wars" were part of a historic ritual, ceremonial and educational <u>process</u> which contributed much to the development of past civilizations in the Americas. During their highest state of spiritual evolution, they were true representations of collective choreographies with the specific goal of "raising the consciousness of the collective/people" and individuals by educating them and making them <u>responsible</u> for having a real space and time ruled by the stars and the cycles of nature.

In the Flowery Wars, armies of spiritual warriors confronted each other to dramatically represent precise movements of celestial events. Powerful participants were associated with "bringing on" plentiful harvests, severe changes or foretold upcoming disasters. Their montage contributed to unmask the mismanagement of governors, the wrong actions of high priests or the Gods' unhappiness with the excesses of humanity. These rituals were true initiations which awakened sleeping archetypes in the general population's subconscious. They were a mourning (*Uayebs*) for dark times, the loss of loved ones, sadness and winter time – or literal festivals to <u>celebrate</u> the end of harsh times, the beginning of spring or to re-ignite the New Fire to celebrate the new cycles of their calendars.

The Flowery Wars in Chiapas emerged at a precise time in the ancient cosmic calendars, when the prophets (*Balams)* and wise ones recognized the sign for the ending of "The Path of Tears" or "The Nine Hells"-- when a long cycle of misfortunes for the Indians of Mexico which started with the "conquest" of Mexico had finally come to an end. This was the time when the "Time Keepers" let the Maya communities know that they were starting a new turn of the "Sky Belt", a new cycle of "Thirteen Heavens", and that it was time to say: ENOUGH!!!

For the Mayas, the life of a culture, plants, the stars and the suns are also subject to a natural process of birth, growth, maturity, old age and death or re-birth, like the cycles of the seasons and all that exists in the universe. The Flowery Wars, like the arts, social organizations, harvests, habits, costumes and even the development of cities, have their time of splendor and their times of decay and corruption. Therefore, it is possible to understand how in our times, as in the past, some social movements have been guided by high values, humanist ethics, the search for social and spiritual justice, while others have been and continue to be guided only by material wealth, petty interests, ambition, unconsciousness, abuse and perpetuation of the power of a few individuals, social classes, the church and political parties.

The Indian Wars and peace of Chiapas are a clear example of a Flowery War in the stage of awakening of the consciousness of Mexico and all of indigenous American Indians, Afro-Americans and *mestizo* people. A theatrical war to end all wars, a masked army to end all armies, an armament of words, jests, humor, play, poetry, collective choreography, pilgrimages, caravans, peaceful takeover of public squares, cities and even the very Congress of the Union, was held in order to call attention to the justices being demanded -- denied for five centuries -- by the original inhabitants of our continent, giving voice to indigenous people around the whole planet Earth. Our leaders are rooted in history and indigenous families: those who have been here before all of us.

Mass ideologies, be them of a socialist or neoliberal style, always belong to the Era of the Herd. We can view them historically through stages in which "out of control" habits of mass consumption, debasement, violence, collective unconsciousness, individualism, competition, ostentatious acts, fanaticism and a deep fundamentalism reigns in society. These are signs of what we are experiencing today with fashion mania for the masses, the lack of spiritual values, massive and manipulated control of information, fundamentalist religions, desire, need, fear and insecurity -- these are signs of the Age of Neoliberal Globalization.

But there is no eternal inferno. Just as a few years ago, when the walls, beliefs, monuments and repressive structures that upheld the East European Block for more than half a century came "tumbling down", it is now also possible to identify specific signs of breakdown in the apparently indestructible paradigm of the Western world. The Maya's "Flowery Wars" are one of these unmistakable signs. That is why it has caught the attention of the mass media and of hundreds of thousands of thinkers, activists, artists, women, youth, intellectuals and Indians from around the globe. We are dealing with the first successful social movement of the 21st century! And this is quite differently from the successful revolutions in Russia, Mexico and China in the last century, this one does not follow a mass ideology, it is not a call for destruction and death of the "enemy" and it is not based on revenge, hate or class struggle.

Subcomandante Marcos has synthesized characteristics of the charismatic peasant leader Emiliano Zapata (for whom the indigenous army is named), the magic spirit of Votan (mythical character of the Mayan cultures of Chiapas), the bravery of Don Quixote (eternal champion of lost causes) and of the incomparable Che Guevara. He has also taken inspiration from the great military strategist Pancho Villa and the great spiritual strategist Mahatma Gandhi. His mentor in Rainforest wisdom is a simple man, a Maya Indian with a deep knowledge of life and the cosmos called "Old Antonio". He undertook a long apprentice relation with him, similar to that of anthropologist Carlos Castaneda and the legendary Yaqui Shaman, Don Juan Matus.

The unmistakable Sub Marcos, without falling into the hero-martyr syndrome of Che Guevara, turned himself in just a few years into an admired gallant cultural figure for women from all ages, the hero of numerous ballads, the envy of many right and left wing intellectuals, and the object/subject of a media phenomenon that has generated a mind boggling and vast market of products that sell his charismatic image. He has become a legendary, mythic, surreal, real and magic human being -- an enigmatic masked synthesis which even the best of contemporary theater, movies and TV directors and actors recognize and respect for being one of the best director, actor and poet of our times.

The Flowery War of Chiapas, by using weapons like poetry, humor, masks, coded messages, enigmas, surprises and creative ferment has been able in just seven years to unleash, without a single shot, a national catharsis all over Mexico which ended over seven decades of the "perfect dictatorship" of the PRI (Institutional Revolutionary Party of Mexico), has totally ridiculed the image of two outgoing presidents (Salinas de Gortari and Ernesto Zedillo), profoundly shaken the foundations of the leftist opposition party in Mexico (PRD=*Partido de la Revolucion Democratica*) which it wisely never joined (nor supported without great reservations) and finally it has unmasked the racist and reactionary elements of the conservative party (PAN *Partido de Accion Nacional*) which rose to the presidency in the surprising election results of July 2, 2000.

Additionally, the EZLN has forced presidential candidate Vicente Fox, who has been in the presidential seat since January 1, 2001, to protect the Clandestine Indigenous Command, Marcos and a Caravan of several thousands EZ sympathizers on a historical month-long pilgrimage through the main capitals of the country ending in the very *Zocalo* (Central Plaza) of Mexico City on March 11, 2001. There, after much opposition from the PANistas senators, they were finally allowed to speak to the highest political authority of the country, the National Congress, on March 28, 2001. The cultural and ceremonious welcoming events widely celebrated in 12 states and the Nation's capital were overwhelming and heavily attended, bringing together hundreds of thousands of people from all walks of life and professions, age, religious leanings and social standing, in addition to representatives from all ethnic groups of the country and many more from around the world.

After various episodes charged with tension and discourse, as is expected of any successful cosmic soap opera, the insurgent commanders, along with representatives from the indigenous groups from all over the country gathered in the chambers of the National Congress, in the presence of witnesses from other ethnic groups and nations and for the first time were able to let the whole world hear their voices and demands. This was a historic event without precedence, not even before the times of the Mexican Conquest of 1521.

A crowning triumph for the Flowery Wars of Chiapas started over twenty years ago in the Lacandon Rainforest. And still, this great feat was accomplished without spilling a drop of blood, without kidnapping anyone for ransom, without destroying public or private property and especially without tying the EZLN to any political party, church, World Bank, Transnational Corporation or drug cartel. Something apparently miraculous or unexplainable without taking into account conditions that have something to do with the natural process of cosmological cycles on the one hand, and to the deep knowledge of these cycles that some of the wise Maya guides -- *Halach Uinics* or "True Men"-- held on to and passed on from generation to generation until reaching the right moment to initiate this historic undertaking.

The serious and respectful dialogue and the profound, heart-felt messages of the 23 Zapatista Commanders and one Sub-commander have been heard, translated, gathered and sent to all corners of the Earth and in every language, for "The People of the Color of the Earth, For People of all Colors." The process unleashed by these voices is already having its first repercussions, even among the most irreconcilable revolutionaries, who have recently begun recognizing that their war strategy is ever less effective based upon violence. The deeper message will also have increasingly similar effects among all individuals, groups and movements who recognize and resonate with a proposal that demands of the dominant society an attitude of <u>respect, justice and dignity for the indigenous people</u> of the Americas and world.

The popularity of these Maya warriors has increased with time, and their demand for the approval of the San Andres de los Pobres Accords (a peace accord agreed upon by both the EZLN and the Mexican government in 1995) to arrive at the constitutional changes that would give them their rights and autonomy in their own territories, which they should already have given the simple fact that they are native and Mexicans, are the very same demands for which millions of indigenous people from all over the planet have been fighting for over five hundred years.

In one of their last big public events, held in the heart of the jungle in August 2003, the indigenous commandancy of the EZLN declared an end to the delimitation of rebel territories, or *Aguascalientes*, and exhorted all the indigenous communities of Mexico to defend their rights of survival, to maintain their resistance, and to consolidate the autonomy of their nations in the whole country. The new form of parallel authorities were baptized before more than 5,000 assistants to the event in Oventic, Chiapas, "*Juntas de buen Gobierno*" (good government councils), and the Zapatista's leaders also declared that the new free autonomous Municipalities would be called *Caracoles*, and would be governed by indigenous civilians elected by their own communities.

The process started when a council of thirty Zapatista autonomous municipalities informed the commanders of the EZLN that they had built their own houses of Good Government, and where ready to take over the governing role that the rebels had until then. They also let the nation know that they would eliminate the taxes to all those crossing their territories, and would continue prosecuting the traffic of alcohol, drugs, weapons and illegal harvesting of wood in their communities.

Marcos has slowly backed from the front line, and married to an indigenous woman, they are raising their children to continue the path they undertook twenty years ago. And in one of his last communiqués, he informed the nation that the EZLN had accomplished the main tasks given to them by the indigenous Mayan nations, and they would continue talking and defending the people, "those who are the blood, heart and though of the nation," and "that armies, even revolutionary armies are there to defend the people, not to govern them."

He also declared that "there were many good people in Mexico and the rest of the world following the example of the Zapatistas, " and he concluded that "in their eyes he could see that respect and hope would continue prevailing" and that "he trusted that the resistance against the bad governments that still hold the reins of power in the planet would continue as well."

To conclude this testimony about the Flowery Wars, I would like to just quote something I read on a great big banner hung on some building of the Zocalo of Mexico City on the magnanimous welcoming for the EZLN on March 11, 2001. It said something very important that we often forget: "WE ARE ALL INDIGENOUS OF SOME PLACE ON EARTH". Think about that.

Excerpt translated/reprinted with author's permission from the book: _Hay Tantos Caminos (Una Crónica Zapatista)_ (Mexico City, Mexico: Editorial Colofón S.A., 2004).
****

Subcoyote Alberto Ruz is a lifetime peace activist who lives in Mexico and travels extensively with his "Rainbow Peace Caravan" of activists throughout Central and South America. He has *been a well-known activist in bio-regional, permaculture, and peace events throughout the Southern Hemisphere,, including the latest event, EL LLAMADO DEL CONDOR, a Vision Council for Bioregional Action, that brought together more than 700 representatives from 34 different countries for a whole week of sharing of experiences, wisdom, ceremonies, multicultural activities, love and magic at the feet of Machu Pichu, in the highlands of the Peruvian Andes.*

From Preparation to Leave the Earth

for Mars, to Stewardship of a Peaceful Planet

by Brian O'Leary

A physicist trained as a NASA astronaut during the Apollo program

Loja, Ecuador

****

As the new millennium dawns, I see hope for us and for reversing the human-caused pollution of the Earth. The changes and adventure will be exciting and challenging for us, yet time is running out. I believe solutions are there, and can be enhanced if we transcend our denial of emerging truths based on suppressed experiments in new science, new energy, healing, consciousness, hemp production and evidence for contact with nonhuman intelligence and our eternal being. I believe we have the potential to make the needed changes, but we are going to have to let go of many worn-out, vested interests and begin to empower ourselves toward solutions.

The birth of this process, as almost always, comes from "necessity being the mother of invention." It is clear to me that we as a species must begin to come back into balance with the biosphere. We must create a sustainable future so that we may once again inherit the Earth. Not to do so will be a deterioration of the quality of life for our children --or global extinction.

As a little boy, I always wanted to go into space. But there was no space program then! Many of my teachers thought I was just a dreamer. Then Sputnik went up in 1957, when I first entered college. Ten short years later I became an Apollo scientist-astronaut destined to go to Mars. Soon after, NASA cancelled the Mars-exploration part of the program. I went on to other things, but I got to experience the feeling of anticipating what it would be like to go to the red planet.

The Apollo Moon program taught me many valuable lessons. I saw it as a crowning human achievement, an example of what we can do as a culture when we put our minds to it. This was an extraordinary, historic achievement -- "one step for a man, one giant leap for mankind". To me, the Apollo program epitomized the best of our collective human potential and authentic power. It gave me a valuable reference point for the future, which I'll explain soon.

Some years later, as a faculty member in the Physics Department at Princeton University, I began to have some personal experiences that I couldn't explain within the traditional science I was teaching. At some risk to my credibility as a mainstream scientist, I began to dream again like the little boy looking through the telescope at Mars and wanting to go there. I questioned the beliefs of materialism and reductionism as being the most general case of our reality. As I stepped ever further out of the cultural box, I grew and groaned tremendously, losing my visibility and credibility among colleagues.

I asked, "How can the scientific method be applied to studying experiences such as psychic healing, transcendental consciousness, survival after death, communication with nonhuman intelligence, crop circles, and many other things that demand unbiased examination?" I was at first surprised to discover that these fields were scientifically further developed than I had imagined, but none of them had yet been integrated into the mainstream. Some of them had, in fact, been suppressed.

I began to learn that many basic principles of consciousness and our multi-sensory being are being confirmed by experiments in quantum mechanics, psychokinesis, alternative healing, clairvoyance and zero point energy generation. I am encouraged that more and more scientists are breaking ranks with their materialistic biases to take the courageous stand that our consciousness is the ground of all being. In my opinion, materialism is but a limiting case of reality and we are on the threshold of a new paradigm which will provide the means for a new renaissance in human affairs. We can learn a lot from what many spiritual leaders and mystics have been talking about for a long time.

My current passion is to release our enormous human potential to balance the Earth's environment. This massive task needn't necessarily force us to immediately adopt radical new technologies before they are thoroughly researched and debated. Free energy is a dramatic example of what could be done to transcend our polluting ways, but we will need to learn to use this resource wisely. Just in case this is abused by military interests, I support low technology solutions as backup, for example, hydrogen, biomass, solar, and wind power.

I have witnessed and researched a dazzling array of solutions to our global challenges in laboratories of innovators worldwide, who want to work for world PEACE, not 'energy wars'. Citizens require an increasing awareness of clean technologies, ever further probing our potentials as multi-sensory beings, and socially inventing those structures and procedures with which to make the necessary changes.

We in America inherit a revolutionary tradition of freedom, one which is threatened by environmental neglect. Our people enjoy unprecedented abundance. We therefore have an opportunity as never before to empower ourselves into bold resolutions. Do we have the will to join in community to dare to dream of a mega-Apollo project <u>for the environment</u>? I believe we do, but we need to examine the ways in which we can come together to discuss and debate our millennial solutions. This will require an inner-motivated authentic power, free of the ego-traps of greed, denial and self-interest. This is 'peace work'.

This new project could spin off many others, such as world peace circles, abundant food, and the opportunity to evolve to higher states of being as citizens of the universe. Many more of us may soon discover that we are not alone in the cosmos as sentient beings, and that our awareness never dies!

Governments will have to change radically, and learn how, at last, to convert swords to plowshares. Private industry will have to change, too, so that the ecology and all humanity will profit from every successful business endeavor. We must re-invent what is meant by the collective global interest, and keep refining it so that our new direction will be felt enthusiastically by all. We could convene a council of elders, based on an inspired *Declaration of Interdependence*, to oversee this project.

I believe the global situation calls for decisive social action. It is time to consider and debate all reasonable solutions. Then we will be on track. Most of all, we need not be afraid to feel our feelings, to grieve the past and then to look at transcendent solutions based on our greater essence. They will require nothing less than our most inspiring, inner-directed compassion and love for all creation. We are at a critical crossroads now, and we must act now. It is time to walk through the void to the miracles that lie ahead, together.

Later: upon moving from Hawaii. What a difference a few months make! When I was writing my manuscript for the book Re-Inheriting the Earth late last year, people seemed oblivious about our energy problems and now it's in the headlines every day. Yet the press omits any mention of the inevitable demise of the fossil fuel age, which will become necessary because of dwindling supplies and increasing pollution. In the long run, the issue will be joined between two opposing forces. The one now in power will certainly lead our culture into a state of such disarray, there may be no way out. The other offers sustainable solutions.

The Bush administration has wasted no time offending the rest of the world with its insistence on nullifying the Kyoto agreement on global warming emissions, drilling in the Arctic National Wildlife Refuge, forestalling renewable and clean energy research, building new fossil fuel power plants which would contribute even more to America's lead in carbon emissions, protecting the interests of the rich and big business, and promoting a costly and destabilizing missile defense system.

Unfortunately, in the eyes of the mass media, discussion about ending pollution and global climate change has been abandoned. The debate has narrowed to political and short-term economic considerations rather than the long-term physical facts and technological directions which would surely prompt a serious discussion of a sustainable future, as described in my new book. Innovation and even talk of innovation are stifled at almost every turn. A recent example is a USA Today cover article "Six Ways to Combat Global Warming" (July 16, 2001 issue). No mention is made at all about the real solutions such as solar, wind, hydrogen, improving efficiency and new energy research. Instead, we only heard about political steps like ratifying the Kyoto agreements (too little too late, but a still an important step towards international cooperation) to non-steps such as trading emissions credits for the privilege to pollute, doing more studies, or doing nothing at all. How could these be considered ways to combat global warming?

Is this neglect of considering the clean, renewable options a reflection of the dumbing-down of America, is it greed, is it fear of the loss of power? Or has the energy cartel joined ideological forces with the media and government to buttress the status quo at any cost? In my more than forty-year history as a senior energy analyst, I have never seen a debate narrow to such non-solutions which appear as propaganda. Since my childhood, I learned how the USA was a land of invention and opportunity, not an energy-hungry empire which suppresses solutions and is an embarrassment to the rest of the world. This can be very disquieting on the home front and invite ever more denial of our responsibility.

The only global option we have is to cut our toxic emissions to near-zero--a measure which not only prevents global suicide but is cost-effective in the long run. Over the coming decades, petroleum and natural gas will become more scarce and expensive, and certainly not cost-competitive with clean renewables. The only beneficiaries will be the giant energy companies, related infrastructure and the very wealthy. The rest of us will suffer from more toxic pollution of the air, global climate change, escalating prices and more dependence on foreign oil. We can end our addiction to fossil fuels by first acknowledging that they have dominated our international economy and that now we must find ways to replace them through innovation and active civil participation. Once this becomes more widely understood, coal, oil and natural gas will go the way of tobacco, but on a much larger scale and a greater toll of lives. I hope my new book will help you understand the depth of the situation and inspire solutions.

We must expand the debate to embrace the real answers. Fortunately, those answers do exist and need to be presented to the public. Our silence in this matter suggests a more insidious aspect of control in the exercise of power. "The most successful tyranny is not the one that uses force to assure uniformity but the one that removes the awareness of other possibilities", said Allan Bloom in his book The Closing of the American Mind.   Noam Chomsky stated the problem this way: "The smart way to keep people passive and obedient is to strictly limit the spectrum of acceptable opinion, but allow very lively debate within that spectrum - even encourage the more critical and dissident views. That gives people the sense there's free thinking going on, while all the time the presuppositions of the system are being reinforced by the limits put on the range of debate."

So what can we do? In my book <u>Re-Inheriting the Earth,</u> I propose with many others the establishment of a global green democracy which would have jurisdiction over unbridled competition and growth of giant multinational corporations and their friends in politically high places. These forces of globalization and "free trade" encourage the very powerful to step into those countries that have the cheapest labor and most relaxed environmental standards in a vicious cycle of pollution and competitive stress. These unregulated actions make a mockery of authentic free trade which could deliver the needed goods and services for a green future.

I present in my book the case for the most urgent measures, ones upon which the preponderant number of citizens of the world would agree. Included would be the shift of public subsidies from polluting to clean enterprises, enforcing strict emissions standards, controlling the excesses of economic globalization, protecting workers, ending nuclear technologies and other weapons of mass destruction, and taxing international currency speculation for the relief of Third World debt and for the creation of new enterprises which would protect, restore and sustain the biosphere.

In order to do this job as quickly as possible, I have become aware of a brilliant idea proposed by John Bunzl in England. It is called the Simultaneous Policy (see www.simpol.org). Under this plan, measures such as those listed in the previous paragraph would be adopted in principle by any individual, organization, city, state or nation that wishes to do it. (I am already on board as an adopter.) Meanwhile, business-as-usual would continue to prevail, so adoption would pose no immediate threat to existing policies. By the sheer force of attraction, the Simultaneous Policy would then be adopted by more and more nations, until every country has done so. At that moment, the new measures would be implemented simultaneously by each nation to enact the needed paradigm shift. Ideally, this would be the first step for global green democracy in action, without needing yet to establish the new governance structures themselves, which might take a longer time than we have to reverse the accelerating deterioration of life on the planet, as chronicled in my book.   This innovative solution could also allow us plenty of time to debate appropriate measures upon which a majority of people in the world would eventually agree.

The idea could be likened to responding to the outbreak of a serious fire. Whereas pouring buckets of tap water on the fire would never do the job (our current situation of legislating incremental solutions), calling the fire department and waiting for their special equipment to arrive would be what the Simultaneous Policy could do: It would give us the chance to put out the fire once and for all, but at a later time. Our global civic responsibility is to call the firemen to come out quickly, at which time decisive action can reverse the damage. We have been asleep at the wheel of democracy while the fire rages on. It is time to awaken to sustainable solutions and have the courage to embrace them.

There is a deeper spiritual crisis lurking: current power structures are effectively blocking the need to transform our ethics from ruthless competition to cooperation, from selfishness to selflessness, from separation to unity, from greed to generousness, from staying inside a box of the false security of bread-and-circuses to embracing greater truths of our being. President Abraham Lincoln said: "Nearly all men can stand adversity, but if you want to test a man's character, give him power." Power is vested in the wrong places now, and the necessary shift will need to be returned to the people by a global consensus which has no precedent. The design of a new world governance structure will be one of our greatest challenges and opportunities in human history.

The quest for new knowledge of our being is also a birthright which has been diverted to a mass culture that has arbitrarily separated church and state, has confused dogmatic religion with individual spiritual transformation, and has overlooked the enormous potential of a new science of consciousness. I have noticed that many leaders of the sustainability movement have not gone much further than our political, business and religious leaders have in understanding this point, and so are sometimes missing the full range of solutions and spiritual openings - sometimes called miracles. I'm sure some environmentalists will take issue with my attempts to bridge the gap between sustainability and greater truth. Yet my discussion is well-grounded in collective human experience and scientific study. Perhaps, in those moments of inspiration, we could turn crisis into opportunity. Perhaps we could express our grief first and then move into responsible and compassionate roles. I hope my book <u>Re-Inheriting the Earth</u> will help shed some light on some of the basics to ensure an enduring civilization on our dear Planet Earth.

****

Reprinted with author's permission from the book, <u>Reinheriting The Earth, 2nd edition</u> © (2005). *Brian O'Leary received his Ph.D. in astronomy from the University of California at Berkeley in 1967, and was a NASA scientist trained as an astronaut during the Apollo program. He has published over 100 peer-reviewed articles in the scientific literature in planetary science and astronautics, served on the faculties of Cornell University, California Institute of Technology, UC Berkeley, and Princeton University. He was deputy team leader of the Mariner 10 Venus-Mercury television science team, and the author of* <u>Mars 1999</u> *(Harrisburg, PA: Stackpole Books, 1987);* <u>Exploring Inner and Outer Space: A Scientist's Perspective on Personal and Planetary Transformation</u> *(Berkeley, CA: North Atlantic Books, 1989),* <u>The Second Coming of Science</u> *(Berkeley, CA: North Atlantic Books, 1993),* <u>Miracle in the Void</u> *(CA: Knowledge 2020 for DVD and video). His latest* <u>Reinheriting The Earth, 2nd edition</u> *(2005) has been published in Spanish as* <u>Re-heredando la Tierra</u> *(Bridge House Publishers, 2006) and in Portuguese . See* www.brian-oleary.com *to order books & videos. For more information on the Free Energy movement and 21st century research, see* http://www.brianoleary.org

- -

"The environment desperately needs our help. In this groundbreaking and powerful book, Brian tells us how. He uses his unique credentials and expertise as a physicist, new scientist, author, speaker and energy adviser to bring forward concrete solutions to our global dilemma. He boldly states that we can end the fossil fuel age by converting to a new energy economy, using a mix of hydrogen, solar, wind, cold fusion, and zero point energy options. His words are so easy to read and reflect a rich creative imagination which is welcome in such a serious subject. But <u>Re-Inheriting the Earth</u> *is more than a recipe for sustainability. It is a wake-up call for civil action and for developing a new science of consciousness which will surely provide global healing."* Maury Albertson, Ph.D., Professor of Civil Engineering, Colorado State University; Co-Founder of the U.S. Peace Corps

Remembering Tiananmen Square:
An Eye-Witness Account

by a Chinese University student (anonymous by request)

****

In 1989, I was a sophomore studying Aerospace Engineering in a Beijing University, and many in our large campus became active in student protests that spring. I observed and took part in rallies, which grew so large they were held in soccer fields – triggered by the sudden death of the former Chairman of the Communist Party, Hu Yaobang, who had been extremely sympathetic to student concerns and was forced to step down in 1986. Most students felt that he deserved a fair treatment and evaluation of his actions during the 1986 student movement for democracy and openness. . .

The mourning events in downtown Beijing began to draw large numbers of people from across universities in Beijing. The students wore black armbands and gathered in the large Tiananmen Square. As far as I know, these protests were quite and peaceful. However, there was escalation one night: police moved in to 'clear out' the students and began to beat them. I was a total bystander, witnessing these protests because I did not want my mother to worry about me. My mother went through the Culture Revolution, and is extremely timid about doing something against the Communist Party's will. There was much in my own history books about protests and students getting shot and killed before the Communist Party came into power. My opinion was that protest was pretty futile – if the government is corrupt and does not care what the people think.

The burial ceremony took place for the former Chairman of the Party, and police were going to block all traffic in the huge Tiananmen Square. Hence, thousands of university students decided to camp over night near the People's Hall on the side of Tiananmen Square – almost 100,000 students were there. They wanted to submit a petition of request to give the 1986 events a fair evaluation. They waited patiently for several hours but no body came out to accept the petition. Out of frustration, some of the student leaders knelt down in front of the People's Hall, holding the petition above their head.

Eventually, a very low-level official came out and took their petition. The students felt strongly that they were ignored and went back to campus calling for a nation-wide strike. I felt the anger of the students and several told me how humiliated they felt -- that their student leaders had to kneel yet no one even came to hear their protests. Some started to raise money, and protests and rallies became common place in our university. The university administrators were almost invisible during this period of turmoil, contrary to their usual role of having a strong hand on student events.

The media did not report any of the student movements, as if these were not happening. As time went by, the students became more and more impatient and frustrated, feeling that we were totally ignored despite our best effort to draw attention to our concerns. What shocked us all, however, was suddenly out of blue, the official Communist Party newspapers had a headline describing student groups as "mobs" and menacingly affirmed: "We need to crack down on this anti-communist radical movement: they are disturbing the social stability of our country."

April 27th, 1989: The media was broadcasting a very one-sided view and the student leaders were shocked – most thought that they had initially asked for very simple things: a fair evaluation of a former national leader. But language in the Party newspaper was getting harsher: we were now described as "criminals" and anyone who participated was being warned of "repercussions". This fanned the fire with students who felt completely misrepresented and unheard.

Several days before the historic visit of then Soviet Union leader Gorbychov to Beijing, the students decide to have a hunger strike at Tiananmen Square. At the beginning, the people participated in the movement were mostly students. As the sirens of the ambulance rushing students who had fainted to the hospital became more frequent, more and more Beijing citizens joined us. People donated coats to the students to fend off the early morning chill and restaurants catered the students with truckload of foods.

In the daytime, millions of people streamed through the Square to show their support and demanded that the government to have a dialogue with the students to end the hunger strike. Even the media started to report the student movement. I spent many days and nights in the Square, feeling the power of the people. I was so proud to be part of the movement because I believe the movement has helped the ordinary Chinese step out of the shadow of the Culture Revolution and feel free to express their opinions publicly. All these hopes were shattered when the Communist Party declared a curfew and announced that they will bring the troops in to "restore stability." Even though the troops were blocked outside of Beijing by the regular citizens, the tone in the media changed. People were warned **not** to go to the Square any more. More and more people began to ponder about the direction of the movement. Students started to leave Beijing to other cities as the standoff between the students and the government in the Tiananmen Square had no end in sight.

I went home, deeply troubled, in late May. It was with shock, far out in the country where we lived, that a telegram came delivered to me from a fellow student: "Come back to the University! Classes will start again on June 1st." So, knowing the consequences for not attending my engineering classes, I dutifully went back to crowded Beijing. However, most of the dormitories were still empty. I have no idea why the school office want to re-start the class on June 1st as the demonstration in Tiananmen Square was still continuing and had no sign of ending. On June 3rd, I decided to go alone to Tiananmen Square.

It looked _very_ different: there were tents and yet the number of students who were occupying the side of the Square was much smaller. However, public transportation wasn't running that early in the morning, so I was walking along, and heard rumors that soldiers had attempted to advance towards the Square the night before -- with their combat weapons! On the street, Beijing citizens were talking about how they spotted the plain-clothed soldiers and stopped them way before they reached the Square.

I decided to head over towards the government complexes, about a block west of Tiananmen Square, and the students there were displaying the knives, helmets, metal chains to choke students, and other wretched devices they had taken from the plain-clothes soldiers earlier. Not far from the government complex, a bus full of weapons was being surrounded by the angry crowds. Why would they use these against our own students? Machine guns were displayed on top of the roof. While I was watching, a policeman came forward and told the students that "You must turn these weapons to the police --- these are military weapons!" However, the student leaders just brushed him off – they ignored him.

In hindsight, I wish the students had listened to him because one of the excuses for the troops to open fire the following night was that the "mobs" had taken weapons from the soldiers. I decided to head back to the university --- but suddenly I saw people running, frightened, towards us. I was told tear gas was being used, and soldiers with clubs had come out of the government complex, beating people on the way, and took all the weapons on display back to the government complex. People were trying desperately to wash their faces and man-powered tricycles were rushing the wounded to the hospital.

At that time, I didn't think things had gotten that bad. So, I started briskly walking back to the government complex. When I got there, there were two rows of soldiers guarding the entrance. The police had drawn their clubs, but now people in the growing crowd were shouting. I was curious as well as afraid, but it seems that nothing happened in the 'stand-off' between police and the citizens that day.

By evening, back at the university, the official school broadcast station started to broadcast the announcement from the government through the loudspeakers across campus, "Students! Everyone must remain on campus! If you go out, you are responsible for your own life!". My roommate, a small woman like myself, knew that I had gone to Tiananmen Square so she left in a hurry on her bicycle before sunset to find me -- at the same time I was walking BACK to the campus. How ironic, I thought as I asked our friends where she was.

However, I decided not to go back to the city and break the curfew, but grew more and more concerned for my kind roommate. No one could fall asleep that tense night. About 2AM, my roommate finally arrived, exhausted, back at the University. She told me she had been 'hanging out' until about 11PM in Tiananmen Square until things got very tense there. She decided to leave, but it became increasingly difficult....

On her way back, she had looked up – and saw huge military tanks approaching! The tanks were going so fast that she jumped off her bike and hid in a doorway, crouching there with several other frightened Beijing citizens. One woman had already been hit by tear gas and was crying. Later, my roommate told me in a shaking voice that night, if she had not jumped out of the way, she would have certainly been crushed by the oncoming tank...

As dawn broke, we began to check who came back to campus and who was not yet back... It was a very emotional day. The students have taken over the school's broadcast station and those who came back from the Square described how they nearly escape death or how people risked their lives to save other people, through the loudspeaker. Students and teachers alike gathered around, tried to understand what happened the night before. As time went by, we became more and more worried about our classmates who had not came back to campus and our teachers began riding bicycle to other campuses to see if the bodies collected there were their students...

If anything, before this week, I still had some hope for the Chinese Communist Party. I heard from my parents about the horrible acts the Communist Party had conducted during the Cultural Revolution of the 1960's. However, I believe they have learned from their mistakes and it is their genuine interests to serve the people and the country. In the summer of 1989, I was awaken to the harsh reality that the Party just wants to stay in power, no matter what the cost. Considering that how many people have lost their lives during the Culture Revolution, the "few" lives lost in 1989 does not mean anything to them.

Years have passed. The international media showed photos of several solitary, brave Chinese students in Tiananmen Square, standing up to the tanks. How many around the world, however, knew that there were <u>literally millions</u> of us, standing up to the corrupt government, that summer in the Square? Our old leaders had passed but the corrupt ones are still in control. I realized with a heavy heart that protest doesn't work if the government doesn't want to change.

Hence, I began to prepare to immigrate, and am now writing this from an American coffee shop. I am now 35, preparing to move from one university to another university, to continue my engineering research as a professor. Even if I had known that the Communist Party and military would have 'cracked down' through violence (and we now know that many student leaders are still missing, either in prison alone or dead) – I myself would not have resorted to violence in my protest. It is not worth it! Each loss of life is a tragedy, no matter this loss come from the students, the citizens, or even the soldiers. What still puzzles me is that how can the soldiers blindly follow the order of the government and kill innocent people who were demanding a better government for all of us -- including the soldiers <u>and</u> the soldiers' families.

In terms of peace, I have reflected that we need new ways to "change" governments that don't want to change. I lost my faith in the Communist way of governance and now wonder about America and its wars….It seems that each government has a means to make the people believe in their propaganda and to die for their "just" course. Sitting in a U.S. coffee shop, I wonder if it is possible that we can teach our next generation about independent thinking and to judge between truth and propaganda. A government can not do evil deeds without the support of the people who blindly believe that the government is doing the "right" thing.

****

Narrated by a 38 year old Chinese female Engineering Professor, reflecting upon her memories, who wishes to remain anonymous.

Making Peace Work an Integral Part of One's Lifetime

By Charles Mercieca

President, International Association of Educators for World Peace (IAEWP)
Professor Emeritus, Alabama A&M University History Dept.

****

Ascetical writings tell us that minutes before our life comes to an end, we receive a bird's eye view of our entire life. We see how many good things we did in life that would fill us with consolation. We also see how many bad things we did in life that we wish we had not done. We then feel the desire to reverse the "clock of history" to undo the unpleasant things we did. But then we realize that we cannot reverse the clock -- under no circumstance whatsoever.

However, there is a way or approach that we could use that would eventually enable us to reverse the clock of history to do things that were thoroughly beneficial to the welfare of all people without exception. Beginning *at this very moment*, let us examine what we did so far in our lifetime. We need to retain all those things that are viewed as blessings and we need to proceed to amend all those things we did that caused others to suffer in a number of ways.

Relative to newer actions in life, we need to put ourselves into the future before taking such new actions and ask to ourselves: How would such an action look ten to twenty years from now? Would I be proud of myself? Would the world be better as a result of me? If the answers are positive then we may proceed with the action we plan to take. If the answers are negative then we should refrain from taking such actions by all means whatsoever. Let us always keep in mind that prevention is better than cure.

One of the greatest injustices in the history of human experience lies in the waging of wars of one kind or another. In the recorded history of 6,000 years, there has never been a war that proved to be beneficial afterwards to a particular region and the world at large in the long term.

Yet, we keep on waging wars, killing and maiming thousands of innocent people that mostly consist of women, children, the elderly and the sick.

On August 14, 2004, Larry King of CNN interviewed Heather Mills (ex-wife of Paul McCartney from the Beatles), who is very much involved in the elimination of landmines from the surface of our planet. She talked of the hundreds of children in the city of Basra in Iraq that had one or both legs amputated as a result of the war waged by the United States. It was very sad and quite emotional to see these dear and lovely children struggling to lead a normal life the best they can. It is certainly criminal for any nation to take the initiative to wage wars when so many innocent people are killed or maimed for life.

However, since those in power assumed the authority to do what they like, nothing could stop them from performing the most beastly and savage actions in the world. They are convinced that no one would dare to punish them because of their heinous acts. In fact, government officials involved in the atrocities of war speak of such infernal actions of theirs as acts of "heroism" and "patriotism" and as a means of "defense" of one's country! And to turn an insult into injury, they refer to innocent Americans killed in the hands of terrorists as "victims" yet to the innocent Iraqi people killed or brutally maimed with American ammunition as merely "collateral damage!"

As Pope Pius XII said on the eve of World War II, "In a war no one is a winner; everyone is a loser." Both Germany and Great Britain had their respective nations devastated; their infrastructure destroyed; and millions left dead. On virtually the eve of the Iraqi war, Pope John Paul II warned US President Bush that waging a war against Iraq would prove to be a great mistake. He underlined that terrorism, instead of being brought "under control" would eventually be augmented and that the world, as a result of this war, would be less safe.

In Iraq, the USA is trying to win one battle after another, but it is losing the war at a more rapid pace than anticipated. Most nations view US military actions as a sign of arrogance and abuse. As a result, they feel now quite alienated from their "ally". Thousands of young Moslems, who never thought of ever resorting to war, are now giving a second thought to joining forces to align with Muslim leaders. Confronted with such brutal realities that the innocent Iraqi people are facing, many young Moslems are now determined that their only purpose in life would be to do something harmful to the USA! Would it be the destruction of a nuclear plant that might cause the death of some two million Americans almost overnight? Or worse? Who knows!

The year the United States invaded Iraq, the South African statesman, former President Nelson Mandela said: "The United States is emerging to be the most dangerous country on Earth."   Most people in the USA have never had the _experience_ of a war fought in its own territory, with numerous cities literally reduced to rubble and with countless millions of innocent people killed or maimed. Hence, the American people do not have the direct experience of the ravages of war. This means, they are not, as a whole, in a position to put pressure on their own government to avoid waging wars by all means whatsoever. To make things worse, they seem all to have been indoctrinated with the idea that the American waging of wars is done for self-defense purposes, and that young Americans fighting wars in other countries are to be viewed as heroes.

My Story of War and Peace

I was born and raised on the Island of Malta, which served as a strong military fortress of the British in World War II. In fact, our island was so heavily fortified by the military that the mighty NAZI military forces could not take it, even though they blockaded it for three years. The Germans also bombarded it with 30,000 bombs weekly during this same period. In fact, three-fourths of the island was virtually wiped out and every single Maltese family had relatives killed and/or maimed -- that applied to our family as well. During this horrible time of utter devastation, I was merely six years old. By age 9, I had seen a great deal of the horrors of war.

When World War II started in 1939 between Nazi Germany and Great Britain, the people in Malta became highly alerted, since Malta then was a British territory. To make things worse, Italy joined NAZI Germany against Great Britain. Considering that Malta was so small, just 144 square miles consisting of three major islands, and considering the vicinity to Italy, barely 60 miles, the Maltese people were very much afraid. They prayed to God every day from morning until night to save the island from annihilation that would involve the death of thousands of its inhabitants.

My father had two jobs to make ends meet in some way. He worked as a custom officer whose job was to verify all the food imported to Malta and then report it to the government. He also was a Special Constable during the war. As such, he had to work as an extended arm of both the military and the police. Among other things, he would help and assist to save those whose houses were hit by bombs where people might have been buried alive. Of course, my mother was busy taking care of the three little children. World War II was a terrible experience, and I learned early that war that is not worth it, even for a billion dollars.

Needless to say, with that heavy Nazi bombardment day and night, we had to sleep in shelters deep underground for three years. Among other suffered inconveniences, we may mention the sleeping on shelves squeezed with other people, the lack of fresh air, the absence of toilet facilities, and the lack of food and water. Of course, the schools were closed because they were used as hospitals to house numerous injured people. One of the awful experiences I had was when someone sleeping near you dies during the night and you find yourself stuck with a dead body until the morning with nothing that you can do.

A cousin of mine, who was 17 years of age, just eleven years older than me, joined the military to help the British fighting the Nazis. During the week he often came down to the shelter to play with little children of my own age. He really entertained us and we loved him dearly. Three months later, he was machine-gunned by the Nazis and died shortly afterwards. In the meantime, some of my close friends who happened not to make it to the shelter on time during air raids, died buried in the rubble of their own houses. At age six and seven I could not understand why my good friends who were so little and so good and so harmless were killed so brutally.

Confronted by such reality, I decided that if I were to survive the war I would spend the rest of my life studying, especially foreign languages, and traveling to see what could be done to contribute toward the avoidance of the repetition of a senseless and brutal war. World War II came to an end in 1945 when I was 12 years old. This personal experience of war gave me some unique insights that those who never witnessed a devastating war in their own country could never have. I may speak about one experience, which may help us to realize and understand the fallacy of any nation's approach to the solution of world problems through the use of the military and the waging of wars.

I recall every evening people hugging and kissing each other and saying to each other with tears in their eyes: "This may be the last time that we may be seeing each other. Today we are alive, tomorrow we may be dead." And then they would turn to their children with tears in their eyes, hug and kiss them and press them to their heart while asking God to keep them alive. People were so afraid that you could see some of them literally trembling. As the months passed by, there began to be a great shortage of food. The Maltese government created what was termed "victory kitchens." All groceries were closed and the government created several victory kitchens in each city. People would form lines in the morning, at noon, and in the evening for breakfast, lunch and supper.

The food distributed was little but there was enough for everyone to just survive. From 1940 to 1943 Malta was bombarded through air raids some six to seven times a day. As the infrastructure of the island was destroyed, and as more than one half of the nation was obliterated, the Nazis presented the Maltese people with an ultimatum: They stated: "If you surrender, we will feed you: we will give you all you need, and we will help rebuild the island. If you choose not to surrender, we will continue to devastate the rest of the country. You have only one week to think about it and to make your decision."

I recall there was panic in the initial hours following this ultimatum. But then I noticed there was complete calmness among people who prayed from the bottom of their heart to the Blessed Virgin Mary in particular to be delivered from this dilemma. Then it took the Maltese people not one week to come with a decision but merely 24 hours. And the reply to the Nazis was unanimous: "DEATH but No Surrender." And I recall, from that moment every single fear that the Maltese had of the war, of annihilation and death disappeared completely.

Each time the Nazis came to bombard Malta, many of the people, including children, did not go down into a shelter for fear of being killed. On the contrary, they remained out in the streets to watch air fights between the British and the NAZI planes. Moreover, children played what was termed to be the "ladder game." This game consisted of children climbing on the shoulders of each other while holding themselves against the wall and then with a black chalk in their hands would write at the various levels of the wall in large block letters: DEATH BUT NO SURRENDER.

I recall I felt so good to see my relatives and friends for the first time since war started three years earlier with radiant faces, serene, and literally fearless. This is something that the American government officials cannot realize and understand simply because they never had a devastating war taking place on their own soil where entire cities would be annihilated and with millions of Americans left dead. This means, the American government is incapable of understanding that when you use the military, weapons of mass destruction and serious threats to control a population, it will all fire back. People become even more determined than ever before to resist you and to fight you.

The United States should have learned from Vietnam, Cambodia and other small nations that a strong military equipped with the most sophisticated weapons of destruction cannot obliterate an ideology. They can destroy the infrastructure of a nation and kill of maim thousands, even amounting to millions of people, but unless the ideology is destroyed the US can only win battles but never a war. Ideology could be overcome only through education which is based on the promotion and protection of the universal welfare of all people without exception.

In 1966 General Westmoreland, commander of the US military forces in Vietnam, made a special trip to the University of Kansas for the commencement address there. I happened to have been there present since I was then graduating with a Ph.D. Among other things, he remarked: The Americans in Vietnam have the most sophisticated weapons you can imagine to literally win the war. At the same time, the Vietnamese come to confront us with rifles that we use in the USA to hunt for rabbits or birds. Yet, we just cannot subdue them. We cannot bring them under control. And we know the rest of the story. The United States lost the war because they could not bring under their full control an ideology through the military and weapons.

We are all familiar that you can catch more flies with honey. One of the most conspicuous problems in the United States lies in the fact that there is a strong tendency in the nation that those who had been involved in a war by fighting in it, are more qualified to lead the nation because, they say, they can understand the nature of war better. This is a false and deceitful assumption because when American soldiers are involved into a war overseas, they are fighting a war as invaders and occupiers. They are not fighting the war as being invaded and being occupied.

This means that the American soldiers, who later may run for a political office including the Office of the US President, do not have a clear understanding of the psychology of war as it exists in the mind of the people whose country was invaded and occupied, like the recent case with Iraq. They cannot understand, by all means that the presentation of a so-called strong military and more weapons will only amount to strengthening the people's will and determination to fight back, using other means at their disposal and different tactics. We view such means and tactics as terrorism but they view these same means and tactics as the only element they have to threaten the USA for their self-defense purposes.

We all recall what the Master Teacher of Nazareth said regarding the rich who were hopelessly attached to the material things of this world. He said: It is much easier for a camel to pass through the eye of a needle than it is for a rich man to enter the kingdom of heaven. Regarding the US government, we may formulate with accuracy a similar statement by saying: It is easier to bring to life a dead man than it is for the US government to realize that the military, wars and weapons will instigate more enemies in the long range and that the USA will be more vulnerable. Since the USA is built on a capitalistic system, where money is viewed as the God of the nation, the situation becomes even more complicated.

The weapons industry has emerged as the most lucrative business in the nation where many, including government members, have invested interest. Hence, many believe that the US government has agents whose job is to create turmoil around the world through more struggles between nations and factions within the same nation, the purpose of which is the justification of the manufacture and sales of more and more weapons. In fact, many notice that while US government officials, by word of mouth they speak of "peace", but in action, they constantly promote the causes of wars.

Since 1967, I had the opportunity to visit almost every state of the American nation and well over 90 countries. During such visits, I conducted lectures and discussions in more than 50 universities in the USA alone and in over 100 universities across every continent on a global scale. My purpose was to explore what kind of interest teachers had all over the world in using their profession for the promotion of international understanding and world peace through education. I found that all teachers and all students were very much concerned with the culture of war, which they wanted to replace with the culture of peace.

President Eisenhower's Warning

This reminded me of the words former US President Eisenhower spoke to the entire assembled US Congress in his "Farewell Speech". He said emphatically: "Remember that all people of all nations want peace: only their government wants war." As a result of these world-wide educational tours of mine, the International Association of Educators for World Peace came into existence upon its legal incorporation in the USA on April 25, 1969. In 1970, it was declared a tax-exempt organization and in 1973, it became a Non-Governmental Organization (NGO) under the United Nations, linked with the Economic and Social Council and UNESCO. Later, it also became linked with the UN Department of Public Information and UNICEF as well.

We are all familiar with the scriptural saying: Judge a tree by the fruit it gives. This means that if a tree is viewed as an orange tree but it produces lemons, then we have to call it a lemon tree. The United States is virtually the only major nation in the world that hates to see nations being demilitarized, that detests seeing nations inserting in their constitution a clause that would prohibit rearmament and the involvement in wars. The United States views all this as loss of profit from its unlimited manufacture and sales of military weapons.

Recently, Japan has been considered by the United Nations to become a member of the UN Security Council. That would be very appropriate for a number of reasons. Japan's population is well over 100 million. Besides, this country is very advanced in both education and technology. In addition, it has written in the constitution that Japan cannot build an army and get engaged into wars. Confronted with this reality, the United States had the arrogance to ask Japan recently to change its constitution in a way that it could start rebuilding an army that could be engaged in numerous wars.

In recent years, the USA sent top officials to visit as many countries as possible where the military and the purchase of weapons happen not to be a nation's priority. The purpose was to instigate such nations to purchase modern weapons and to develop a strong military. One example was the island of Malta that was completely devastated in World War II. This nation secured its independence from Great Britain in 1964 and one of the first things it did was to abolish the military. The money that would have gone for the military and to purchase weapons went for the education and health care of the people where now the Maltese enjoy free education and health care.

Even here, the United States, one of its top government officials tried to bring Malta's President under its tight control by urging him to ignore the nation's constitution and proceed to rearm this peaceful island. Because of the fact that in the United States, the news media is heavily censured, the American people have no way to know how belligerent their nation has become on a global scale! They are not aware that the censorship of the press in America is very similar to that same type of censorship that was witnessed in the former Soviet Union under Stalin and the Chinese nation under Mao. Such censorship differed only in style. The ultimate goal of American censorship has been to prevent people from learning about the belligerent foreign policies of the US government.

The International Association of Educators for World Peace has now branches in more than 90 nations. Its members come from every walk of life and profession. They work hard to secure common objectives that promote progress, stability, prosperity and peace. Among such goals we have: 1) Promotion of international understanding and world peace through education, 2) Protection of the environment from pollution, 3) Safeguard of human rights in accordance with the UN "Universal Declaration of Human Rights", and 4) Disarmament and development of the human resources for positive and constructive purposes.

For over 30 years that has been my job and the job of thousands of my colleagues from across every continent. No matter how difficult our task may be to bring about peace in the world, peace workers will never give up. They will keep on moving forward knowing for sure that world peace will eventually become a tangible reality at one time or another.

This has been a brief story summarizing a lifetime involvement in peace work. In telling my story, I felt compelled to write about the rationale that instigated me, along with many colleagues of mine from around the world, to study quite a few languages, to travel across the world, and to dedicate all of my energy to the good cause of peace for the entire human race. Those who spent their lifetime working for the welfare of all people without exception, like Mother Teresa and Mahatma Gandhi, in addition to numerous others, have made an enormous difference in our world. Because of such altruistic human beings, there is great hope which lies ahead in the horizon --- and we will eventually reach our hope for world peace before we even know it.

****

Dr. Charles Mercieca is the President of the International Association of Educators for World Peace, which is a non-governmental organization (NGO) of the United Nations since 1973. To date, this organization has branches in more than 90 countries, including the USA. Its members come from every walk of life and profession and they are all *volunteers.*

The objectives of this organization may be summarized as follows: peace education programs, environmental protection, organization of peace conferences, safeguarding of human rights, disarmament education, and development of the human resources for positive and constructive purposes of communicating about peace around the world.

International Association of Educators for World Peace (IAEWP) is an NGO and is an official *"Affiliate organization"* of the United Nations' Economic and Social Council

(ECOSOC); United Nations' Educational, Scientific and Cultural Organization (UNESCO) *and* United Nations International Children's Educational Fund (UNICEF).

Dr. Mercieca is a Member of many educational organizations including the Russian Academy of Pedagogical Sciences, National Education Association, World Council for Curriculum and Instruction, and the Philosophy of Education Society. He is the author of six books including Crucial Issues Facing the World *(2004),* Marian Spirituality: Key to Eternal Happiness *(2004),* The Way of Love and Repentance in the Church of the Third Millennium *(published in Russian, 1997),* Marian Apparitions: Meaning and Purpose *(published in English and Russian, 1997),* World Peace and Spirituality of the 3rd Millennium *(published in both English and Russian, 1996), and* Mismanagement in Higher Education: A Case Study *(1986).*

Dr. Mercieca can be contacted at mercieca@knology.net *and see* www.iaewp.org *for upcoming events of the International Association of Educators for World Peace.*

Practicing 'Compassionate Listening':
A Trip to Israel and Palestine

by Lung Ogle

A Vietnamese-American Peace Activist

****

I view my first trip to Israel and Palestine as an "eye-opener". I would like to relate my impressions as a woman, a U.S. citizen and peace activist, and discuss some of the highlights and organizations which are working very hard on reconciliation between Palestinians and Israelis. I am of Chinese origin, born in Vietnam, and truly felt amazed at the situation (and tensions) both Israelis and Palestinians face on a daily basis in their land.

On November 7, 2004, we visited Israel and Palestine as a group to practice "compassionate listening". We listened to both sides' stories. After we came back, we hoped to influence our government to make clear decisions, which will assuage the divisive feuds and enmities of both sides and help them live side by side in peace.

We were a group of ten: seven women and three men, six American Jews, three Christians and one American Buddhist. We ranged in age from 50 to 83. Our trip was sponsored by the organization Promoting Enduring Peace (PEP), which was established in 1952. This organization advances the cause of peace by seeking ways to bring people together, to encourage dialog and to promote mutual understanding. Our goal is to change the social paradigm from one of competition to one of cooperation, from a culture of violence and war to a world devoted to its peoples' mutual benefit and peace. Compassionate Listening training is one of the programs of PEP, and it is an important peace-making tool.

While we are listening to others, we stay present. We don't offer advice, don't try to fix anyone or situation, or give any suggestions. The skill of *deep empathic listening* is an ability which can be learned! It is also a vital skill to bring people together as they recognize their common needs, fears, hopes and humanity. We listen with our hearts, not with our ears: true peace work, from inner to outer.

On November 8th, we arrived at Tel Aviv at 10:30 p.m. and transferred to the Old City section of Jerusalem, to the sector where many Muslims live. Taxi drivers refused to take us there because insurance doesn't cover them. The first thing that came to my mind was that we might be blown into pieces. We negotiated with the drivers and they finally agreed to take us -- but only dropped us off outside the Old City. We had to haul our own luggage on the narrow rocky road about one third of a mile to the convent (called "Ecce Homo"), where we stayed with Catholic nuns for two nights. The stone wall surrounding the convent is very thick and high. There is a TV security monitor, by which the people inside can see everything outside very clearly. We had to ring the bell before we entered. They do not open the door unless they recognize the person. The rooms are very simple but this place is safe.

In the afternoon, we walked up along the famed Via Dolorosa, the path where Jesus walked when he was crucified. We visited the Holy Church, where we saw places where Jesus was taken down from the Cross, where he was laid down and where he was buried. After dinner, we went to the Wailing Wall, where Jewish men pray on the right and women on the left. Every morning we were wakened around 4:30a.m. by the Palestinians' Muslim dawn prayers. What a holy city Jerusalem is!

Everywhere we walked, we saw soldiers pointing their rifles at us, which made us very nervous. What was going on today? While we having dinner at a Palestinian restaurant, we saw thousands of Palestinian civilians and suddenly, Israeli soldiers as they stormed into the Old City, which made us even more nervous. While I was shopping with other ladies at a store, the owner told us that "Arafat was finished". The moment I heard it, I dropped everything and rushed back to the convent. I didn't want to find myself in the middle of an confrontation or riot that might ensue. However, the transition was a peaceful one.

On November 9, we drove to Samaria, as it was called during the time of Jesus. The program was facilitated by Rabbi Ascherman, who belongs to the organization Rabbis for

Human Rights, the only Israeli organization comprised of Reform, orthodox, conservative, reconstructionists, and Renewal Rabbis. Our American group and Rabbinical group leaders climbed a rocky hill for about a mile to an Oliver grove where we helped a Palestinian family pick olives. Picking olives in occupied territories is not like picking oranges in the United States. It was a very strenuous day! Most Palestinians rely on olives for their living. We had to stop at a one or two checkpoints halfway to our destination, and Israeli soldiers questioned us briefly. Our work for peace was simple: we were down on our hands and knees by the end of the day, and scraped the small black oliver from the ground. Although we do not speak Arabic, we communicated with our *hearts* and made many Palestinian friends.

On the morning of November 10, we arrived at Hebron, an old city where Palestinian Muslims live. They are constantly under the surveillance and control of the Israeli soldiers. This city has about 120,000 Palestinians and about 500 Jewish settlers. There are two kinds of roads: one paved road is for the settlers and the other, a dirt road for the Palestinians. As we were holding American passports, we could walk on either one: that was a metaphor for our entire trip.

We met with an organization called the Christian Peacemaker Team (CPT). The team is a program of active peacemaking supported by Church of the Brethren/Menonite Church of Canada, the Menonite Church USA and the active Quaker Friends organization. They walked us through the market and showed us the soup kitchen, which was established by donations from the local people and which provides food to Palestinian children. The poverty in Hebron hit us as we wandered through the streets. Almost all the shops were closed except stalls in narrow alleyways. Member of CPT usually escort Palestinian children to school and to the soup kitchen, since the children are often harassed by Israeli soldiers and settlers. The impoverished situation struck us to the point where we gave up our food allowances to them.

Arrangements were made for nine of us to stay overnight with two different Palestinian families. Our leader, Yael Petretti, stayed with her Palestinian friend. Five of us -- four women and one man (three of us were Jewish) -- stayed with one Palestinian family. The host has a beautiful wife and two lovely young children. All his brothers and sisters, nephews, and nieces live nearby. After dinner, their cousins, neighbors and friends, who were all males, came to spend time talking about the problems they faced with the occupation. Our hostess (who speaks good English) then retired to her room and we women, as tradition is the norm here, were not allowed to engage in the men's conversation.

Around 9:00 p.m. that night, we heard big trucks running on the road and our host said, "The soldiers are here again to search houses." In order not to arouse the Israeli soldiers' suspicion, our host let the windows remain open. Peeping out of the windows, we saw the soldiers search every house across the street and drag children, men and women out the house. Several men were stripped to their waists for the search. The soldiers made the Palestinians they pulled out of the house stand behind them as a human shield. We heard gunfire and we were scared. As the Israeli soldiers already ransacked out host's house in the morning, we escaped being searched again. This scenario was never published in the newspapers. All we read in the U.S. newspapers often is that Palestinians may be suicide bombers or "terrorists". We need to open our hearts and minds to all possibilities about both sides of this conflict, and become conscious of the fact that all things have cause and effect. In Israel and Palestine, both sides have their own agendas and both sides have made mistakes.

During our conversation, one of the ladies from our American suddenly spoke up: "You Palestinians have suffered as much as the Jews suffered from the Holocaust years ago." Our Palestinian friend immediately refuted her, saying, "There was no such a thing as a holocaust and the Jews are liars." This accusation made me jump to the edge of my seat. One of the Jewish ladies already wanted to defend herself and the atmosphere suddenly turned tense.

Fortunately, I managed to placate her. Listening compassionately sometimes is not easy, especially when what other people say conflicts with what you know to be true. The next day we had difficulty walking through the checkpoints and it took us more than three hours to walk to the place where the bus was waiting for us. While we were driving back to Jerusalem from Hebron, we ran into thousands of Palestinian men walking in procession, chanting and mourning for Arafat's death. The atmosphere at that moment made our skin crawl. However, we were in the midst of "history in the making"!

We felt so relieved when we arrived at Jerusalem and we forgot we might run into a suicide bomber on the street or at a restaurant there. One of the ladies was so scared that she cried, saying that she would never come back and that she had the right not to submit herself to this dangerous situation.

During the next few days, we visited several organizations, which are working hard on reconciliation. One of my favorite highlights of this trip was attending Shabbat service at *Kol HaNeshama* conducted by Rabbi Kelman. During the service, people chanted and sang in Hebrew from the beginning to the end. Rabbi Kelman was chanting and singing while his hands were tapping on the podium. There were no musical instruments. Non-Jews visit their congregation regularly and I learned that the Latin Patriarch, Micheal Sabbah, attended a Shabbat service. His entourage included the Bishop of Nazareth and nuns and assorted priests wearing large crucifixes on the chest and purple *kippots* on their heads. After the service, I was quite surprised to hear the announcement that the discussion on the subject of the "end of the occupation" would be on Sunday. It seemed that all Jewish members of this synagogue supported the creation of a Palestinian state.

Many people are working very hard building bridges through peace work. I wish to be one of them and do something good for a better tomorrow. We often hear people say, "We die for nothing if nothing good comes from us." During this trip to Israel and Palestine, I certainly learned that we must strive to listen to "both sides" if we are truly to do good for this world.

****

Lung was born in 1941 in Hanoi, a city in Northern Vietnam, second of five children. After the fall of Dien Bien Phu during the civil war in 1954, the whole family moved to Cambodia in 1956, where she met my future husband, Wayne at the age of 15. Shortly before Cambodia's government became unstable, her parents sent her elder sister and Lung (their family was of Chinese descent) to Taiwan for high school and college education. From that time, they never saw their father again.

In 1975, the Khmer Rouge took over Cambodia. She recalls vividly: "My younger sister's whole family were executed the moment the communist soldiers broke in. Our parents starved to death on the road while trying to flee for their lives during the infamous evacuation of all Cambodian cities. My brother was sent by my parents to France, but we have not been able to locate him. Growing up in French Indochina, we went through several civil wars during my childhood in Vietnam. This prompted me eventually to become a peace worker for life."

Lung Ogle earned her Bachelor's degree in English and Master's degree in Linguistics at National Taiwan Normal University, and also took additional classes at the University of North Carolina in Charlotte and Chapel Hill. She belongs to the Tai Ji Men Qigong Academy in Taiwan, and was also an active board member of an organization known as Promoting Enduring Peace in Connecticut. She has visited more than 60 countries for conferences or pleasure. She affirms: "I am especially interested in visiting countries where there is political unrest. I went on a trip to Vietnam in 2002 and one to Israel and Palestine in 2004, both of which were sponsored by Promoting Enduring Peace. Not having gone through war, most of the children and young people here in the United States do not know what pain and suffering taste like. We sometimes do not value what we have." You can correspond with Lung via lungogle@aol.com.

Why Do Men Make War? The Art of Peacemaking: A Human Necessity

By Michael Whitty and Dan Butts

University of Detroit-Mercy Graduate School of Business

Detroit, Michigan

****

Historian Alexander DeConde has written a book, <u>Presidential Machismo:</u> <u>Executive Authority, Military Intervention, and Foreign Relations</u> (Northeastern University Press, 2002), that explores a dimension of warfare that is not well-understood, yet helps explain the policies, behavior, and rhetoric of Bush, Rumsfeld, Powell, Perle, and other superhawks. As the <u>Oxford English Dictionary</u> states, "machismo" connotes an exaggerated masculine pride, an admiration of physical aggressiveness, and an entitlement to dominate, often associated with military violence.

DeConde adds that social scientists now recognize that the macho stimulus runs through much of American society, war is one of the most rigidly "gendered" activities known to humankind. Until recently most societies viewed the contest of arms as providing proof of male vigor, and that other societies (though not all) have similar attitudes toward masculine behavior and dominance. In his book, DeConde examines the foreign/war policy records of every American president through Bill Clinton. He describes how many presidents aggrandized their war powers and engaged in the unrestrained practice of unilateral executive war-making, often undertaken for personal, political, and power considerations. Often, however, this military recklessness heightens presidential approval ratings.

War is the most destructive of all human activities (injustice, especially poverty, is a close second). Very few societies (or tribes) in human history have not engaged in war. Hence, this is an exploration of these tales.

Historical and Evolutionary Possibilities for Justice and Peace

Jean Houston, philosopher and master teacher, has written <u>Manual for the Peacemaker: An Iroquois Legend to Heal Self and Society</u>, based upon the work of Deganawidah who founded the Iroquois Confederacy of five Indian nations between 1000 and 1500 A.D. at the end of several generations of bloody and divisive warfare between the five nations. The democratic ideals and organization of the Iroquois League, which accorded women relative equality, influenced the great social theorists of the Enlightenment, like Rousseau and Voltaire, and Benjamin Franklin who began publishing the Pennsylvania Gazette, one of the first American newspapers in the 1730s.

Franklin later incorporated Iroquois principles into the Albany Congress plan that had a major impact 20 years later on the Articles of Confederation for the Colonies and was the key in creation of the U.S. Constitution and formation of the young American republic. Deganawidah, who had a severe stutter, Hiawatha, and their allies used a combination of healing methods, including singing and dancing, massage, realigning of energies, a medicine ceremony, and political persuasion. They sang a peace hymn that is still sung today. The peace hymn, a hymn of thanksgiving, was also known as the "Six Songs." In her book Houston adapts eight steps, and processes (rituals), in becoming the Peacemaker.

- *Embrace the Open Moment and Do the Impossible.* Deganawidah was able to float a stone canoe. We can work from our inmost truth and accomplish seemingly impossible tasks by discarding outmoded, limiting beliefs about ourselves.

- *Embrace the True Message and Stop Nourishing the Toxic Raiders.* Wholeheartedly affirm the good news of peace and power, and stop feeding the negative forces in our lives.

- *Welcome the Consciousness that Carries the Mind of the Maker and Become a Partner of Creation.* Find symbols, metaphors, and other ways of accessing our whole brain/mind (and Great Mind) to find new solutions to old problems.

- *Go Toward the Sunrise, See the True Face of the Other, and Admit Your Handicaps.* See everyone as a deep ally in the soul's journey. To embrace the New Mind, "we must look fearlessly without denial at what we have been and, perhaps, to some extent, still are."

- *Risk the Fall into a New Form and Hack Away the Tree of Falsehood.* Your truth will be tested again and again. Welcome opportunities, even when there's opposition, to confront lies and speak your highest truth.

- *Lift Grief and Allow Your Griefs to Reveal their Full Story.* Telling our life story deepens and enriches its meaning, and energizes and clarifies the potentials of our path. A partner can witness our grief and use condolence beads to touch our throat, ears, and eyes to lift the darkness with new vision.

- *Work with a Larger Circle of Allies, Heal the Crooked One, and Invest the Crooked One with a Higher Usefulness.* There are many tools to help heal our enemies and the debilitating lies in our profession.

- *Meet in Councils of Cooperation and Co-creation and Plant and Nurture the Great Tree of Peace.* Create new forms of authentically democratic community based on the desire for justice, health, and spiritual power.

- *Peace is Potent.* It diffuses fear and hate. It energizes "deep knowing". It calls us to remember who we really are and that we can do the impossible -- "dream the impossible dream and then go out and do something about it."

Contrary to common belief, the number and intensity of wars has risen in modern times with the development of technical civilization; it is highest among the powerful states with a strong government and lowest among primitive man without permanent chieftainship, according to Erich Fromm (see his famous analysis in <u>The Anatomy of Human Destructiveness</u>).

In the 20th century -- the most violent in history, writes Fromm --over 100 million people died in war (in recent decades since, over 90% of the casualties have been civilians). Over 50 million lost their lives in World War II. Over 3 million Vietnamese perished from 10 years of military assaults that ended 30 years ago. Our brief, but brutal, war on Iraq in 1991 killed over 100,000. U.S. sanctions have led to another 600,000 deaths.

American soldiers have hardly been immune from the horrors of war. Over 58,000 were lost in Vietnam. Hundreds more committed suicide after the war. Tens of thousands more were ravaged by Agent Orange, suffered homelessness, or were afflicted with post-traumatic stress syndrome, including many who became alcoholics, drug addicts, or (up to 1/3 of combat veterans) committed violent acts, often against their loved ones (see Hendin & Haas <u>Wounds of War: The Psychological Aftermath of Combat in Vietnam</u>). The second war in Iraq has once again illustrated the power of male elites utilizing anger and fear to sanction hatred, violence and war. Men's history shows little progress toward outer peace (or inner peace).

Political and Economic Goals of War

World War II was the one classic major war of self-defense in the 20th century. The U.S. and many other nations had been attacked, invaded, or threatened by Germany and Japan. Yet, our strafing of Tokyo, and our obliteration of Hiroshima and Nagasaki with nuclear bombs, and other aerial assaults in Germany (including civilian targets) -- which killed over 300,000 and initiated the nuclear age -- were arguably immoral and unnecessary (see Lifton & Mitchell, <u>Hiroshima in America: Fifty Years of Denial</u>).

Political and economic war priorities are well-documented, though not always widely understood by the general public (largely due to inevitable mass government propaganda), as was the case in the U.S./NATO 78-day aerial war against Serbia in 1999 or in our war against Iraq (even Walter Cronkite condemned our biased media coverage of the Gulf War in 1991--see John MacArthur's <u>Second Front: Censorship and Propaganda in the Gulf War</u>).

For thousands of years nations (tribes and factions) have engaged in war to gain access to more land or other valuable resources like oil or diamonds (as we're seeing in Africa), or water "wars" (which have begun in the U.S.). As history buffs can recall, in the mid-19th century it was our "manifest destiny" to "acquire" Texas from Mexico.

The U.S.-driven "New World Order" (corporate globalization) constitutes class/economic warfare against much of the planet. George Bush's extreme right-wing policies (supported by numerous Democrats, Wall Street, and other plutocrats) are clearly a war against the poor, people of color, immigrants, American workers, political dissenters, democratic principles, the environment, and especially, a war against dozens of poor nations and over 1 billion world citizens trapped in absolute poverty (almost 3 billion make less than $2 a day). As some are predicting, future wars may be fought over access and control of information and knowledge; i.e., cyberwarfare.

War, strangely, appears to satisfy a wide range of psychological needs. War fulfills patriotic impulses, including the desire to serve one's country and help defend it against a (real or perceived) enemy. War presents many opportunities for high-risk adventures, courageous acts, heroic feats, and deep human bonds. Combat soldiers richly deserve great credit for risking their lives in the most horrendous circumstances. Warfare is almost unique in providing ordinary men (and women) with the opportunity to achieve fame and glory (especially among their friends, families, and in their home towns).

There are darker, sometimes evil motives at play in war such as ethnic, racial, or religious hatreds as we've seen in the Balkans, Northern Ireland, Central Africa, or between India and Pakistan. Ideologies and rhetoric demonize the enemy. In the 19th century in the U.S. (and on American TV into the 1960s), Native Americans were "savages." In the 1950s the Chinese and North Koreans were the "yellow peril." The Vietnamese were labeled "gooks."

War Triggers Many Passions

The lust for revenge or retaliation is another war-inducing motive, as we see in the centuries-long war between the Catholics and Protestants in Northern Ireland. The 9-11-01 terrorist attacks on the World Trade Center and the Pentagon triggered widespread calls for revenge among Americans that continue to fuel the Bush junta's "endless war on terrorism."

Vietnam veteran and journalist William Broyles, though non-violent by nature, vividly described the conflicting human forces in war (Esquire, 11/84). "The constant rush that war junkies get; a great intensity to the point of a terrible ecstasy and endless exotic experiences, enough 'I couldn't fucking believe it's' to last a lifetime." "Most people fear freedom; war removes that fear... the difficult gray areas of life gain an eerie, serene clarity, especially who's your enemy and who's your friend... War is an escape from the everyday into a special world where the bonds that hold us to our duties in daily life -- the bonds of family, community, work -- disappear... it's the frontier beyond the last settlement, it's Las Vegas." "War is a brutal, deadly game, but a game, the best there is.

And men love games... if you come back whole you bring with you the knowledge that you have explored regions of your soul that in most men will always remain unchartered... no sport I had ever played brought me to such deep awareness of my physical and emotional limits... I was terrified, I was ashamed, and I couldn't wait for it to happen again" (blasting the enemy with heavy weapons). "The enduring emotion of war, when everything else has faded, is comradeship. A comrade in war is a man you can trust with anything, because you trust him with your life... possessions and advantages count for nothing; the group is everything... it's a love that needs no reasons, that transcends race and personality and education -- all those things that would make a difference in peace. It is, simply, brotherly love... isolation is the greatest fear in war." "Love of war stems from the union, deep in the core of our being, between sex and destruction, beauty and horror, love and death... the closest thing to childbirth for women: the initiation into the power of life and death. The love of destruction and killing in war stems from that boyhood fantasy of war as a game. There is true joy in being alive in death's presence -- not a great step to the joy of causing death." "War offers intense beauty, heightened sexuality, great decisions, but can also destroy empathy for the suffering of others. Men love war for love and war are at the core of man. We must love one another or die. We must love one another and die." "To overcome death, our love for peace, for life itself, must be greater than we think possible, greater even than we can imagine."

Masculinity and War

War is, in fact one of the most rigidly "gendered" activities known to humankind, according to Barbara Ehrenreich, <u>Blood Rites: Origins and History of the Passions of War</u>. Among traditional cultures, the passage of boyhood to manhood often required successful participation in war, meaning often the killing of an enemy. Ehrenreich describes a group of Fang men (in the Congo) who, after shooting someone down in an ambush, came home shouting, "We are real men, we are real men, we have been to town and shot a man, we are men, real men." And the Naga warrior in the Papuan Gulf who has to bring home a scalp or skull before he is qualified to marry. She suggests that war in fact may have originated as a substitute occupation for underemployed male hunter-defenders. And, that early man was driven by the need to become a predator to avoid being a prey to large, killer animals. Thus, war becomes a response to a primal fear of being destroyed by a more powerful adversary.

President Johnson felt he could not withdraw from Vietnam because he would be considered weak and unmanly. Remember, too, before Bush Sr. declared war on Iraq, pundits were calling him a "wimp." Thus, although most men are non-violent and many oppose war, many men, and a lingering cultural mythology, regard war as an important test and proof of masculinity, especially strong male leadership and the traditional role of heroic defender/protector.

The Hague Appeal for Peace (HAP) Conference, which took place in the Hague, Netherlands, in May 1999, has set a "Global Agenda for World Peace" in the 21st century. Over 1,000 groups, from 100 different countries, intended to voice their suggestions on how to make international peace possible. The four-day event yielded a turnout of over 8,000 people and resulted in ground-breaking initiatives and resolutions. One of the many new campaigns launched at the conference was the "International Action Network on Small Arms" (IANSA). The IANSA goal is to encourage tracking, protesting, and publicizing the sales and shipments of weapons (from 1989 to 1996 the U.S. sold $119 billion in arms, some 45% of the world's total).

The Hague Global Agenda calls for recognition and enforcement of World Court rulings that over 150 countries have endorsed (but not the United States which fears being charged with war crimes). A long-term project put in motion at the conference is the "Global Action to Prevent War." Its purpose is to establish a coalition of organizations that will build a permanent body of Non-Governmental Organizations (NGOs), individuals, and eventually governments to support world peace. The good news is that the number of international NGOs has increased from 6,000 in 1990 to 26,000 today.

The Global Agenda outlines 10 "fundamental principles for a just world order":

1. Every government should adopt a resolution prohibiting war.

2. All states should accept the jurisdiction of the "International Court of Justice."

3. Every government should ratify the "International Crime Commission" and implement the "Land Mines Treaty."

4. All states should integrate the "New Diplomacy" -- the partnership of governments, international organizations, and civil societies.

5. The world can't ignore humanitarian crises, but every creative diplomatic means possible must be exhausted before resorting to force under U.N. authority.

6. Negotiations for a "Convention Eliminating Nuclear Weapons" should begin immediately.

7. The trade in small arms should be severely restricted.

8. Economic rights must be taken as seriously as civil rights.

9. Peace education should be compulsory in every school.

10. The plan for the Global Action to Prevent War should become the basis for a peaceful world order.

While the conference was covered by Associated Press and released worldwide, the United States media ignored it, with coverage in the back pages of only a handful of small regional papers (see Peter Phillips & Project Censored, Censored 2000: The Year's Top 25 Censored Stories).

World peace is indeed a critical and achievable goal with vast personal, social, national, and global benefits. A significant reduction in military spending ($300 billion annually in the U.S.) will promote world peace by freeing billions of dollars to invest in overcoming major social and environmental problems such as poverty and pollution, and shifting to a solar-based economy.

The Art of Peacemaking: A Human Necessity

For many men peace is elusive and nearly impossible to achieve. For others peace is too passive and even boring. Conventional thinkers regard peace as merely the absence of war or serious conflict. Human conflict, though inevitable, can be creatively resolved with what the Buddhists call equanimity -- balance, inner calm, and deep understanding.

We cherish peace-of-mind for its many gifts. There is the serenity and contentment with our life and choices; and the sense of sufficiency -- of having, doing, and being enough. When minds are calm, like the surface of sea, one is able to discern greater depths of meaning and understanding. Meditation has helped to gain inner peace and mental clarity.

Forgiving ourselves for any real or imagined mistakes, failures, or shortcomings; forgiving and accepting our past and parents, and others that we felt had hurt us; a deep psychological, spiritual healing is needed on an individual level in order to achieve inner peace. Once humanity has evolved to a higher level of inner peace then the groundwork for a just world will be in motion. Inner peace can lead to outer peace. Mankind's genetic and childhood memory can be modified over time to evoke peaceful feelings including love and gratitude. From a childhood of appreciation, respect and joy can come a new human consciousness and a win-win world.

Further research is needed into the deep, primal roots of human hatred, violence and warfare. Is the psychology of men evolving in a humane direction? Are men capable of overcoming their fears and negative responses to threats, real or imagined? Does power holding by men contribute to status fights, holy wars and scape-goating of resented or feared minorities (such as gay bashing and religious extremism)? Why do men love or make war?

****

Michael Whitty, futurist, is the Director of Institute for Building Sustainable Communities and also a Professor at the University of Detroit-Mercy campus MBA Program. As the Chancellor of the International Association of Educators for World Peace U.S. branch, he can be reached at: whittymd@UDmercy.edu

Dan Butts, author of How Corporation$ Hurt Us All: Saving Our Rights, Democracy, Institutions and Future (Trafford, 2003), *is a therapist, writer and healer.*

A South African University Becomes Real:
A Vision of Success

by Gayatri Erlandson and Louisa Dyer

Editors, 'Spirit in the Smokies' Magazine

Asheville, North Carolina

****

Journalists describe Taddy Blecher as a grown-up Harry Potter, living a charmed life and exuding positive energy and childlike innocence. Yet he clearly has a most intelligent mind. Dr. Blecher was wealthy, white, in his thirties, earning a big salary in financial services in South Africa, and on the verge of taking a job in the United States when Maharishi, leader of the TM movement, called South Africa to say, "No TMers should leave this nation."

Taddy had practiced TM (Transcendental Meditation) for many years and that night, he decided to stay. He was stunned by visits to black townships around Johannesburg. "I'd never been there before. I'd always just made money and gone on nice holidays."

He saw 20 people living in one house, while many homes were cardboard shacks, and people had no shoes or adequate clothing, with shockingly run-down schools. His first reaction was to give money but quickly saw this as creating dehumanizing dependence. So he began teaching TM.

Peace Inspires Brilliant Ideas

"After a few years of teaching TM to 9000 students, crime fell over 80 percent. The whole area changed. Suicides stopped completely. After the students learned TM, they came out of grade 12 so pumped up. But unable to afford to go to University, they ended up unemployed. Unemployment is 40 percent in South Africa, structured by Apartheid by taking math out of the schools. Millions of blacks had no math or science, a cruel education."

Taddy and four friends decided to create South Africa's first _free_ university. Knowing nothing of how to start, with no books, computers, teachers nor buildings, they wrote to 350 schools. After two weeks, they had five prospective students. But soon they had 40 applications!

Using an old fax machine as the only equipment, the University began. Four thousand students applied to this university that didn't exist. Dr. Blecher says, "Two weeks before school was to begin, we got a building downtown. It was terribly dark inside, awful. On the fifth floor we found 400 chairs so we invited 350 students.

And So We Started

At our inauguration, we had no idea what we were doing. We introduced the students to the five of us, the management. Then, to introduce the faculty, we stepped back, then forward. So they met their teachers for statistics, math, Human Resources management, finance, Internet Technology. We each taught five subjects, which we didn't really know. We sweated late every night to learn what to teach students the next day.

"By day two we had lost 100 students, but the 250 who remained were amazing. We talked of consciousness-based-education. It didn't matter that we had no library. To teach about computers, we made 250 photocopies of a computer keyboard, and for three years taught every student to type on a piece of paper.

"We had no textbooks, so we used donated financial magazines to learn investments, finance, English, and stock markets. Our students come in shy. They know no one. They have heard their whole lives they are nobody. Yet there was so much energy in our school, you cannot imagine. All these students–so happy, meditating every day.

"In every case, they were the first in their family that had ever been to university. In South Africa 97% of adults never go to college. We brought one student from every village. Now our graduates go back to teach their village how to create businesses, farm and manage money. In their first year in jobs, these students earned four times the entire cost of their four-year education.

"Our first graduation was so touching, a thousand faces of parents whose lives and whole villages were changed. In the middle of the graduation, the students began dancing and sang for fifteen minutes—on prime time TV. These kids came in unemployed, and nobody believed in them, and they became enlightened, bright citizens with jobs.

"To get accredited took four long years, working eighteen hours a day, seven days a week. Now our university is a household name in South Africa. The government does not understand how we have done it. Our kids are doing brilliantly. Many visitors come in, spend time with our students, and start crying. They can't believe it. All our kids have learned TM.

He recalled: "We got American companies to donate $15 million dollars worth of books! But these weighed many tons. How to get them to South Africa? We learned South African export ships return empty after delivering their cargos, and were allowed to fill these. We now have 300,000 books, with a business library better than most universities! We now have 1,400 computers and a Foundation College, where students come and live. All the college tutors are our graduates."

The university - CIDA City Campus - has become a remarkable success story, with a campus and a reputation for innovation. Five years later, it has taught 1,600 students. Apart from being available to poor students, who get a virtually free education, students run and maintain the university buildings, and on their holidays they teach young people in their home villages, reaching hundreds of thousands.

When they graduate, they pay the university costs of another student who will follow in their footsteps. "In one year, these students will be earning more than their families could earn in their entire working lives," says Dr. Blecher.

"The Dalai Lama visited us. We put one thousand students in front of him. He was to stay 40 minutes. After 10 minutes he told his helpers, 'Cancel my other appointments. I am not leaving.' He stayed three hours and now sponsors a student. Oprah, who meditates every day, came in 2003 and talked to giant groups of students. She gave $1.3 million to build a ladies residence and sponsors students as well."

Dr Blecher concludes by saying: "This is what it's like to do Maharishi's work. It's not easy. Nobody shakes your hand every day. But you keep on. Every day you just have to be in the Self. Just tap into what Nature's telling you, that desire deep inside your heart. So you just start. Just out of nothing."

****

For photos and information, contact CIDA CITY Campus,
www.safrica.info/ess_info/sa_glance/education/taddy-blecher-200605.htm

Gayatri Erlandson, Ph.D. and Louisa A. Dyer, M.A., are editors of <u>Spirit in the Smokies</u> *Magazine and compiled the information on Taddy's work and the Campus from various websources such as BBC News Johannesburg, South Africa. This article was first published in the January, 2006 issue, pp.26-27: see www.spiritinthesmokies.com for other uplifting, true stories. Contact the writers at editors@spiritinthesmokies.com*

On Editing Benazir Bhutto's <u>Reconciliation: Islam, Democracy and the West</u>

by Mark A. Siegel

Author/Journalist,
Washington D.C.

****

This book was written under extraordinary circumstances. It was my privilege to work with Benazir Bhutto on this project over the last very difficult months. This period of her life included her historic return to Karachi on October 18, 2008, which attracted three million supporters to greet her, and the unsuccessful assassination attempt on her in the early minutes of October 19 that killed 179 people. In the midst of all this tumult Benazir and I collaborated on the book, at times while Benazir was under house arrest by the Musharraf regime and under the constraints of emergency rule, tantamount to martial law.

Despite the events swirling about her and her responsibility of leading Pakistan's largest political party – the Pakistan Peoples Party – in the parliamentary election campaign, Benazir Bhutto remained focused on <u>Reconciliation: Islam, Democracy and the West</u>. This book was very important to her, and she threw herself into it with the complete attention and intensity with which she did so many things in her life. Benazir was convinced that the battles between democracy and dictatorship, and between extremism and moderation, were the two central forces of the new millennium. She believed that the message of her cherished religion, Islam, was being politicized and exploited by extremists and fanatics. And she believed that under dictatorship, extremism festered and grew, threatening not only her homeland of Pakistan but also the entire world.

That's why she wrote this book. That's why it was so important to her. And that's why she devoted herself totally to this project, quite literally under the early morning of her death, when I received her final edits of the manuscript.

Although I helped Benazir research and write this book, it is her work from beginning to end: a positive statement of reconciliation among religions and nations; a bold assertion of the true nature of Islam; and a practical road map for bringing societies together.

Benazir Bhutto was the bravest person I have ever known and a dear, irreplaceable friend. She was assassinated on December 27, 2007, in Rawalpindi, Pakistan. I find some solace in knowing that the last memory of her will not be the bloody carnage of the murder scene, but rather the legacy of this book, which manifests the strength, optimism, and vision of a great woman. *Mark A. Siegel*, Washington DC

[In Bhutto's own words, from her book: <u>Reconciliation – Islam, Democracy and the West</u>]

N.Y., N.Y.: Harper-Collins Press, 2007

THE PATH BACK

As I stepped down onto the tarmac at Quaid-e-Azam International Airport in Karachi on October 18, 2007, I was overcome with emotion. Like most women in politics, I am especially sensitive to maintaining my composure, to never showing my feelings. A display of emotion by a woman in politics or government can be misconstrued as a manifestation of weakness, reinforcing stereotypes and caricatures. But as my foot touched the ground of my beloved Pakistan for the first time after eight lonely and difficult years of exile, I could not stop the tears from pouring from my eyes and I lifted my hands in reverence, in thanks, and in prayer. I stood on the soil of Pakistan in awe. I felt that a huge burden, a terrible weight, had been lifted from my shoulders. It was a sense of liberation. I was home at long last. I knew why. I knew what I had to do.

I had departed three hours earlier from my home in exile, Dubai. My husband, Asif, was to stay behind in Dubai with our two daughters, Bakhtawar and Aseefa. Asif and I had made a very calculated, difficult decision. We understood the dangers and the risks of my return, and we wanted to make sure that no matter what happened, our daughters and our son, Bilawal (at college in Oxford), would have a parent to take care of them. It was a discussion that few husbands and wives ever have to have, thankfully. But Asif and I had become accustomed to a life of sacrificing our personal happiness and any sense of normalcy and privacy. Long ago I had made my choice. The people of Pakistan have always come first. The people of Pakistan will always come first. My children understood it and not only accepted it but encouraged me. As we said good-bye, I turned to the group of assembled supporters and press and said what was in my heart: "This is the beginning of a long journey for Pakistan back to democracy, and I hope my going back is a catalyst for change. We must believe that miracles can happen."

...Within the Muslim world there has been and continues to be an internal rift, an often violent confrontation between sects, ideologies, and interpretations of the message of Islam. This destructive tension has set brother against brother, a deadly fratricide that has tortured intra-Islamic relations for 1,300 years. This sectarian conflict stifled the brilliance of the Muslim renaissance that took place during the Dark Ages of Europe, when the great universities, scientists, doctors, and artists were all Muslim. Today that intra-Muslim sectarian violence is most visibly manifest in a senseless, self-defeating sectarian civil war that is tearing modern Iraq apart at its fragile seams and exercising its brutality in other parts of the world, especially in parts of Pakistan.

And as the Muslim world – where sectarianism is rampant – simmers internally, extremists have manipulated Islamic dogma to justify and rationalize a so-called jihad against the West.

. . .The terrorist assassination attempt against me on October 19, 2007 [weeks before her death – editor's note] underscores the issues troubling me about internal strife within the Islamic fold and the intersection of Islam and democracy. The Muslim-on-Muslim massacre that took place in Karachi in October is consistent with the Muslim-on-Muslim fratricidal sectarian violence that is raging in Baghdad and other parts of Iraq in the early 21st century. The Talibanization of the Federally Administered Tribal Areas of Pakistan and the growth of extremism within the North-West Frontier Providence of my country highlight my central concern and the reason for writing this book. The potential exists for the radicalization of Muslims around the world in a political environment of dictatorship and authoritarianism.

. . . I will argue that the fundamentals of democratic governance are part of the Islamic value system and debunk the myth that Islam and democracy are mutually exclusive. I know from my own experience that democracy is an integral part of Islam. The core of my being as a Muslim rejects those using Islam to justify acts of terror to pervert, manipulate, and exploit religion for their own political agenda. Their actions are not only antithetical to Islam but specifically prohibited by it.

The central message I would like to convey….is of the two critical tensions that must be reconciled to prevent the clash of civilizations that some believe looms before us. There is an internal tension within Muslim society, too. The failure to resolve that tension peacefully and rationally threatens to degenerate into a collision course of values spilling into a clash between Islam and the West. It is finding a solution to this internal debate within Islam – about democracy, about human rights, about the role of women in society, about respect for other religions and cultures, about technology and modernity – that will shape future relations between Islam and the West. But both clashes can be solved. What is required is accommodation and reconciliation.

Reprinted under negotiation with HarperCollins Publishers, all rights reserved © 2008

****

Mrs. Benezar Bhutto was assassinated in December 2007. She was the Prime Minister of Pakistan from 1988 to 1990, and her second term as Prime Minister was from 1993-1996. She was the Chairperson of the Pakistan Peoples Party. Born in 1953 in Karachi, Bhutto was the first woman to ever lead a Muslim country. She had to live in exile with her husband and children since 1999, and returned to Pakistan in October 200 and was assassinated two months later. The world was shocked to lose this great, courageous leader. (The Editors)

From the Berlin Wall to Pharaoh's Hall:
Crossing Borders for Peace

by Patricia Rife

President, Writers Express
Washington, D.C.

****

Peace is an inner state of equilibrium, a divine alignment with the First Source and Center which is at the core of every human being. Hence, peace begins <u>within</u>, 'radiating' outwards! This spiritual peace is a state of "being" and can radiate <u>to all</u> around you, as well as affect one's point of view, attitudes and actions towards others and towards the world. Martin Luther King Jr. and other spiritual leaders throughout time have taught us this "nature" of peace. Our current political state of un-rest and war is a mirror of the human condition at this time in history, but is not the end-state – oh no! We are making slow but certain progress towards world peace as we develop ourselves spiritually and serve our brothers and sisters in many ways around the world, finding that "peace which passes beyond all understanding"......

My work and research as a historian of science has taken me to many places around the world. It was a hot, sultry afternoon in West Berlin, 1988: a dank smell wafting over from coal-burning generators across the Berlin Wall in East Berlin cast a pallor over the city's atmosphere, but in general, the mood was pleasant. It was a summer holiday weekend, so I decided to take a break from my historical research on Einstein, Planck and Lise Meitner's discovery of nuclear fission in 1938 to visit a History of Science conference being held at Humboldt University located "on the other side of the Wall". Imagine my delight when I learned that I could even walk <u>through</u> the Berlin Wall that sunny day!

The checkpoints would be crowded with tourists taking gifts of food and other "western items" to their friends and relatives trapped in Communist East Germany, so I packed for the University conference with only a 1 day visa: perhaps the guards would let a majority of us walk in, through the rooms, and out to the other side (East Berlin) across without hassle. The Wall kept us apart but most Westerners, including Americans, could easily travel over on day-visas or for short visits, as long as the curfews were not violated: their relatives had, since 1961 when the Wall was built, been begging them to bring over supplies, Western books and the 'banned' music often confiscated by the mean-looking, but very young, blonde East German border police. Only those living under Soviet oppression for 40 years could understand how tense the situation was, and how dismal the poverty, Russian-style, truly was on "the other side of the Wall". Yet there was a festive feeling in the air that day, as many hundreds waited to cross the Berlin Wall on foot.

When I got up through the crowds to the sullen blonde-haired guards, one surveyed my passport and then asked me rudely: "What? YOU, a professor? And so YOUNG? And .." -- here he sneered in my face -- "and…a woman?" Yes, I explained, I am a woman Professor -- and I wasn't feeling so "young"on that hot afternoon, loaded down with books and gifts for my physics colleagues on the other side of the Wall! I was finally permitted through the highly-guarded Checkpoint, and gazed up at the barbed wire snaking across the Berlin Wall as I entered into East Germany. That day, I realized with a deep spiritual shock: *walls which try to separate us have no meaning* for those who "walk the talk" *of world peace*! We can cross psychological barriers; we can work to cross physical restraining walls; and we can open our minds and hearts to cross deep walls of resentment, misunderstanding, and misperceptions about peace. As the old prophets and spiritual songs tell us about Jericho: "… and the walls came/tumblin' down"…

The other side of the Berlin Wall was another world. It was like going back in time, into the early 1920s…..literally. Old Soviet-made cars whizzed along the streets, most art was literally forbidden, and fashions? Mostly a drab grey. East Berlin remained underdeveloped under the dictates of the rigid Soviet Union, including making us change our currency (and leave some with the guards) while forbidden to stay with colleagues in the comfort of their small apartments. I walked through the Check Point, and a shadow darted into an alcove – my goodness, I thought quickly: was I being followed? Well, there was no time to lose. I must find my way across East Berlin to the Humboldt University, and meet up with the many international guests who were expected for dinner preceding our History of Science Conference. I took in all the architecture and old-fashioned clothing as I inquired, in my rusty German, for directions to the University: young people stared, women with kerchiefs over their hair pointed, riding Russian-made bicycles; and your normal types of students, thin and intellectual, discussing theories and ideas on their way to cafes', nodded to me, not knowing I was an American. But I had no time for 'kaffee café' today....

I had received a grant to work in the Nobel Prize archives after many years as a professor in the California State University system. Hosted by the Swedish Institute and the Royal Institute of Technology, I was happy to take time off from my teaching in the California Bay Area and return to my research in Sweden. I was missing a key piece of the puzzle about the interpretation, then dissemination of the news of nuclear fission in 1939. Even <u>nominations</u> for the Nobel Prize in Physics as well as Chemistry then had been forbidden by Adolf Hitler. Albert Einstein had been persecuted and hounded out of Berlin. It was illegal in the Third Reich for any German scientist to submit names of Jewish colleagues, such as Lise Meitner, for the Nobel Prize. As the Nazis grew in power, censoring Jewish scientists work, they kept few records so I had to travel to East as well as West Berlin archives and review dusty old letters and boxes for clues. It was plain to me that I would have to live in Berlin to continue my post-doctoral research, trace the lean existing correspondence which lay resting in dusty archives and kept meticulously by German science institutes. As a Professor, it was not only "publish or perish" that drove me, but a sincere desire to know the story of how Albert Einstein, Lise Meitner, Niels Bohr and others had made their <u>ethical decisions</u> during the dark war years after escaping Nazi Germany – decisions about world peace as well the splitting of the atom, knowing that either Hitler's scientists or the Allies would harness it to produce weapons of mass destruction.

My memories suddenly returned to the present, in drab East Berlin. Who <u>was</u> that who following me? I turned around quickly, as a secretive woman darted into an alcove on Karl Marx Platz, East Berlin. Well, I reflected, picking up my pace, the Secret police would have a hard time keeping up with <u>me</u> on this trip! I asked in my rusty German dialect for directions to the History of Science department, and was guided by a young soul through the old staid academic hallways to a new office. There were Atari computers there – I smiled, since I had just been teaching in the Silicon Valley, California some months prior, and in the U.S., those computers would now have been relics of a 'bygone era'…. But I held my thoughts and comparisons between East and West, and put out my hand, which was shaken warmly by the young colleagues, and was introduced all around to the younger professors at the first stage of their careers. It was 1988 – not 1938 now…

We "younger generation" colleagues hit it off, chatting and laughing, and by the afternoon, had exchanged articles, books, and promises to correspond. One memory stood out: a young, proud scholar told me defiantly that he "had <u>no</u> interest coming to the West" and had **no** desire to cross the Berlin Wall. He boasted loudly: "We can see by the glitter from our airport that your Western culture is over-materialistic, and why would people in the Communist block <u>ever</u> want to go there?" So I was happy to simply be escorted by him to our Academic Banquet that evening: we walked arm-in-arm, a blonde American with my proper young Communist scholar-friend. We made quite a pair! And yes, we spoke about world peace in a 'nuclear' era.

Imagine, to my embarrassment that evening when, surrounded by esteemed East Berlin professors (many of whom praised my work and writings on Einstein, Meitner and the Nobel Prize), I simply lifted a glass of the fine German wine up to make a toast to our hosts. Heads turned in horror, scholars hissed at me and the younger men turned red – what, an American making a *toast* at a formal academic banquet….and a <u>woman</u> no less! Quickly, the moment disappeared but the whispers did not. I managed to make peace over desert, red-faced, and all was forgiven….

Returning that evening, escorted by my colleagues, I made it across the Checkpoint at the Berlin Wall, through the guards and their questions, before midnight, and waved back at my hosts. It was a bit eerie, re-entering the noisy gaudy-lit streets of West Berlin, with its fast cars, futuristic fashions and post-modern architecture, all alone. That night, as I lay digesting all I had seen and heard, the international rock band "Pink Floyd" was blasting their song "The Wall" across the Berlin Wall, as a fitting protest to all divisions which are artificial and government contrived….

It was hot and still that night: the same summer evening on both sides of the Wall, but so many differences divided us…including my sense of freedom, compared to the sorrow of colleagues who were not permitted to leave the Soviet bloc.   I was happy to be in this 'other world' – but suddenly, I flashed back to my first trip – far more trying – across the Berlin Wall seven years before. I remembered the barbed wire, guards, and … just then, Pink Floyd played their crescendo, and my mind drifted back to 1981…

I was younger then (weren't we all?) and my doctoral (Ph.D.) research was in process. The warm Swedish countryside had a smell of thousands of gorgeous wild flowers that summer. I was still a graduate student, and had been living in Stockholm, Sweden, writing my dissertation from a comfortable tiny office in the Physics Department, Swedish Royal Institute of Technology. My intent was to interview as many older physicists who lived through World War II who remembered the discovery of nuclear fission (1938) and my dissertation subject Lise Meitner's escape from Hitler's Nazified Berlin.   My Scandinavian colleagues well-understood my dedication to world peace and my reasons for writing the history of nuclear fission and development of the world's first atomic weapons as an original Ph.D. thesis. It was hard work. They had welcomed me when I first shyly wrote from Harvard University, asking to conduct archival research about Hitler's forbidding of any German to accept the Nobel Prize, or nominate their Jewish colleagues. It was my year in the MIT "Science, Technology and Society" program, however, that firmed up my resolve to interview retired physicists before many of them died, their stories and memories untold, and the scholarship to Sweden was like a dream come true. The interpretation of fission became my quest, and interviews, my methods of diving into the past swirling around Nazi Germany… Even then, I drew parallels to future work for world peace, and historical research on those, like Einstein, whose courageous voice spoke out against war for over 4 decades.

I met the grandson of Nobel Prize winner Otto Hahn that summer, and we agreed to meet in Berlin and cross the Berlin Wall together during the summer of '81. We would walk, not drive, in order to meet and interview our physicist hosts in East Berlin, crossing through the tight security of the Wall on foot.   When I arrived, smiling, modern Dietrich Hahn was in a hurry. "Come on, we only can get a one day visa – that means we have to be back by midnight!" he exclaimed in German.   I well remember a pair of nuns watching us in amazement as we huffed up to the guards (no lines that day) and began to be interrogated: literally, <u>the guards led us away,</u> to the astonishment of those Westerners still waiting in line. Little did I know that in his briefcase, Dietrich was carrying all sorts of history books on nuclear weapons and uranium fission. After all, it <u>was</u> our on-going research focus and the purpose of our trip!

Unfortunately, Dietrich's top-of-the-line tape recorder -- and the fame of his grandfather and other Nobel Prize winners in his address book -- was enough to alert the young East German guards. Strictly, they motioned to their superiors and we were whisked away …into separate interrogation rooms inside the Berlin Wall. I imagine no one has ever told you before that the Berlin Wall was actually filled with small rooms! Mine was filthy, with a bare light-bulb. A rough speaking woman guard made sure I was not smuggling currency, and questioned me at length about who I was visiting (elderly nuclear physicists?), their addresses, and of course, since I spoke little German, my contact addresses in West Germany and America. When I was let out, there was a surprise: no one was there to meet me, during my first moments in communist East Germany! I was practicing Zen Buddhist meditations in those days as a hectic grad student, so I just breathed in.. and out… in… and out….until over an hour later, Dietrich emerged into the dirty station, huffing and swearing, telling me animatedly how they had copied his entire address book and confiscated his history books on atomic fission and Hiroshima!

We let the trauma of the intense interrogation process slip away when a very friendly elderly man suddenly hobbled up to us, shook our hands warmly, and welcomed us to East Germany – apologizing for being tardy since "the damned police" had given him a parking ticket on Karl Marx Platz!   That was a day to remember. We talked about everything under the sun, while our elderly hosts shared stories of Nazi Germany over German cakes and strong coffee. It was hard to say goodbye, after meeting with other historians that evening. My stomach hurt!   I still have a photo of the clock in the grungy East Berlin station, at five minutes to midnight: quickly, we had to leave or would be in violation of East German law.   We bid our physicist hosts a tearful farewell. They had grown up in the sector now know as West Berlin, and when Hitler's Army began to draft young boys, one of our hosts had been shot in the leg – and, still walking with a limp, led us to that late night deserted train station to say goodbye, as we journeyed to a place across the Wall where he had not been allowed to travel to for 40 years.... He swore to me that if he could "get out", he would come to visit me in America....someday.... My stomach ached...

The ripples of time shifted and receded.... I had to have an emergency appendectomy in West Berlin a few days after we had all waved goodbye. Some doctors said it was the stress of the interrogation in the Wall which brought it on...who knows, for fate is a fickle companion, and peace often emerges 'after the storm'... Interesting, as I laid in Spandau Hospital, the former site of concentration camps (now only a peaceful suburb of then-West Berlin, surrounded like an island by East Germany), I reflected on the meaning of it all..... And during those Zen moments, breathing in, breathing out.....I made my spiritual vow to commit my life and time *to work for world peace*. Only in times like these, alone, do you know the power of your faith and spiritual practices...and if more would 'shift' their focus from war or trauma to work for peace, we could literally transform our planet.

Some say they make decisions gradually about their 'life-mission', while others feel an eye-opening, like a flaming sword cutting their former life from their new one. All I can say is that I survived the 'near miss' of my appendix bursting, learned how to struggle up and walk again (no nurses spoke English!) and returned to my writing, completion of my doctoral studies, and life in America with a renewed sense of purpose, to become an educator ~~ teaching, via whatever subject, about peace, conflict resolution, management and its complexities.

The most satisfying part of this 'peace story' memoir is that yes, indeed, I did have the pleasure of hosting one of my elderly East German physicist colleagues in the U.S., before the Wall came officially down. Yet the strangest things then began to happen. Months after my retired physicist Professor-colleague had visited, and even gave a talk in the Ethics course I was instructing at the Oakland, California, I began to receive phone calls. By then I was very busy: actually, had come home from my second trip to Berlin and could still hear the band "Pink Floyd" booming its haunting strains against the Berlin Wall! But imagine my ears ringing when I was told it was the San Francisco division of the FBI calling: they wanted to ask me "some questions" about my research. Patiently, my temper rising, I told them that I was teaching in both the California State University system <u>and</u> a history course on a Naval Base. If they wanted to question me about my history work, they would have to come to my campus!

They sent out a gum-shoe, fumbling FBI agent to interview me, and for several hours, I had to simplify my tale of research, coursework and interviews with physicists about the topics of Albert Einstein, Lise Meitner, World War II, and the 1939 discovery of nuclear fission. I insisted to him: everything I had been researching was over 50 years ago! This truth failed to interest the FBI – but again and again, I was questioned about my visits across the Berlin Wall.

Resigned to my work, I returned home crestfallen. What had I done? My family was not supportive. I was told "Well, you <u>went</u> to a communist country: our government has the <u>right</u> to ask you questions!" Years later, when the internationally-illegal US invasion of Iraq occurred, I was told by my family (in a similar tone of voice) that it was "my fault" I was injured in a small Egyptian village. Which brings me to an important juncture in my peace story – dealing with the resistance of our blood family to our global commitments and *responsibilities* as we work towards peace for our *global* family.

We must each face this subtle family resistance to our commitments to non-violent peace work: often those we love the most will often <u>not truly understand</u> our drive, our dedication, to standing up for the values of human equality, world peace and cooperation across borders and nationalities! So we must persevere for the *global family*, in compassion for their suffering as well as in determination to 'see our mission through'.

When Martin Luther King Jr. was assassinated, Bobby Kennedy was already deeply involved in his own Presidential campaign. Weeping, he found himself on a street corner of Indianapolis, in a poor neighborhood, and told black supporters assembled that he too felt their pain: that he had lost a brother who had been assassinated, and felt their grief. He quoted Aeschylus: *In our sleep, pain which cannot forget falls drop by drop upon the heart until, in our own despair, against our own will, comes wisdom through the awful grace of God.*

Many times as a child, I wondered about the "Sunday-go-to-church-all-dressed-up" syndrome – amnesia of sorts where people were nice for several hours and then emerged to continue to talk badly or negatively about others – other races, places, nations, even family members! It will be very trying and taxing to many of you to find your own "house divided" as you shift your allegiances, time and focus to *serving the world* and your global family via peace work. Perhaps your family will not understand, and it will pain your heart. But the 'awful grace of God' will shine through!   Be consoled – Jesus had these same struggles, and spoke gently and firmly about this many time, in favor of serving the broader 'family' and so…we must press on, with a smile and quiet joy in our hearts.

I thought my load had lightened by the late 1980s when I finished my book chapters on uranium fission, and rose to prominence as a Professor. I received an award for teaching in the California State University system in the widely varying (but interrelated) subjects of philosophy, women's studies, humanities, education, science & society, ethics and history of physics. Imagine my surprise, however, when I received a second call from the FBI: this time, to report to their Marin County headquarters, north of the Golden Gate Bridge.

I put on a lacy dress and a nervous smile, and went to meet a very smooth-talking gentleman, who bragged to me about his foreign language abilities and that he too was a Professor. "Not many women in our field, however", he grinned, oblivious to his cut-down.   I was nervous: did I look innocent enough, I thought, as he shuffled papers or would he interrogate me, like in the Berlin Wall?   After all, I had done nothing wrong…   Then he changed the subject: "Let's go into this other room".

There was that familiar bare light bulb, and many files on the table: a blue one was marked "TOP SECRET". He has originally been asking me about my visitor from East Germany, and my trips to Berlin. Where had I crossed the Berlin Wall?   But I slowly realized, after an hour of questioning, that those FBI files on his desk were not about my retired physicist friends, but about ME! The FBI interrogator looked at me coyly: "Well, Dr. Rife, you see a lot of students, don't you? And you have taught at several military bases… have you ever had a chance to meet with foreign students?" No, I innocently replied, the sweat forming along my neck. "Well, what if one of them approached you someday… for information, or some scientific data? What *would* you do?" The room grew silent. I recalled my moments in the Berlin Wall. I knew I was not a scientist, just a humble historian.   Breathe in…and out….in and…..I suddenly realized that, if that file was indeed about me, that I had better answer wisely ("be wise as a serpent, gentle as a dove.."). "Well, Sir… if anyone from any foreign country would ever approach me about the history of physics or Albert Einstein's life…. I would certainly call YOU! May I have your business card?" And with that, his face turned all red…. and the session drew to a close. No letters ever came in the mail again; no phone calls, and no 'return invitations' by the FBI. Whew!

Peace becomes the frame of mind you maintain under all circumstances, if dedicated to this state. Years later, as one of the only Americans conducting historical research in a small Arab village near the Pharaoh's tombs in Egypt during the winter and spring of 2003, I kept my 'cool' when Iraq was invaded -- and became known and respected by the entire circle of Arabic-speaking family members I grew to know and love. I speak a smattering of Egyptian Arabic, but like my German language skills, I first learned the *key* phrases of respectful greetings, acknowledgement, respectful thanks, and praise.   Friendship and respect are <u>human</u> characteristics ~~ and as a woman in a Muslim culture, learning such phrases demonstrates sincere interest in those you are meeting.

Such gestures of peace break down walls of misunderstanding and bring smiles wherever one travels. I was always greeted kindly in the Internet cafes' in Egypt cities and rural villages, where many Muslims were puzzled at why a blonde American woman would spend so long on the Internet! I kindly explained that I was a Professor of e-Business as well as history ~~ certainly the 'commerce' resounded as a global, common theme, even if the e-business and Internet terminology did not! A smile and yes, even terms like "e-mail" are often understood around the world, and a peaceful disposition soon wins friends…. It was not my expertise that mattered, it was my *peaceful presence*, whether crossing the Berlin Wall, working in an Arabic-speaking village during the start of the Iraq war, or surviving US governmental agency questioning.

Blending in while living in a Muslim village was a challenge. As hundreds of men in turbans gathered 'round shabby televisions throughout Egypt the day that the U.S. invaded Iraq nearby, smoking their *hooka* pipes and animatedly discussing the American surprise invasion, I knew that my peaceful presence in their village, a blonde scholar, was accepted. Like destiny, history was unfolding before my eyes as news of Iraq grew increasingly dark, day by day. Being "present in the present" often brings one <u>clarity</u> to make the right decisions and bring a peaceful state to those around you. I pray my presence touched Muslim hearts as well as lives that year. While the Pharaoh's tombs remind us of the grandeur of a Kingdom, televised war brings news immediately around the world, and hence even powerful leaders may be 'exposed' when not pursuing pathways towards peace. . .

Yet we don't have to cross such dramatic borders for each of us to <u>learn</u> peaceful practices at home, work, or in our relations with others. While some may *not* know how to treat us respectfully or in a peaceful manner (due to our race, gender, religion or national differences), we can defer potentially volatile, dangerous or hurtful situations by our attitude – and our gratitude! My friend John Lilly, who was an expert on dolphin communication, use to tell me from his deck with ocean views in Maui, Hawaii that many times, he had experienced dolphins *communicating* "cooperative signals" to one another in a 'relay' fashion, so that the entire pod could avoid danger. Our human will has <u>choice</u> as its mandate and crucible – and hence, which path will we choose?

The world presents us with an awful mess, a daily carnage on our TV screens. It is our human challenge to try to make "meaning" in a world torn by war and conflicts. Historians strive to interpret meaning from events, and poets do their best to grasp for word-images which convey the irony and the ecstasy of our Soul's path towards God. Slowly, I have emerged from my research trips to the past to confront my own spirit-choices, and reach out to serve others humbly. I have focused my work into useful global educational programs striving to teach conflict resolution and negotiation skills to future leaders, Graduate students and managers around the world. I have met and lived with *kahuna*, shamen and diplomats. I have volunteered in San Quentin Prison's education program and conversed with several Nobel Prize winners about war and peace. All confided in me about the *same hope*: each sought <u>peace</u> somehow, from within and without, just as I did inside those interrogation cells in the Berlin Wall. Again, this quest is universal – and as many spiritual paths point to, the answers lay within, like jewels waiting to shine in the light of the world. Each of us, dear readers, hold the keys to world peace in our hands and life-choices….. There will be new horizons and borders to cross – which ones will you surmount?

As global communications networks shrink due to Internet horizons, the world indeed 'becomes flat', and I take comfort in knowing that, over the years, the *practices of radiating peace* might also reflect the wisdom and radiance of others in their spiritual choices and life-paths whom I meet along the way. The prince of peace, Jesus Christ, is my guide, rock and role-model. Crossing borders, religious differences, cultural challenges and government interrogations, I've share the vision of world peace with many who also <u>share the same aspirations</u>. We know it is difficult work: yet we embrace the "walk of peace" as our life path nonetheless. I am reminded of the quiet refrain by poet Robert Frost, who once eloquently wrote: "…*And miles to go..before I sleep…. And miles to go..before I sleep…*" Peace be upon you, all my brothers and sisters around the world!

****

Dr. Patricia Rife is an Associate Professor in the Graduate School of Management and Technology, University of Maryland University College, where she teaches Global E-Marketing and Conflict Resolution/Negotiation courses in Master's Degree programs for graduate students around the world. She was a Professor in the University of Hawaii-Manoa system for seven years, and taught inter-disciplinary courses for the Matsunaga Institute for Peace, including "Sources of Conflict: An Ethical Approach", "Biographies of Peace Leaders", *and* "Science and Spirit: A Historical Exploration". *She was a 1990 and 1993 Templeton Foundation University Lecturer on the topic* "Einstein, Ethics and the Atomic Bomb" *in Honolulu as well as New York City's largest synagogue. During the Einstein Centennial Year, she was an invited Lecturer at Boston University's Physics Dept. and the Nurenberg Trial Archives, Center for Human Rights, University of Connecticut/Storrs, hosted by the Physics Dept. Dr. Rife has presented Hiroshima memorial lectures at the University of Hawaii campuses, Honolulu and Maui; the San Francisco Goethe Institute; the Jimmy Carter Center Peace Program, Atlanta, GA; and*

Morehouse College's International Educators for World Peace 'Science & Spirituality' conference, held at the Martin Luther King Jr. Chapel. She is happy to share her courses and correspond with any interested educators and can be reached at RifeAssociates@gmail.com

She is the author of The Messenger's Daughter: A Woman's Journey Through Islam and Three Spiritual Plays, (British Columbia, Canada: Trafford Publishing, 2007, available through *www.TraffordPress.com*); I, Count Francesco: Love & Intrigue in 16th Century Venice (*www.story-writing.net*); Lise Meitner: Eine Leben fuer Die Wissenschaft (Frankfurt: Claassen Verlag, 1989) *and* Lise Meitner and the Dawn of the Nuclear Age (Boston & Berlin: Birkhauser, 1999, available through *www.Amazon.com*) and a forthcoming book entitled "Empowerment Circles: Practical Social Action to Empower Social Change". *Patricia has been a busy Professor for 25 years in over 7 universities worldwide, and encourages all to embrace the joys of sharing through the art of teaching effective, action-oriented communication methods.*

The International Peace Garden:

2,300 Acres of Beauty between Canada and the U.S.

By International Peace Garden Board

North Dakota, USA and Manitoba, Canada border

****

The International Peace Garden was the 1928 dream of an Islington, Ontario, Canada Horticulturist, Dr. Henry Moore. He wanted a "garden" somewhere along the International boundary of Canada and the United States that would recognize and commemorate the peace and goodwill between these two great countries.

He presented his idea to the National Association of Gardeners of the United States when they met in Toronto, Ontario, Canada in August of 1929. The idea caught on and money began to be raised over the next 3 years. Location became the question. In July of 1931, Manitoba, Canada and North Dakota, United Sates of America offered adjoining tracts of land free of cost in the scenic Turtle Mountains. One look convinced Dr. Moore.

"What a sight greeted the eye!" he exclaimed after viewing the location from the air. "Those undulating hills rising out of the limitless prairies are filled with lakes and streams. On the south of the unrecognizable boundary, wheat everywhere; and on the north, the Manitoba Forest Reserve. What a place for a garden."

The site was approved at a meeting in December, 1931 and on Christmas night that year Dr. Moore made this statement on a Toronto, Ontario, Canada radio station:

The Great Garden will be on the Canada to Canal Highway at a point on the International Boundary between Dunseith, North Dakota, [United States of America] and Boissevain, Manitoba, [Canada] and 60 miles south of Brandon [Manitoba, Canada]. The location is almost the exact center between the Atlantic and Pacific and but 30 miles north of the exact center of the North American continent, which is at Rugby [North Dakota, United States of America].

The highway extends from a point 200 miles north of the boundary to the Panama Canal and is to extend north to Churchill [Manitoba, Canada] and south to Cape Horn, [South America] upon this Main Street of the Americas and which will be the longest north and south highway in the world, will travel millions of people in the days to come.

July 14, 1932, more than 50,000 people gathered to witness the dedication of the International Peace Garden. Unveiled that day was the only piece of construction at the Garden, a simple cairn made of native stone which carries the inscription:

To God In His Glory,
We Two Nations
Dedicate This Garden
And Pledge Ourselves
That As Long As Man
Shall Live, We Will
Not Take Up Arms
Against One Another.

This cairn still stands today on the international border in its original location.

Early Development

The Civilian Conservation Corps, (CCC) a United States government work program established in 1934, began clearing roads, constructed an artificial lake, picnic area, shelters, bridges, fences and a magnificent lodge made of Canadian timber and United States granite. During the 1940's, growth and construction at the International Peace Garden was reduced to maintenance because of World War II. In the early 50's work began again with governmental funds coming in from both countries for work on the formal area and the garden panels that straddle the international border. Rock retaining walls were built as well as cascading waterways, flagstone terraces and reflecting pools.

Youth Camps

The Civilian Conservation Corps dormitories, built back in the 1930's, were transformed and International Peace Garden began to be the focal point for a variety of youth camps. In 1956, the International Music Camp was founded. Six years later the Royal Canadian Legion Athletic Camp was formed and now the International Peace Garden is recognized as one of the top youth centers in North America. These two youth camps abound with thousands of students from around the world each summer, advancing their skills and talents in almost all the performing and athletic arts. Noted instructors and coaches provide leadership and training to these young people during the summer.

Size of the Garden and Facilities for Banquets, Hiking, Auditorium Events and "Peaceful Camping"

The International Peace Garden encompasses 2339 acres. Of those 888 acres are in the United States, and 1451 acres are in Canada. Souvenirs and food concessions are open May - September, Banquet/Buffet Sundays during summer. There are Campgrounds, Picnic areas, Bike Paths, Hiking Trails, a lovely Chapel, Bell Tower, Pavilion, Masonic Auditorium, Arboretum, Meeting and Conference facilities.

Visiting The Park Open all year. Gate attendant Mid - May to Mid - September. Peak flower season end of July through August, all weather related. All visitors must pass through either Canadian or United States Customs/Immigration upon departure from the International Peace Garden.

Time Needed to Visit

If you plan at least 2 - 4 hours, you will have time for driving and walking self tours. A detailed map to our large Peace Gardens with directions from the North Dakota U.S. border as well as directions from the Manitoba, Canada border is available at: • www.peacegarden.com Reservations for camping or events can be made via 1-888-432-6733 (or from Canada, 1-204-534-2510).

****

Steven F. Gorder, is the Superintendent/Treasurer of the International Peace Garden. He welcomes any visitors to come camping and relax at the Peace Gardens, and explore Manitoba as well! See http://www.boissevain.ca *and if you are interested in reservations or information on the International Peace Garden, contact* kathy@peacegarden.com *Phone: (Canadian call) 1-204-534-2510*

Creating a Peace Studies Degree Program in the American South

by Timothy Hedeen and Tom Pynn

Kennesaw State University Philosophy Department

Kennesaw, Georgia

****

Part I: Tim's Story

I found my way into collaboration with my colleagues in the Georgia State University system's "Peace Studies Certificate" working group through various commitments to social justice, environmental preservation, and educational reform. From my elementary schooling in the Montessori tradition through my undergraduate degree in Nonviolent Conflict and Change from Syracuse University, I have learned the theories and methods of cooperation for social change. In my work in neighborhood dispute resolution and service on the board of the National Association for Community Mediation, I realize the value of dialogue and self-determination. I presently teach in Kennesaw State's innovative Master of Science in Conflict Management program and coordinate the university's Alternative Dispute Resolution certificate program. This was a big step for the Georgia State University system, as well as for me!

Part II: Tom's Story

The Vietnam war, the civil rights movement, the women's rights movement, the American Indian Movement's standoff at Wounded Knee all introduced me to our inhumanity and at the same time were the catalyzing events that prompted me to ask whether a better, more humane world was probable or even possible. While college, both undergraduate and graduate, strengthened my questioning and gave me ample opportunity for education as well as direct participation in peace oriented activities, I came to believe that peace work and academic study were separate activities. Even when I went to work for Greenpeace in 1992, I assumed that my work at Greenpeace was distinct from my responsibilities at the college where I was teaching at the time. Yet, I somehow knew, or hoped, that there was a connection. When, in the spring of 2003, Dr. David Jones sent around an email inviting faculty who were interested in establishing a Peace Studies program at Kennesaw State University to meet, I soon began to see that my academic responsibilities are inseparable from peace work. They are not distinct areas of interest, but are mutually informing activities enhancing my life, the lives of my fellow colleagues, and the lives of those students who are engaged with me in our ongoing education. I saw that when brought together, education and peace work can be transformative.

Some Background about Kennesaw State University

Kennesaw State University, the third largest university within the State of Georgia Regents system, is a public university of some 17,000 students located in the northwest suburbs of the metro city of Atlanta. Ninety percent of students are undergraduates, and nearly sixty percent of these are of non-traditional age. Approximately twenty percent of all K.S.U. students are non-white, while Cobb County is thirty- percent non-whites. Furthermore, it is noteworthy that Cobb County boasts a high household income and a high percentage of citizens who tend to vote Republican.

K.S.U. is a university in transition, as the past decade has seen tremendous growth: total enrollment has jumped forty-seven percent, while the combined total of full- and part-time faculty has grown by nearly seventy percent. Founded in 1963 as a junior college with an emphasis on teaching, the school has transformed into a Master's degree-granting university of six colleges. As the University continues to expand, new programs, such as the Peace Studies Certificate, are being developed.

Currently, while there are some private and public colleges and universities in the state of Georgia offering some mix of ethics-based curricula, religious studies minors/majors, international studies degrees, there are no programs of study focused solely on peace.

The Peace Studies Certificate Takes Shape

The Peace Studies Certificate initiative has emerged as the product of interdisciplinary collaboration among faculty at Kennesaw State University. In the summer of 2003, philosophy professor David Jones worked with faculty and staff of the Hiroshima Peace Institute and this experience spurred him to action at Kennesaw. Convening a group from departments of history, foreign languages, philosophy, political science, and conflict management, Jones breathed life into the concept of an academic program related to peace.

The faculty group met regularly throughout the academic year to design the Peace Studies Certificate Program. As peace education is often noted to be both a philosophy and a process (Harris and Morrison 2004), the group adopted a consensus-based collaborative process. As Gandhi (1938) has written, "The means may be likened to a seed, the end to a tree; and there is just the same inviolable connection between the means and the end as there is between the seed and the tree." For the end product to reflect our shared commitment to constructive, nonviolent ways of living we wanted to operate through a collaborative, respectful way. To that end, we employed rotating responsibilities as meeting convener and facilitator as well as the use of consensus decision making.

These steps proved invaluable for at least three reasons: it reinforced each member's high level of commitment to the project through shared responsibility; it accommodated the diverse interests and expertise of our interdisciplinary group; and it established a context of procedural justice that allowed for a close working, peace-oriented relationship among the members. In retrospect, we recognize this ethos of participation to be both unusual for our campus and beneficial for our future work together. Indeed, several faculty members have already commented upon how they feel they have benefited from this collaboration both professionally (in terms of getting a different perspective on committee work and gleaning ideas for their respective courses) and relationally (in terms of seeing sides of their colleagues not ordinarily apparent).

Our strong commitment to the program is documented nowhere more clearly than within our draft proposal. Given the fiscal limitations throughout public education today, the university administration has indicated that adding new courses to the curriculum is a tall order; given the school's tremendous expansion of late, the pressures of delivering even the existing courses are high. Thus, to ensure that the envisioned capstone course will be available, the Peace Studies faculty group agreed to the following: "should enrollment in PEAC 4480 dip below the 'make' level [the minimum enrollment for the university to pay for the instruction and overhead], members of the Peace Studies Certificate Advisory Coordinating Committee will collaborate to deliver the course without receiving teaching credit or remuneration."

The Peace Studies Certificate curriculum was built within the existing undergraduate course offerings of the university, drawing on relevant classes from nine departments, fulfilling our desire to create an interdisciplinary program. To complete the Peace Studies Certificate program, students take five courses; in addition to two required classes, students select one each from three areas ("pods") that correspond to the normative orientation of the certificate: ethics, social identity, and application. Ethics is foundational to the study of peace, as it focuses on human identity and interactions with others, their environments, and the planet at large. The study of social identity is critical, too, as it develops students' awareness of the dynamics of creative and destructive tension within and between social groups. The application pod directs students to courses that emphasize the application of theories, methods, or philosophies related to peace studies from global perspectives.

The capstone course consists of 100 hours of experiential/service learning, followed by a month of classroom seminar meetings. Students will design their own capstone learning projects in consultation with faculty; it is anticipated that many students will participate in internships with peace-oriented organizations. The goal of the capstone is to integrate prior coursework, practicum experience, and readings into a coherent picture of peace studies.

Introduction to Peace Studies: Philosophy 4490, Spring 2004

It might well be asked, "Why philosophy for an introduction to a peace studies certificate program?" Philosophy is not simply an exercise of logic, but is first and foremost a passionate, *engaged* pursuit of wisdom. Fundamental to the pursuit of wisdom is knowing one's self because knowing one's self has a direct impact on how we act in the world. In knowing myself I am less likely to fall into the trap of what Hans-Georg Gadamer has called, "the mere prejudices of prevailing conventions," the ubiquitous unexamined beliefs and desires that tend to inform our lives and are, more often than not, the locus of conflict.

The preeminent philosophical way of not taking things for granted is to pose questions, but they are very different kinds of questions from those we ask in the demand for an answer. In our introduction to the Peace Studies Certificate, Philosophies of Peace, when we pose a question such as, "What is the meaning of peace?" we call into question the very meaning structures that have dominated western society for over two millennia especially the meanings and possibilities of peace.

For the better part of 2,500 years in the West, peace has been conceived of primarily as negative peace, a peace based on an institutionally coerced absence of conflict. This is an old way of conceptualizing peace that is predicated on at least three assumptions: retaliation, self-possession, and the exclusivity of love. In the ancient view of retaliation, there are at least three ideas that form its core: one's position in the social group supersedes performative competence (and, *a forteriori*, that one's own social group supersedes all others), that violence is the best way to solve problems, and that mere survival trumps a life that is lived well. Self-possession is two-fold, the privileging of one's own *I* over the other; and maintaining the superiority of the family, clan, tribe, or nation over all others. Self-possession is the direct cause of retaliation. Finally, the exclusivity of love reflects an old way of thinking when the idealized form of relation, love, is reduced to the exclusive property of *the couple in love*. All the above reflect archaic thinking that is always divisive, confrontational, and destructive. Given the pervasiveness of this conceptualization, skepticism about the probability of peace has not only survived, but has thrived. So, in designing the Peace Studies Certificate, we acknowledge that calling into question old ways of thinking opens windows reviving not only the possibility of peace, but also the probability of attaining peace.

For the Peace Studies Certificate in general, and the "Philosophies of Peace" introductory course in particular, to instantiate global awareness, students must encounter other cultural orientations other than their own familiar ones. Encountering other worldviews yields an awareness of cultural difference. Cultural difference, the tendency of a culture to ask particular questions and to think about particular things, is our way to understand others. Since all cultural orientations are, in effect, ways of relating, by coming to know others' differences, we broaden our capacity for and experience of relationships. Being able to draw on different cultural orientations enables us to be effective in working for and bring about peace on both the local and international levels.

In designing the "Philosophies of Peace" course we understand that we cannot simply assign readings, discuss writings, administer examinations and then expect the students to bridge the gaps between an academic grasp of, working for, and experiencing peace. Thus, we are challenged to conduct the course in accordance with the stated goals of the course—"*In the classroom, as in the rest of the world, means and ends must cohere*". We find Martin Buber's philosophy of authoritative democratic education useful in our teaching philosophy: the teacher instructs with *authority*, yet is not the only one in the classroom with *power*.

Sharing power in the classroom does not mean that the teacher abdicates the authority from which he/she speaks and conducts the practice of philosophy. Authority necessarily speaks from the humility of understanding that one's own education is a work in progress; therefore, the teacher models life-long learning. It is a sign of authority that the teacher speaks with strength of purpose, knowledge, understanding, compassion, and encouragement; hence, the classroom space, is a practice space in which *all* persons are empowered to take responsibility for their own education. Each person within the classroom contributes to the overall democratic ethos of the classroom, defining its limitations as well as its possibilities. The end result of not only this course, but also the Peace Studies Certificate, it is hoped, will be the emergence of an authoritative confidence in each student. An authoritatively confident student is more likely to embrace and work toward the probability of peace.

The design of both the Certificate and the "Philosophies of Peace" course takes into consideration five principles of peace education: building a democratic community, teaching cooperation, developing an ethical sensibility, promoting critical reasoning, and developing confidence. From an unabashedly normative perspective, the Peace Certificate in general, and the course in particular unify means and ends in order to educate the whole person by fostering a peace-centered relationship between students and instructor(s), and between students and members of the community. The use of a discussion-based classroom, seating in a circle, and the subject matter itself served to orient the students towards these goals. The addition of optional field trips to peace-oriented sites (Our Lady of the Holy Spirit Monastery in Conyers, Georgia, the peace murals in Little Five Points, Atlanta, and the Ann Frank exhibit at the KSU Center in Kennesaw) gave the students opportunities to cultivate deeper levels of understanding and relation.

"Philosophies of Peace: also introduced students to the transformative goals of peace education: conscientization, the expanding of one's horizons by understanding the causal links between meaning structures and action in culture, and the development of global awareness. Peace Education philosopher Betty Reardon (1988) has summarized these goals succinctly: "profound global, cultural change that affects ways of thinking, worldviews, behaviors, relationships, and structures that make up our public order. It implies a change in the human consciousness and in human society." Providing a space in which conscientization and the development of a global consciousness might emerge is of paramount concern in "Philosophies of Peace"; therefore, course activities are structured to facilitate deepening levels of understanding of the inherent connection between theory and *praxis*.

To this end, students read past and present works on peace as well as thoughtfully engaging each other about the topics raised in these works. Students also have the opportunity to engage members of the community in dialogue about peace issues. Several students took the opportunity to interview members of their respective communities and came away with a deepened sense of a larger world around them and other human beings grappling with realizing peace. One student, who interviewed a Muslim refugee from Bosnia, wrote,

> *I noticed that as I spoke to him, he seemed to want to talk less about his personal feelings and tragedies than he did about political events. It seemed the anger and resentment were still too close for him to relate it to himself personally; instead, he tended to frame his memories in terms of worldwide Muslim oppression, the Bosnian people, or in ways you would expect a news caster to relate the tale . . ..*
> *As I interviewed him, I became painfully conscious of the fact that I didn't have the skills to do the interview justice. I was merely tainting the sacredness of his story.*

Reflecting upon his interviewing experience, the student noted that "it is easy to sit in an air-conditioned classroom in a prosperous American suburb and talk about peace being more than the absence of war and the responsibility one holds for all human beings, but what does one say to someone who has seen war, whose youth was forged under siege?"

Another student in the course interviewed a Vietnam veteran and noticed that in preparing for the interview, he became sensitive to asking questions of others: "having foreseen that Mike might not wish to speak about such things (and being already more interested in the sorts of questions that I ended up asking him than in descriptions or accounts of battle and warfare itself), I prepared my questions so that he could answer only to whatever degree he felt comfortable."

The interview option afforded the students to ask others about the central focus of the course, getting beyond a negative conception of peace and moving toward a positive understanding of peace. One student arranged an interview with noted American historian and longtime peace veteran, Howard Zinn. Zinn told the student that "the fundamental character of peace rests in a need of human beings for peace. War does not result from 'human nature' because people must be manipulated, propagandized, coerced, seduced in order to mobilize them for war. Our problem is to cut through the propaganda and get people to think and feel back to their basic desires."

Student Thoughts about Philosophies of Peace

"You go through life knowing that change is necessary, but you don't have the knowledge to know *why* change is necessary or *how* to go about change. This class has helped me to begin to know what is necessary for change of the world and my inner being."

"I feel that I've regained hope in peace. Learning about the different philosophers and peace activists opened my eyes to a different way of life."

"I think my idea of peace has changed from not thinking about it as idealistically as I used to. I now think that I can be at peace and try to help others to be at peace even when there is conflict. The class has made me realize how important self-awareness and self-knowledge is."

"I already had a pretty positive idea from reading Thich Nhat Hanh; however, being exposed to the writings of such people as Winona Laduke was very helpful. If anything, this course served to make my ideas of peace well rounded."

"Why isn't this class mandatory curriculum? We *have* to learn about the history of each war in history class, so why isn't it mandatory to learn about peace? Education for change begins in the classroom. If it's mandatory to learn the history of Hitler, Stalin, and Vietnam, then why isn't it mandatory to learn the opposite, how not to have war—peace?"

Closing Reflections

The certificate program is a promise yet to be fully realized on our campus, just as is peace in our individual and collective lives. So, it feels a little strange sitting down to write a closing section for this essay. As one student observed in the transcript after interviewing a Bosnian Muslim, "How do you write a conclusion to an event what has yet to end?" We might appropriate his question here as "How do you write a conclusion to an essay about a peace studies program that has barely begun?" This is one of those questions that does not demand a direct answer, but instead calls for an on-going and deepening consideration.

The collaborative efforts of our faculty group, and the enthusiasm and excitement generated from students and administrators alike, is a strong and hopeful beginning. It is our hope that students who enroll in the Peace Studies Certificate Program will find strong direction through their studies that will lead them to work for peace in whatever they choose to do. We hope that faculty who teach courses in the Peace Studies curriculum will find a deeper understanding of the relationship between their own educational efforts and peace work. And it is our sincere hope that in choosing to study peace we may all find our way deeper into own our hearts and the hearts of others to realize the promise that peace holds for all.

References

Gandhi, M. K. (1938). *Hind Swaraj (or Indian Home Rule)*. Ahmedabad, India: Navajivan.

Harris, Ian M. and Mary Lee Morrison. (2003). *Peace Education*, second edition.

 Jefferson, NC: McFarland.

Harris, Ian M. (2004). "Peace education theory," *Journal of Peace Education*, 1, (1), 5-20.

Reardon, Betty. (1988). *Comprehensive Peace Education: Educating for Global responsibility*.

New York: Teachers College Press.

****

Dr. Thomas Pynn can be contacted via the Philosophy Department, when he is not traveling in Africa or promoting peace projects worldwide, via TPynn@kennesaw.edu

Stalking Interpersonal Peace

by Two Lifetime Offenders

By Cynthia Moe and Mark Feinknopf

Co-Founders, Sacred Space Inc.,

Atlanta, GA

****

Would you read further if you knew the authors of this story had been and still are committing violence most days of their lives?

Would you believe it if it was suggested that YOU have perpetuated some violence most days of your life?

As two seasoned travelers in a culture riddled with violence, we had perceived ourselves as peaceful, peace seeking – and certainly not violent! Discovering Dr. Marshall B. Rosenberg's characterization and comprehensive description of passive, everyday violence, however, has been eye opening and relationship changing!

We have come to acknowledge (sometimes <u>very </u>abashedly) that we each have participated (and regrettably sometimes continue to participate) in every category of passive (covert) violence that is characterized in the book <u>Nonviolent Communication ℠: A Language of Life</u>." (Puddle Dancer Press, 2003).

If, in my arrogance, I believe myself to be "most right," the authority over the life and actions of another deserving of or entitled to a particular style of treatment, or insistent on "my way" to the exclusion of consideration of the needs of others, I am exhibiting violent behavior, according to Dr. Rosenberg:

I can thus pretty much expect that any communication *delivered from that self-absorbed position* will elicit resistance and defensive protectiveness from the recipient.

If, on the other hand, I am consistently aware of my own needs while **equally** interested that the needs of the other be met, communication from that position offers opening and possibility for respectful and harmonious outcomes … **peace.** Arun Gandhi, writes and reflects that learning such a new language of connection and respect for the needs of others is indeed what will foster peace on our planet and in our everyday transactions – and, in fact, is the only thing that can. He, as his legendary grandfather, M. K. Gandhi, deeply believes that it is compassionate communication that offers the possibility to preclude passive violence that will in turn eventually eliminate physical violence.

Our own current late-life alliance has graced us with the opportunity to begin moving beyond the trauma and limitations of earlier life in search of the kind of respectful, egalitarian, compassionate relationship that we eventually found modeled by Marshall Rosenberg's 4-step Nonviolent Communication ℠ (NVC) process. We both strongly suspect that we might not still be together had we not begun practicing Nonviolent Communication two and a half years ago.

Our initial togetherness emerged out of a void left by broken marriages and spousal death respectively.

As we scanned each other from across a small circle of new-found healing school classmates, we each were intrigued by the other's energy. "Who is that interesting woman?" Mark wondered. "I wonder why he is looking at me so intensely?" Cynthia queried.

Thus began the dance which continues today, eight years later, as we position to navigate as gracefully as possible between our individual needs for independence and autonomy and our shared need for connection, partnering and making a difference in the world.

We, as all humans, come to each relationship opportunity a product of our-life-until-then. Mark had enjoyed a 35-year marriage in Columbia, Ohio until cancer took his wife's life and ended that dance. Determined that her death would not be his, Mark strongly suspected that in six months he would meet someone from a different city who was unlike anyone he had ever known. When that occurred across the healing circle, his new journey began.

When we met in '96, Cynthia had experienced two thirteen-year marriages and was now determined to do whatever was required to manifest an authentic, supportive and egalitarian long-term connection with a man. We both had childhoods that seem characteristic of the late 30's/early 40's – financially concerned, controlling, emotionally remote and authoritarian Fathers in locally respected professional positions; stay-at-home and do-as-dad-says (but resent it!) bright and creative mothers; and one talented, sensitive and co-cowering sister.

Eventual travel and college experience provided release from early life confinements and the foundation upon which to begin building independence and fostering individual interests. Mark's interests led to architecture, urban design, community building, healing work and family life with a son and daughter. Cynthia's interest led to teaching, community service, dream work and energy healing facilitation, art, and family life with two sons.

While we had studied and done clearing work in a great variety of healing modalities, NVC offered something additional that was missing elsewhere – tangible, simple-to-remember and totally reliable tools for restoring ourselves to a place of compassion and connection when differences separated us and skewed our perceptions.

Though we consider ourselves to be bright, well-educated and articulate, we had ill-developed understanding and language for expression of our feelings, needs and values – the very things most critical to a person's sense of well being and ability to maintain connection with another.

The NVC (Non-Violent Communication) model offers discernment tools and invites us to get in touch with those characteristics in order to help us get our needs met. Our own connection, as well as all our relationships, has been unbelievably enriched by the use of this tool. Our everyday transactions are rewarding and satisfying to the extent that we maintain consciousness in the way we are expressing ourselves.

In our own relationship, as the initial glitter has worn off to expose our "rough edges," we have been challenged to grow beyond our previous capacities for connection. This has also required excavating the old trauma that is underlying especially strong angry reactions. Thanks to our Non-Violent Communications study, we have been able to clearly see that each person's anger is about them and what lies unhealed within them. We now recognize that most people have past experience that impacts them still.

We can, therefore, be more compassionate toward others when we realize that their anger is simply telling us that some old wound has been reactivated by a current stimulus. It has therefore become easy to see that each person is always doing the best they can do to get their needs met – whether we appreciate their strategy for doing so or not!

We have come to deeply understand and accept that anger is not about an outside action but rather about what we are telling ourselves in our heads about that action or behavior. Our own anger is about us and our history and what we are telling ourselves about some outside stimulus. Your anger is about you and your history and what you are telling yourself about some outside stimulus.

When we can perceive anger – ours or others' – as an ally that is masking an early fear or unmet need, we can respond differently. We can view anger as "the tragic expression of an unmet need," as Dr. Rosenberg sometimes characterizes it, and extend ourselves to respond more nonviolently and peacefully.[3]

Offering deep empathy at this juncture, to our self or the other or both, can initiate connection to the positive essence that is available in all of us instead of connection to the anger/past trauma.

Recently Mark felt his anger building while traveling on a long trip with Cynthia. He continually heard directions regarding his driving that sounded like demands. He felt he was being corrected at each turn and each stoplight.

Going inward he realized how Cynthia's voice resembled his Mother's and then others who had apparently criticized his driving. He realized how sensitive he was about his driving skills related to several recent incidents.

Mark began listening to his own self-empathy process and quietly worked himself through his issues. He also realized that Cynthia was nervous possibly due to some of her previous experiences and began empathizing with her. Over the next week what may have become a very unpleasant trip became a connecting and peaceful time together .

———————————

Just last night we experienced a time of "violent" disconnection because each of us had unmet needs that were so intense we were unable to be present or empathic to the needs of the other until we'd provided ourselves with extensive "emergency first-aid empathy."

So, our pursuit of peace and nonviolence continues as we journey in companionship with intense commitment to expand, enrich and maintain our ability to be compassionately connected – with one another and all others. In so doing, we hope to become the mentors of respectful, egalitarian relationship that we sought in vain at the beginning of our relationship in order that others on that quest might meet with less frustration and greater possibility.

****

Authors and Workshop Facilitators Mark Feinknopf and Cynthia Moe are co-presidents of Sacred Space Inc., a consulting practice based in Atlanta dedicated to building healthy community and fostering nonviolence. They conduct numerous workshops: see
www.sacredspaceinc.com (770) 934-2787
info-sacredspace@mindspring.com

Organizing a Persian Festival

in Sydney, Australia

by Dr. Kurosh Parsi

Medical Hospital, Sydney, Australia

****

December 1993. I received a phone call from my ever-enthusiastic friend, Homer Abramian. He told me he was convinced that the Ethnic Affairs Commission of New South Wales, Australia, would approve a hefty grant of $50,000 for a Persian Festival! He said he had been corresponding with the Chairman and he was given a personal guarantee about the grant. He also added that one of the very rich Sydney-based Iranian merchants had accepted to cover the other $50-60,000. He said that it was time to organize that "ideal Persian Festival." Well, this is the way it started. For the sake of brevity, we will have to ignore the minor insignificant details which followed (for instance, the detail that the EAC granted us $15,000 instead of $50,000 and the merchant gave us $6,000 instead of $60,000). Yes, the budget for the Festival reached $200,000! We will also ignore the insignificant detail that a good number of the Iranian population of Sydney turned against us when they found out our plans for the biggest Persian Festival ever held overseas: yet we carried on in New South Wales, far from our Iranian homeland.

It was pretty ambitious all right. The program spanned over ten days, with a magnificent opening ceremony in the majestic Curzon Hall AND a grand performance of Persian Music and Dance in the Sydney Opera House! There were seven intensive days of Seminars regarding Persian culture, arts, literature, history, archaeology, religion and other issues with participation of more than 20 scholars from all around the world; a special festival for children; dance performances in the middle of the city of Sydney; and as a highlight, a special Persian Traditional Music concert by the Dastan group who were brought to Sydney direct from Iran.

This was not exactly what we had planned back in December 1993. This was what *actually* happened. We wanted a much more harmonious festival. The reality was much harsher

Back in December, one of our friends, still agitated by Shamloo's account of Ferdowsi and Zahak, suggested we erect a statue of Ferdowsi in Sydney. He was quite convinced he would get approval. Despite my utmost respect for Ferdowsi, I knew that no Western government would approve of a statue of a turbaned man to be erected on its land. The connotations and the physical resemblance to the usual attire of the now-ruling clergies of Iran would not pass by unnoticeable. I had a better idea.

This was not because we had the same name. It was not even because I had always liked him and had made him my role model . It was simply a pragmatic and possible, <u>achievable task</u>. I believed we should erect a Bas-Relief of Cyrus the Great in Australia instead of Ferdowsi!

Why? Well, first, he was an accepted international figure associated with peace and freedom. Second, he is considered a key figure in the Bible and referred to as "Zol-Qarnain" in the Koran , so no religion would be offended by his statue. Third, he was the first inventor of the "policy of Multi-Culturalism", also widely embraced throughout Australia. Lastly, he was the first Emperor of Iran, the person who "created" Iran from segregated provinces of Parsa, Mede, and Partha. He was an inspirational person who created a nation not by sword but through forgiveness, on the pillars of respect and human equality, with such a vision and commitment thousands of years ahead of his time.

My friend Homer and others accepted my reasoning. We informed Lewis Batros, the Sydney-based Assyrian artist, of our plans and I provided him with some drawings. Since I was in charge of 10 million other things, some members of the organizing committee said they would "look after" everything. Famous last words!

September 1994. Now we have less than 2 months left before the opening, and nothing has been done about the statue yet . They want me to take over the project (still continuing with the 10 million other things and also working night shifts in the Hospital's accident & Emergency Room.) What next?

Now the panic button is pressed! An urgent meeting is arranged with Ms Mary Demech, Head of Community Relations for the prestigious Australia Council for the Arts. Our luck was shining: they approved a grant for $5,000! We still have $9,000 to raise. Urgent phone call to the United States: HELP needed! Soon the Festival, including Sydney Opera House performance, was sold out! Long distance phone calls returned: "Money will come, find a place to put it !"

Homer and Fariborz Rahnamoon had a meeting where they met the chairman of the Bicentennial Park. The minister for the entire nation's Multicultural Affairs, who was our patron, was also there. Fariborz was quick to ask the minister to talk to the chairman of the Park: can a Park authority reject the Australian Minister of Culture's wish? But even in democracies, bureaucracies flourish: in Australia, yes, the Parks rules can override a Council for the Arts request.

One early morning, after having finished another night shift at the hospital, I felt like going for a drive in the Bicentennial Park. The Park was very close to my Hospital. Deep inside, I did not believe that this whole "statue business" would unfold. While I was driving around, however, certain things looked so "familiar" from my homeland. The Persian-style water fountains, the top of the metallic structure in the park (which actually resembled the tomb of Cyrus in Pasargade), and yes, Nature's beauty. So, there was hope after all!

I quickly rang Fereshteh Sadeghi, who is a graphic artist. She came down to the Park with me and understood what I meant. The rest was history. Fereshteh and I worked on the design for the back of our planned statue while Lewis was working on the front. Out of more than 10 beautiful designs, we agreed upon one of them – an interesting process! It depicts people of different nationalities *living in peace and harmony,* symbolizing the concepts and values of Human Rights and Multiculturalism. An outline of Australia embraces the atlas of the world while the whole visual is immersed in the First Declaration of Human Rights by Cyrus the Great. It looked fabulous.

I prepared a proposal to the Park authorities including the full visual design. It was promptly rejected. I will not bother you with details, but it took quite a bit of "flexing" of political muscle to get them to accept our proposal. Even despite that, they wanted to put the statue somewhere out of sight !

An Iranian architect and Mr. Hashem Kamal continued the negotiation with the park, and meanwhile, took up the job of constructing the base .

30 October 1994. This is the day of unveiling of the Bas-Relief. But the statue is still at Lewis' home! Last monies are at last paid, courtesy of International College Spain -- and the statue is carried to the site by a crane. There is only one hour left before the guests of honor arrive and the statue, about 4 meters (12 feet) high, is just now being erected . It is made of a light material and needs to be reinforced with cement. Lewis says there is no time for cement and we just have to make sure it does not fall over!

The honorable guests arrive. Figures like Mr. Bastani-Parizi, Mr. Abolghasem Parto, Dr. Eslami-Nodushan, Mr. Micahel Photios, the late Dr. Kurosh Aryamanesh (who was so happy that day) and so many other scholars, members of the Australian Parliament and media.

The wind was strong and I was truly worried that the bas-relief might fall and even though Cyrus himself did not kill, his statue might kill one of the scholars! Wouldn't that make news? "A great scholar killed in Australia in the unveiling of the statue of Cyrus!": oh, the media would have a field-day!

If there was a spiritual battle between Ahriman and Ahura, and if Cyrus was truly an instrument for Ahura, this is the best opportunity for Ahriman to impart a crucial blow to the forces of Ahura by making the statue fall . While these paranoid thoughts were going through my brain, a strong wind blew and the statue moved slightly, or at least I thought so. That was it: I could not take <u>any</u> chances!

But other forces were at work. Suddenly, with no notice, the Park water sprinkler system started -- and some members of our esteemed audience got very wet ! At the same time, the microphone became disconnected, and hence Ms. Denesh's speech was interrupted .

I was right about my spiritual premonitions. The Ahriman has started attacking and in any second, the statue might fall, marking a drastic end to a long-fought battle. I had to do something! I moved behind the statue. Hashem was standing there, amused at the chaos around the wet guests. I whispered hoarsely: "Hasseem! Quickly! It's going to fall!" The monologue behind our distinguished, chaotic scene went like this:

"No, it's not going to fall! Look, the sprinklers are getting our guests wet!"

"Quickly! Grab Cyrus! The wind is picking up!"

"No, it won't fall!"

"YES! It is going to fall and you will be responsible. Get up there NOW!"

Poor Hashem must have sensed my serious concern. He did get behind the huge heavy statue, and with his strength, supported it. I felt better, and relaxed. And the rest of the ceremony went smoothly. The whole place and setting was so beautiful! The statue was surrounded with more than 30 flags of Iran from ancient times until the recent. To the left of the statue was the ever magnificent *Derafsh* of Kaveh, a symbol of freedom.

Beautiful day, beautiful people! Some of those people are not with us anymore, but their memories will remain with us forever. It is the memories which count, which make a difference. Like Cyrus, gone a long time ago, we memorialize his vision and hence his memory is still alive, still "making a difference." I sometimes wonder if "reality" is only a memory too?

That night, we got a security person to sleep near the statue (to prevent a possible act of sabotage by forces of Ahriman). The base of the statue was made of bricks and fairly ugly. About a year after the festival, The Iranian Cultural Organization (a different group from the one which organized the festival) constructed a beautiful base for the beloved Bas-Relief statue.

Yes, this statue is not just a statue of Cyrus. It is a symbol of achievement. It is a symbol of mutual effort, of Iranians working together and achieving together. It is a symbol of Iranians making their mark on a new land, and it has made us feel at home "down under."

At a time when Iran bashing was the rule and the norm, this gesture by the New South Wales Government was seen as a welcoming sign by the Iranian community and the event has since been annually remembered during the Mehregan Festival each September.

****

To read more about the history of Cyrus, see http://www.oznet.net/cyrus/cyframe.htm   As Prof. Richard Frye of Harvard has reflected (see The Heritage of Persia, *p.151):*

"In the victories of the Persians... what was different was the new policy of reconciliation and together with this was the prime aim of Cyrus to establish a pax Achaemenica.. . . If one were to assess the achievements of the Achaemenid Persians, surely the concept of One World .... the fusion of peoples and cultures in one 'Oecumen' was one of their most important legacies."

Upon his victory over the Medes, Cyrus founded a government for his new kingdom, incorporating both Median and Persian nobles as civilian officials. The conquest of Asia Minor completed, he led his armies to the eastern frontiers. The victories to the east led him again to the west and sounded the hour for attack on Babylon and Egypt. When he conquered Babylon, he did so to cheers from the Jewish Community, who welcomed him as a liberator-- he allowed the Jews to return to the promised Land. He showed great forbearance and respect towards the religious beliefs and cultural traditions of other races. These qualities earned him the respect and homage of all the people over whom he ruled. The Bas Relief statue has a quote from an original document by Cyrus:

... I am Cyrus. King of the world. When I entered Babylon... I did not allow anyone to terrorize the land... I kept in view the needs of people and all its sanctuaries to promote their well-being... I put an end to their misfortune. The Great God has delivered all the lands into my hand; the lands that I have made to dwell in a peaceful habitation...

The monument placed in Australia is a replica of an actual Bas-Relief found in Pasargade, the capital city of Persia which was founded by Cyrus. It depicts Cyrus the Great (580-529 BC). Cyrus was the first Achaemenian Emperor of Persia, who issued a decree on his aims and policies, later hailed as his charter of "The Rights of Nations". Inscribed on a clay cylinder, this is known to be the first declaration of Human Rights, and is now kept at the British Museum.

A replica of this famous Bas-Relief is also at the United Nations in New York.

A G.I.'s Transition from Soldier to Activist

by Bruce Gagnon

Coordinator, Global Network Against Weapons & Nuclear Power in Space

Brunswick, Maine

****

After having grown up on military bases, the son of a career Air Force enlisted man, I took the oath myself in early 1971 and joined the military. The Vietnam War was still raging at the time and when I reported for my induction physical in Oakland, California, I had to wait in a long line of guys who were being drafted. I'll never forget one woman, my mother's age, going up and down the line of new recruits pleading with us in a highly emotional way not to go in the service. Her son had been killed in Vietnam, and she told us in tears: "The war is **wrong**." To this day, I can still feel the emotion from her. What a way to begin your time in the military!

I actually flunked my induction physical exam because of a high school football injury, and had to get a waiver to get into the military. Most of the guys in the line that day were trying to find a way out!

After my basic training in Texas, and then my job training in Mississippi, I was sent to Travis AFB in California for my permanent duty. As it turned out Travis was a Military Airlift Command (MAC) base where GI's would come from all over America to get on planes to fly to Vietnam. When the planes came back from the war zone, they carried the bodies of dead soldiers. I worked just across the street from the flight line, and from my office window could see the rows and rows of body bags lined up on the runway almost daily.

At this point I was supporting the war. I had worked on the Nixon campaign in 1968 and was the Vice-Chair of the Okaloosa County Young Republican Club. My whole life had been a sheltered existence, living behind the fences on military bases, not exposed to much thinking outside of these conservative, "patriotic" environments.

On weekends at the Travis Air Force Base there were usually protests just outside the gates -- typically only a dozen or so people holding signs. Only once was there a big event that drew 500 people and was attended by Jane Fonda and the great band "Country Joe & the Fish". I didn't attend. We were all told to stay away. The military said they'd have the Office of Secret Investigation (OSI) outside the gates taking pictures and if any of us were photographed we'd be in big trouble. It did make me wonder – I thought we were fighting this war in Vietnam for "freedom?"

These protests created a healthy dynamic inside the base for the 18,000 military personnel permanently stationed there, plus the thousands that flew in and out of the base on the way to the war. We'd talk about the protesters and the war in the barracks at night, in the chow hall, and on the job. My conversion to a peace activist came from this process.

After one year in the military I decided that I no longer could support the war and had become a conscientious objector. I requested to be released from the military as a CO but when I was asked about the history of my family (was I a Quaker? did I come from a traditional peace church?), I was turned down -- as the response to each question revealed that I had grown up in a military family.

The one thing that really killed all of my illusions was reading The Pentagon Papers, the secret government history of the war that revealed in startling detail how the government and the CIA had created the pretext to enter the war in the first place. The papers, smuggled out to the New York Times by Rand Corporation analyst Daniel Ellsberg, showed how our own government was capable of deceiving the public, the media, and Congress in order to justify a war. My life was changed for certain after that.

Once I had figured things out, once I knew what was really going on in the world, being in the military was just like doing time in jail to me. After finally getting out of the Air Force in mid-1974 I moved to Florida where I enrolled in college and hoped to "do something good" with my life after spending 3 ½ years doing "hard time" in the military.

Just as I neared graduation from the University of Florida I was recruited to become an organizer for Cesar Chavez's United Farmworkers Union (UFW). I was sent to California for one month, to La Paz, the UFW headquarters where I received excellent organizing training from union leaders, including Cesar. Often at night, Cesar would have the four new recruits from Florida up to his office where he would tell us stories from his career as a union activist. I also spent time taking notes in a contract negotiation while there and from that experience was made the note taker during Florida union contract negotiations with Coca Cola – Minute Maid orange juice. It was a remarkable experience to sit along side fruit pickers as they negotiated with highly paid and trained corporate lawyers. From that experience I learned that just going to law school does not necessarily make one the wisest or most noble person in the room.

In 1983, I became the state coordinator of the Florida Coalition for Peace & Justice, a multi-issue peace organization based in Orlando. In that job that I held for 15 years, I began to study what was happening with the space program, seeing how the military industrial complex viewed space as a new market for the next arms race. I began organizing protests at the space center. We had seven people at our first protest there. By 1987 our ranks had swelled to over 5,000 as we protested the first flight test of the Trident II nuclear missile from Cape Canaveral.

Then in 1989, we took NASA into Federal court trying to block a launch of deadly plutonium on board a rocket. Even though we lost the court case, the enormous publicity that came with an audacious act of bringing a lawsuit against NASA brought many people around the world to our cause and new relationships were born. In addition, it became clear that if we were to prevent the nuclearization and weaponziation of space, we'd have to quickly create a broader and stronger base than we had at that time in Florida and Colorado, the only other place of local anti-Star Wars organizing that was happening.

Thus, in 1992 several of us organized a meeting in Washington, D.C. and created the Global Network Against Weapons & Nuclear Power in Space. Since that time our group has grown to over 150 affiliates on virtually every continent of the world. Each year we have an international space organizing conference and we've since met in Florida, Colorado, New Mexico, California, England, Germany, Alabama, Australia, and Maine.

In 1997 NASA launched another nuclear powered space probe, Cassini, that carried 72 pounds of deadly plutonium-238. In their Environmental Impact Statement (EIS) for that mission NASA acknowledged that in a worst case scenario launch accident, the plutonium could be released into the atmosphere and carried by the winds for a 60-mile radius. NASA's EIS stated that they'd then have to come in and remove all the people in the affected area, remove all the animals, remove all the buildings, all the vegetation, and ultimately they'd have to remove the top half-inch of soil as everything would be radioactive for thousands of years to come. Our global campaign to stop Cassini did not stop the launch, but expanded our membership and our visibility in huge ways around the planet as the public began to realize the dangers associated with the nuclearization of space.

Our purpose with the Global Network has been to create an international constituency around the space issue. The notion of war in space is a new issue for most people, even those in the peace movement. Many people think it is a "far out" notion. How could they ever make weapons in space work? Nonsense, some people say.

Others, who support the idea, say great. Let the U.S. be the country that controls and dominates space militarily. At least we are the good guys! Better us than anyone else.

As I look at the history of warfare what I see is the constant technological progression to more and more deadly weapons of destruction. The cave men had sticks and stones and then humanity graduated to the bow and arrow. From there we went to firearms and then machine guns and airplanes. Then came nuclear weapons, the ultimate weapon. What makes anyone think that given enough time and taxpayer dollars the militarists, scientists, and technologists could not top the nuclear weapon?

As I've become a bit of a "peace movement specialist" by working on space issues, I've tried not to forget my roots. I always try to remember that my first organizing jobs were working with poor people, folks who got very little in government services that could make their lives much better. All my life I've heard the right wing screaming against socialism but the only "socialism" I've ever seen has been for the rich and the corporations.

In order to pay for the Vietnam War, the important War on Poverty had to be "de-funded" and abandoned. Many people believe that the reason behind the assassination of Martin Luther King was his coming out against the war in Vietnam realizing that his "dream" of equality was not possible in a state of perpetual war. King was becoming a leader in the unification of the civil rights movement with the peace movement, something that would have rocked the established powers in the nation.

So as I look at Star Wars today, something that experts believe will be the largest industrial project in the history of the planet Earth, all I see is a further drain on social progress. There will be no money for health care, education, environmental clean-up, public transportation and the like. We can't have guns and butter. Unfortunately many people within the Democratic Party still think we can but the evidence clearly says it is not possible.

Having at one time been a Young Republican for Nixon, I've made a continual transition in my political thinking. In 1972, while still in the military, I volunteered for the McGovern campaign for President and went door knocking on his behalf in the neighborhoods near Travis AFB in California. What I found was disheartening, as I learned that the conservative local Democratic Party leaders thought McGovern too "liberal" and were not putting out any real effort on his behalf! He lost to Nixon in a landslide but ended up winning the moral high ground as Nixon got nailed with Watergate soon after his re-election -- and had to leave the White House, facing impeachment from Congress and the nation.

I then supported Jimmy Carter, thinking he meant it when he said that the "nuclear arms race was a disgrace to the human race" but saw him break his promise to the American people that he would never "lie" when he began cutting social programs and building up the military as he prepared to run for reelection. He lost to Ronald Reagan and lost me too. In 1996 and 2000 I had made the transition to vote for Ralph Nader who impressed me with his honesty and directness. His entire adult life has been a stunning example of service for the public good.

Over the years, I've come to believe that being a political activist requires you to set aside party interests in order to best serve the public. Sometimes you just can't play the party game and be honest to yourself and the issues you have given your life to. I often protested against Bill Clinton's bombing of Iraq and Afghanistan, which I knew were killing innocent people. Many people in the public think that being a peace activist always means that you support the Democrats and hate the Republicans. I think we in the peace movement must show an independence from all the parties. We must be able to oppose war and destruction of the social fabric at home no matter who sits in the White House or controls Congress. If there are good politicians in any party that want to work with us, then by all means we should. But we should not become slaves to any politician or political party.

George W. Bush is, no doubt, the worst president in my lifetime. I've never seen an administration so dedicated to creating an endless war. Not only a war on "terrorism" but also a war on the American people as well. Bush has declared war on our constitutional freedoms and a war on social progress as well. His chief political operative, Karl Rove, says that his favorite president was William McKinley. Why McKinley? McKinley was the last president who presided over the time in America when we had no social programs. We had no social security, no unemployment insurance, no Medicare, no welfare programs. It was just you and the poor house. This is where the Bush team wants to return us. I call it 21st Century Feudalism.

A few years ago, I learned that the space program in the U.S. had essentially been created by 100 of the top Nazi scientists brought to the U.S. after World War II. In a program called *Operation Paperclip*, the brilliant Nazi rocket scientist Werner von Braun, along with 100 copies of his V-2 rocket, were brought to Huntsville, Alabama. Hitler had used the V-2 to terrorize the cities of London, Paris, and Brussels near the end of the war. The entire U.S. space program was seeded with these Nazi operatives.

In the book Secret Agenda, former CNN investigative reporter Linda Hunt tells the horrible story of *Operation Paperclip*. Von Braun and his rocket team had used the slave labor of 40,000 Jews, gypsies, Communists, homosexuals and prisoners of war to build the rockets for

Hitler inside a mountain tunnel called Mittelwerk. By the time U.S. soldiers liberated the slaves over 25,000 of them had perished at the hands of the Germans.

Another fascinating and important part of the *Operation Paperclip* story is the other Nazi's brought into the U.S. after the war. All together over 1,500 Germans were smuggled into the U.S. by the military via Boston and West Palm Beach, Florida. Some of them were Nazi intelligence and came to help create the CIA. Others, who had been doing drug and mind experiments on Jews in Germany, were the ones to do the MK Ultra and LSD drug experiments in the 1960's here in the U.S. We've all heard the stories of people jumping out of windows, having "bad trips", after having been given drugs by the former Nazi scientists. Then there were the Nazi scientists who put Jews in freezing water to find out how the body would react to such conditions. These Nazi's went on to create the U.S. Air Force flight medicine program at Wright Patterson AFB in Ohio after the war.

In his book The Hunt for Zero Point, respected military journalist Nick Cook talks much about the "black" (the Pentagon's secret) budget. For 15 years Cook has been a defense and aerospace writer for Jane's Defence Weekly, which some consider the bible of the international weapons community. Cook spent the last 10 years researching secret military programs in the U.S. and believes that over $20 billion a year is spent on these programs outside the purview of Congress. Cook states, "It (black programs) has a vast and sprawling architecture funded by tens of billions of classified dollars every year."

Cook traced the roots of the U.S.'s secret programs back to the Nazi scientists brought to the U.S. after WW II in *Operation Paperclip*. He states, "We know the size and scope of *Operation Paperclip*, which was huge. And we know that the U.S. operates a very deeply secret defense architecture for secret weapons programs…it is highly compartmentalized….and one of the things that's intrigued me over the years is, How did they develop it? What model did they base it on? It is remarkably similar to the system that was operated by the Germans – specifically the SS – for their top-secret weapons programs."

"What I do mean is that if you follow the trail of Nazi scientists and engineers who were recruited by America at the end of the second world war, the unfortunate corollary is that by taking on the science, you take on – unwittingly – some of the ideology...What do you lose along the way?"

I've come to believe that we will never end war on this planet as long as we have a military industrial complex that has the power to control Congress, the White House, and is a major employer of our citizens. In my own state of Maine, Bath Ironworks is the largest non-governmental employer in the entire state. They make Aegis destroyers that are now being outfitted with advanced "missile defense" systems that will be part of the Star Wars program and will be deployed surrounding China. This will spark a new arms race as China today only has 20 nuclear missiles capable of hitting the continental U.S., while we have 7,500 nuclear weapons of our own.

Our way out of this military madness is conversion: converting our industrial base to practical purposes, and conversion of our hearts. The U.S. is a militarized society, addicted to war, and without dealing with that addiction there will be no end to war. We can protest all we want against this bombing, or that invasion, but as long as our citizenry make their living from killing people we won't have the change we need.

Thus we must take on the conversion issue. Years ago the National Commission on Economic Conversion reported that military spending is capital intensive. That means that for every million dollars, yes we create X number of jobs. But evidence shows that when you take that same million dollars and invest it in any other kind of job creation, in every case you create more jobs. No matter whether it is invested in building schools or hospitals; fixing bridges or roads; hiring teachers or nurses; or building mass transit systems, more jobs are created. And isn't that what we need and want? Good jobs that do something for the society, jobs that put something back for all the people.

This conversion can only happen when we begin talking about it, educate others about it, demand it, and organize for it. This conversion can only happen when we begin to ask about the moral and ethical implications of having an industrial base that requires we keep having wars – just like a drug addict continually needs another fix.

We must ask our fellow citizens what it means to be alive. What does it mean when the only thing we have to offer the future generations is endless war? In this debate we will create the seeds of a positive future. The time is late. We must get to work. We must get organized. Nothing can be more important.

****

Bruce Gagnon is the Coordinator of the "Global Network Against Weapons &
Nuclear Power in Space". He can be reached via www.space4peace.org and their web site has
many informative facts, discussions, blogs and articles on these topics
He lives in Brunswick, Maine and travels nationwide.

Letter from a Visitor to the Era of Light and Life

by Costas Diamantopoulos

Athens, Greece

****

Dear Brothers and Sisters,

I feel compelled to write to you to share with you my recent experience at the Olympics in Greece, which left a deep impression within my whole being!

For seventeen days, I was blessed to have been transported into another planetary epoch where the brotherhood of man was in full manifestation, where altruistic service was the rule and not the exception, where the Flame of Peace was kept sacred in a high altar, where the joy of multiple relationships with different types of human beings from all five continents of our planet transcended all barriers of language, cultures and geopolitical diversities.

Yes my friends, I was not dreaming, although the experience had a dreamlike quality: I was physically there! It was the 2004 Olympics "Opening Ceremony", set against the backdrop of beautiful Athens, Greece.

I feel I was truly blessed to have been among the thousands of others who received and shared the bestowal of the Ministry of The Olympic Spirit. The microcosm of this highly advanced era was bestowed in my very own backyard, in Athens, Greece, and the Ministry of the Olympic Spirit encircuited everyone in the vicinity thanks to the Mercy of the Son.

The prelude of this temporal event started on the 13th of August and climaxed on the 29th of August 2004.

How can I start to impart to you the benefit of my experience? How can I even try to describe to you my impressions from such an event? Let's start from the focal point of the Olympic Games, the Olympic Stadium.

What my eyes perceived was a futuristic but extremely harmonious and pleasing to the eye, architectural marvel inspired by the glorified artist named Kalatrava (who must have been working on this piece under the auspices of Celestial Artisans!)   No doubt you saw the images on your TV screens, but unfortunately you could not have perceived the living energy and the height of emotions such a place generates when being surrounded by 70,000 other dedicated and inspired volunteers. Most of them were young men and women who had left their jobs and their families and had forsaken their traditional summer holidays just to offer their loving and unselfish service to their fellows without any expectation of reward. It was this very presence, and these acts of devotion to serve that were responsible for instilling in me a feeling of unconditional love that permeated through so many different personalities gathered together.

Their smiling and happy faces coupled with patience and politeness proved to me that their choices to serve the Ancient Immortal Spirit had led to a major transformative experience within their minds and souls.

And then it was the opening and closing ceremony and the Lighting and Transference of the Flame that sent shivers down my spine. Those of you who chose to witness those events on your TV screens, namely the opening and closing ceremonies of the Olympic Games, must have formed some kind of an idea of the amount of work that went into the staging of such a complex event, and impact it must have had on everyone involved.

Did you notice on your TV screens during the various sporting events the three concentric circles of the orange and the green variety? Those symbols placed on banners were to be found everywhere in the city of Athens and in the arenas. Obviously they were selected years ago as one of the banner insignia for the 2004 Games but I only noticed their abundance and presence when I became conscious of their use during my heightened awareness in one of the events. This 'peace symbol' was carried throughout the games!

I have no way of knowing which member of the Reserved Corps of Destiny under the auspices of the Angels of Progress succeeded in placing it there. However, I know now of another member of the Reserved Corps of Destiny! His name is Dimitris Papaioannou. He is a 38 year-old choreographer, virtually unknown before these games. He is the man responsible for selecting the concepts and for materializing the ideas in such aesthetic perfection. He is the mortal responsible for transmitting art and symbolism of Truth Beauty and Goodness to four billion viewers of this planet through the TV broadcasting planetary circuits. Here is what he said in an interview with Le Monde:

The opening ceremony is inspired from the Apollo (Light) ancient Greek traditions. The Closing Ceremony is inspired from the Dionysian Festivities (Life). The First Ceremony is the Light, The Spirit, the Ideas. The last one is the miracle and the intoxication of life. The primal ceremony is a hymn to the Human Entity. In the Final Ceremony is the Human Being who celebrates Life. The opening ceremony is like blowing the Kiss of Life to a statue. The closing one is like embracing this very Human Being who came alive. The general idea of the Opening Ceremony is the history of the Consciousness of Humanity, the Adventure of Discovery of what it means to be human, which is the Socratic dictum ' Know thyself'.

Do you also have a visualization of those two ceremonies still imprinted in your memory banks as I do? Do you remember how Love or Eros was depicted as the "unifying Force"? Reflect upon this – love IS! Do you remember how the Clepsydra concept "paraded," expressing the time dependence of our existence? Do you remember how the aquamarine origin of the Human Entity was staged? And finally how our Cosmic Consciousness was also expanded instantaneously by the image of our whole galaxy simulated by 70,000 points of Light held by each one of the spectators within the elliptical boundaries of the "Out–Worldly" Olympic Stadium?

And to complete the transfixing experience, the almost celestial female voice singing a haunting version of Manos Hajidaki's song, "The Dove" while the Dove of Peace was encircling the stadium high above. These are eternal memories for our world!

I do not know if you have had similar emotions like myself, if you were lucky enough to watch this, but I was ecstatic with worshipful tears of gratitude for being human in my eyes for a long period of time. Even if this work of art was not the creation of a Celestial Artisan, I was privileged to have, through this event, a foretaste of what glorious soul nourishing and mind-challenging spectacles await us in our long ascent to Paradise.

In our physical realm of the here and now I received a preview of the feeling such a spectacle can generate within the deeper recesses of the soul, when I saw fellow mortals from 207 different countries and the five continents of our experimental planet assembled together in perfect harmonious coexistence. Their identifying symbols and insignia were diverse but by competing in the spirit of the Olympic Glory side-by-side in the arena and in the spectator seats, they were showing to a divided world that yes, all earthly animosity and racial, cultural and religious differences can be set aside.

Further, in all athletic endeavors the same spirit indwells us compelling us to try to touch the heights of almost superhuman attainments after hard and sacrificial devotion to reach the pinnacle of golden glory. Is it not our ascendant training in the evolutionary arenas that teaches us to surpass our imperfect selves, and to be judged worthy at the end to receive the Golden Medal of an Intergalactic Marathon Finaliter? Or learning further to excel in team work and to become coaches ourselves to younger intergalactic ascending athletes of the personality perfection race overcoming the obstacles inherent in our animal origin earthly careers?

What a spectacle! What an experience to live even for a short period of time within the boundaries of a mini Light and Life planetary epoch! Having said that, the return from such reverie to the divided, hate-filled and relatively primitive current timeframe, was not without physical pain and sorrow. My consolation is though, after my brief visitation to such an era, that now I know beyond a doubt that each one of us brothers and sisters who makes every effort possible to bring to our fellow Earth-citizens a foretaste of the promised Golden Era of Light and Life, also deserves a medal. No doubt this will be bestowed after our graduation from this Mortal Arena of Choices upon our resurrection to the Morontian Shores. This Opening Ceremony medal has the concept "Cosmic Survivor" written all over it! Let's prepare ourselves peacefully for the true Olympiad --- of the Spirit!

Brotherly Love from Your Greek Brother, from the Summer of 2004 and a totally transformed Athens….. Yours, Costas

****

Kostantinos Diamatopoulous is an engineer based in Athens and London,
and can be reached at codiam@aol.com   He is a long time reader of the Urantia Book, and to
learn more about its spiritual inspirational stories and teachings, see www.urantia.org

Buddhism and A Flood of Bridges: Varieties of Peace in Inter-religious Dialogue

by Jeffrey Wattles, Ph.D.

Kent State University Philosophy Department

Kent, Ohio, USA

****

The challenge of Buddhism for me was that it was the most radically different from Christianity of all the major world religions. Two experience-sequences connected with the rock garden at the Ryoanji Temple in Kyoto, Japan, have helped me as a person who professes to follow Jesus to enter dialogue with Buddhists. In the following narrative I pause to comment on the peace of the bright night, philosophic peace, psychic peace, the peace of utter calm, the peace of Jesus, the peace of compassion, and dialogic peace.

The setting

I have to explain some personal background first. Introduced to Christianity as a child, my early devotion waned with the onset of puberty, and I found myself in college searching in Plato and Nietzsche and Husserl; it was a displaced quest for spiritual vitality. In 1970, I had begun the practice of transcendental meditation, repeating a mantra was designed to take the mind to *samadhi*, "pure consciousness." The experience of meditation was attractive and restful, and I felt a number of good results in my life—more relaxed spontaneity, humor, keen perception, heightened mental clarity and concentration, fruits of the spirit. But the experience of *samadhi*, an absolute peace which I call " the peace of the bright night" and which I had for different "durations" on different occasions, raised a question which was for a few years the most urgent question of my life. What is the significance of that experience? What is ontologically disclosed in pure consciousness? Within Hindu philosophy there was a clear answer: it is the *atman*, the Self, non-different from Brahman, the absolutely unitary ultimate Reality. But I could never satisfy myself with that answer, because I was not persuaded by the reasoning I had been given and because I became committed to a concept of a supremely personal God (whose impersonal aspects may be meditatively touched). Thus I could not find philosophical peace about this experience. In addition, I had a question about the psychological effect of different practices in the realm of willing—decision and action. Life is, often, a rugged adventure, whose pleasures and bliss must not unravel our ability for and interest in willed encounter. In other words, there is a kind of psychic peace that seems to mask life rather than to live life.

In decision that engaged my total self, I finally chose to follow a single path of worship and service, rather than a dual path of combining my Christian spirituality with the cultivation of *samadhi*. I have not totally settled for myself the meaning of *samadhi*, but I have had partially clear recurrences of the experience in the context of my deepest penetrations in thought of the Fatherhood of God, of God as absolute, and of the in-dwelling spirit. I have always assumed, however, that there should be nothing to worry about as long as such moments arose spontaneously within devotion and were not themselves cultivated as a religious goal.

The first visit

The first experience-sequence was part of a family visit to Japan in 1986. One day we came to visit friends at Ritsumeikan University, just a couple of hundred yards from the Ryoanji temple, where we went after our visit was over. Like other Buddhist temples in Japan, this one is more than a building: it includes dozens or hundreds of acres of wooded land, with a lake on the grounds and a mountain in the background, and many buildings for monastic use. The Ryoanji temple belongs to a sect of Zen Buddhism, and its garden of raked sand and rocks is world famous, even more simple on account of the absence in it of the small trees which are normally part of such gardens. Getting the feel of the grounds somewhat, I found myself attracted to this lovely center of monastic discipline and study. I had studied enough Buddhism to teach sections in world religion courses, but it had been the religion with which I was least able to empathize. Nonetheless, I had a long-standing interest in Japanese art as an avenue for a certain type of spirituality, and I sat down amid the quiet group of tourists to contemplate the renowned rock garden. I looked; I contemplated; and within a few seconds was suddenly invaded by a depth of peace that left me speechless. This peace I will call the peace of utter calm. The word "emptiness" is equally fitting. Perceptual experience of the scene did not cease, but contemporaneous with this perception was a thorough calm, an absolute calm.

Shortly I began to react to this calm, I became frightened and disturbed. I got up, moved about, put my theological mind into gear, and wandered back with my family to the bus stop.

The rock garden seemed to be carrying me toward that old peace with a velocity that far exceeded that of the mantra meditation. "What is this peace?" I wondered, as I returned to Osaka. All of a sudden, the old issue, resolved only in terms of daily practice, thrust itself forward anew. Let me emphasize that I did not re-enter *samadhi* at the rock garden; I simply felt the calming direction, the profound entry of a peace that did not fit within the context of my Christian religious theory as developed at that time. I also make no claim that my experience at the rock garden gives insight into Buddhism.

The next morning after the disturbing peace at the rock garden, I awoke with an experience of the peace of Jesus, a compassion that had warmth and color, uplift, and, somehow an answer. I had never before felt so strongly this peace that passes understanding with its loving specificity. That experience in no way answered my question about the meaning and value of *samadhi*, the calm anterior to all religious response. But I felt confirmed in what I had devoted myself to years before. It was indeed a striking sequence, but it faded in memory until two summers later.

Later I realized that there is a Buddhist interpretation of my dawn experience of peace: it is an example of the *peace of compassion*, a prominent quality of Buddhism. One can in fact engage endlessly in the intellectual exercise of viewing X through Y and Y through X. There is a certain diplomatic skill in being able to discuss different viewpoints. According to one philosophic perspective the peace of compassion is an essence which is interpreted in one tradition as the peace of Jesus and in another tradition as the peace of, for instance, Amida; these interpretations are viewed as accretions which are not essential, albeit no concrete experience can perhaps be had without some such accretions. Philosophic questions arise, however, that philosophy cannot answer. Are Christian or Amidist views mere interpretations of a more universal experience, or is "the peace of compassion" a name for the universal accessibility of the peace of Jesus (or of the Buddha)? Philosophy cannot resolve the last question, but it should understand what these questions are, rather than assuming one view or another uncritically. There is also the question of how close one person's experience is to another's, especially if they belong to different traditions, and how one could get any answer to that question and how important it is to find out. Intellectual exercise, however, is not where the peace is found. In maturity, the sublime peace should permeate intellectual activity (and all other activities), resulting in an enduring peace in life. And I suppose that sublime peace invades the intellectual life, in part, by being represented in major premises of one's philosophy.

The second visit

In June of 1988 I went again to Kyoto, wanting to meet someone from the Jodo Shin Shu tradition. I had heard of parallels between this sect of Buddhism and Christianity and wanted dialogue with a representative of that tradition. My motives were a mix of curiosity, adventure, enthusiasm, and evangelism.

I was to meet my contact at Ritsumeikan University, and, having arrived nearly an hour early, thought it well to go over to the temple to prepare somehow for our meeting. I did not want my diverse ambitions to spoil our encounter, and was praying to that end, somewhat unable to concentrate my prayer.

Wandering again with other tourists, I came to the rock garden. It looked small, unimpressive as I walked by. The sculptures of Rodin, say, are made to be dynamically attractive as one walks by them attentively; I put the rock garden to this test and found it that morning was utterly lacking in such a feature. But I sat down again for a moment, lacking a strong focus for prayer and opened myself once again. And a second time came an invasion of peace, even more sudden and more profound, if possible, than before.

Getting up, utterly surprised at a repeat performance, at first I felt as though I had been "hit below the religion." (The phrase modifies the idiomatic expression, "hit below the belt," the name for an unfair blow in boxing.) The peace came at a level which could not be reached by my religion. But this time, as I put my philosophic mind in gear, there were more resources.

There was no need to seek a transcending peace of Jesus. I was able to incorporate the experience as a step of growth on my Christian path.

I am convinced that part of what our age is about is the realization of what I still call the brotherhood of man—and by that I mean the radical, spiritual equality of all people, women and men, rich and poor, Buddhist and Christian, etc. Religiously speaking, we are all the sons and daughters of God. It was easy to interpret my experience of calm and to facilitate the continuation of its power through the following thought. The realization of equality is not one that can be fully grasped by the desiring mind; it is a gift. It comes as an abyss that uproots manipulative intention. It heals self-abnegation. The abyss of calm induced by the rock garden brought a certain radical dimension of the experience of equality. I looked forward to the coming meeting not clinging to my religious identify, but drenched with the awareness of the power of the reality of the fact that the person I was about to meet was radically my equal, equal not by any measurement, but equal beyond measurement. I do not believe that all religions offer equally valid accounts of reality, but my beliefs about Buddhism and Christianity as religions have no standing on the abyss of that equality.

In the dialogue that followed, I asked for information about *Jodo Shin Shu* and was generously rewarded. I expressed my desire to build bridges between traditions, and my partner, Mark Unno, encouraged some of my efforts to compare western and eastern concepts. I realized that no theological merger was imminent, but that I was obviously in the presence of a young man of deep spiritual sincerity. As he was speaking about some theme, I experienced "a flood of bridges" rushing over from his side to mine—not just a thread of theory, but a massive spiritual unity. And he became interested in my religious philosophy as well. Thus my evangelistic goals (to share religious thoughts of my own), which had vanished, were satisfied. This experience I call dialogic peace. I have seen this peace make possible the transition from strained to living dialogue. Communion is in fact a much better word than dialogue, because the words, while by no means unimportant, are dwarfed by comparison with the Real that both are recognizing.

For me, then, there is an experience of an abyss of calm different from the peace I identify as having a "Jesusonian" quality to it. The experience of this radical abyss was induced by the Buddhist scene as I opened myself to it. That calm enabled me to succeed with the admonition, "Be not anxious," to be truly brotherly on my own standards, to treat my partner as I would be treated, to love him in openness. Along with the gift of this calm came the privative results: a falling away of hierarchal images of my relationship to my partner, indeed an utter emptiness of self. Through the mediation of a Buddhist garden could I fulfill my goals as a Christian. I have been able to return to readmit this abyss, with at least partial clarity, when I have needed to establish a straight relationship with another person.

I suppose that the drama of the onset of some of these experiences of peace results in part from the energy of submerged hostility which is being transformed in the moments of breakthrough. That hostility, perhaps never permanently released from human life, foments an ongoing need for peace-receiving. Lucid about the structure of the process, those who have received peace can be peace-makers. And the circle is that, our efforts to be peace-makers will, in their mix of success and failure, reveal our ongoing need to continue to receive peace. Furthermore, it is by extending ourselves in peace-making that we open ourselves to the invasion of peace. Finally, it is often through the human other that the divine Other can inject us with peace.

Given my religious commitments, I would now hazard the present organization of these kinds of peace. The supreme peace, the peace of Jesus, manifests the personal love of God, a compassion for all beings. The peace of the bright night is a glimpse of unity beyond all real differentiation. The peace of utter calm grounds equality in human relating (and, for that matter, healing in our ambiguous relation to nature)—a unity that annihilates religious intolerance. At some point effort at systematic philosophy is no longer serviceable. To go beyond philosophy is the only way to find real a beginning for philosophy and for life in peace. At least these experiences and interpretations may illustrate aspects of a typical effort of Westerners to somehow comprehend and/or embrace East Asian . . . and now words already fail: "experience" and "religion" bear connotations that are waiting to be rejected: "experience" sounds too subjectivistic; "religion" sounds too systematized.

****

Jeffrey Wattles is a professor who teaches courses in Philosophy and Religion at Kent State University, and the experiential projects assigned promote life-changing experiences for a high proportion of students. He may be contacted at jwattles@kent.edu, *and his home page is. His first book is entitled* The Golden Rule (Oxford University Press, 1996) *and he is presently writing a book in the philosophy of living in truth, beauty, and goodness (see website) and an eventual book on the multicultural and interdisciplinary concept of humankind as brothers and sisters in the universal family of God.*

CEREMONY FOR THE "SPECIAL CITATION OF THE U.N.-HABITAT SCROLL OF HONOR AWARD" TO PRESIDENT HARIRI of LEBANON

by The Harari Foundation
Washington, D.C.

****

In the opening ceremony of the Second World Urban Forum on 13 September 2004 in Barcelona, Spain, H.E. Rafic Hariri, Prime Minister of Lebanon, was awarded the prestigious "Special Citation of the UN-HABITAT Scroll of Honor Award, 2004" for his outstanding and visionary leadership in the post-conflict reconstruction of Lebanon. This rare award, given only six times in the last ten years, is the highest award given by the United Nations for achievements in the field of human settlements. Acting on behalf of Mr. Kofi Annan, Secretary-General of the United Nations, Anna Tibaijuka, Executive Director of UN-HABITAT, presented the award to Mr. Hariri in the presence of the King of Spain and top international and UN figures, including ex-Presidents Mr. Mikhail Gorbachev of the former USSR and Mr. Martti Ahtisaari of Finland.

A UN-Habitat press release recounts that, "Lebanon lived through one of the longest civil conflicts and regional wars in the second half of the 20th century. The civil war, which encompassed the entire country, resulted in the killing and wounding of tens of thousands of people and displacing tens of thousands more. The economic toll on the country was also devastating in every measure. The World Bank estimated the economic loss of Lebanon to be in the billions of dollars."

"After years of physical and human devastation, rebuilding and rehabilitation need vision and leadership to bring any country back together to restore its political, economic and social fabric. H.E. Rafic Hariri, The President of the Council of Ministers of Lebanon, provided this leadership and vision.

Lebanon's reconstruction and rehabilitation included resource mobilization strategies that began with using more costly domestic and regional financial resources, as a way to attract cheaper long term multilateral funding which was initially not forthcoming. This helped stabilize the domestic financial market and reduce the national debt servicing burden."

During a press conference following the ceremony, Mr. Hariri stated that the award also belongs to the Lebanese people and to those nations that believed in Lebanon during its darkest hours and supported its efforts to rebuild. Mr. Hariri also thanked his wife, Nazek Hariri for "all the suffering she had felt during these difficult times."

In delivering Secretary-General Kofi Annan's speech, Mrs. Tibaijuka praised Mr. Hariri, reading that, "*After years of physical and human devastation, rebuilding and rehabilitating that country needed an outstanding leader with exceptional vision. Yes, a leader with love and commitment to the well-being of all his people and willing to make the sacrifice required to bring a torn society together again and promote a culture of peace and prosperity though cooperation with the United Nations.*" We will all remember him with peace and love.

****

The Hariri Foundation was founded in Lebanon upon a wise decision by H.E Prime Minister Rafic Hariri. Its mission is to make education a means for the development of the young in Lebanon. It is a non-profit institution which responded to a dire national need that resulted from the events caused by the wars in Lebanon, and provides scholarships for Lebanese students to attend universities around the world. See http://www.hfusa.org for more information.

The Hariri Foundation started its mission in Sidon in 1979; it was then called "The Islamic Institute for Culture and Higher Education" but has carried its present name since 1984, and moved to its central offices in Beirut. It opened offices in Tripoli and Bekaa, in addition to those in Sidon and Washington D.C., in an attempt to facilitate the granting of loans to those who -- regardless of their religious or dominational affiliation -- had applied to join institutions of higher learning in Lebanon . Likewise, it opened offices in Paris, London, and Washington, D.C, to keep in close contact with its student protégés who have enrolled in over one hundred universities worldwide. See www.Hariri-Foundation.org for ongoing programs, articles, scholarship information and the Condolences Book entries after Mr. Hariri's assassination.

Empires of the Future

by Loretta A. Scott
President, Global Culture Network

Greeley, Colorado

****
"Empires of the future will be empires of the mind."
Sir Winston Churchill, Speech at Harvard University, September 6, 1943

"Caw, caw," sang the shiny black crow from a tree above the tinkling waters of the ancient spring hidden in the thicket of underbrush along the rocky roadside. As a little girl, age six, I walked home from school along that Anderson County rocky Kansas road in December of 1943. As I walked, I was thinking about my mother and the mailman, Mr. Carrier, who brought those onionskin paper airmail letters, edged in red and blue. Some of the letters made Mama cry and others made her smile, but there was always a look of fear in her eyes as she carefully slit the envelopes with the only paring knife our family owned.. Those precious letters were from two uncles, one Mama's only brother, my Uncle Oliver and Dad's baby brother, Uncle Gene who had lived with us before going to war. Both were soldiers in the army, serving in Germany during World War II. Mr. Carrier also brought those colorful Christmas cards that Mama hung on the Christmas tree.. Most Christmas cards said, "Peace on Earth, good will toward men." And, I wondered, "What do those words mean?"

By age nine, I wondered why those cards came year after year saying the same thing over and over and OVER. Honesty was a big deal in our family. I wondered why those Christmas cards came saying the same thing each year, yet my favorite uncles were away fighting a war I did not understand. World War II was raging. Mother tried to hide her tears from us kids, but I saw her crying silently and often. Every time a B-2 Bomber airplane flew over our house she cried, because it reminded her that her only brother was "at the war front, someplace in Germany." Dad held his head in his hands as he solemnly stared down into his sparsely filled plate, as if the pinto beans spread over a slice of Mom's homemade bread could reveal answers as to where his young brother was to be found.

I wondered where Germany was and why was there a war that required my uncles be away from our home. I wondered, too, why did those Christmas cards comes *every year* saying, "Peace on earth and good will toward men" when that did not seem to be the case at all. Where was the lie? Who was lying? How could people honestly repeat the same thing, year after year? All I could surmise was that the people who sent the cards were not sincere, were not HONEST. I began to doubt the honesty of humankind's attitude toward truly wanting peace. I hoped to see action toward creating peace. This was the beginning of my life as an activist. I wanted to understand what was wrong with people who said untruths. Were they just basically liars or were they deceiving themselves by saying things that they had no intention of doing anything about?

As the years passed into decades, the Christmas cards came with the eternal message, and new wars came too. I grew emotionally, through motherhood, into mature womanhood receiving those Christmas cards and still wondering why war seemed the only solution to international differences. Fortunately, I was born resolute in spirit. Our family's mainstay spirit is to strive, never to relent, but to persevere, to overcome all obstacles. I became a political activist in young adulthood. I learned that I could make the electoral system work for what I dreamed was possible. I learned that participatory democracy is an "alive" entity. I learned how to activate the political process by volunteering in election civic activities. We did not always win but we were a part of the process and it was exciting to be a part of the democratic process. It is thrilling to see the ideas you dream of come true, after years of activist political work. How did this happen in my life years after I left the farm in Kansas?

Dad was a tremendous catalyst in that he taught us, as children, to argue and to fight for what we knew to be right. Being the oldest sister to five brothers, I often had the opportunity to engage in heated debates. We all learned to defend our views and opinions. Mother was the designated mediator when we could not agree or would not give in. She would quietly say, using her soft, yet firm and authoritative diplomatic voice, "Now, that's enough." Her voice and words meant the end of it for that round of debate. The cardinal edict handed down to us all by Dad was, "You must always obey your Mother." She was elevated by Dad, to be the judge, jury and the absolute lawgiver in our family. I learned to argue the most controversial of social, political and cultural topics. Sometimes, just for fun, I would take the side of devil's advocate, to test my debating skills, and to challenge an authority figure, Dad.

Dad liked keeping a lively, interactive, argument (dialogue) going and I liked arguing because I learned to think on my feet and to defend my ideas. Luckily, I always had the natural "gift of vision" for what lay ahead. I learned that my "news," i.e., my vision and intuition, when put into verbal communication, was not always understood or welcomed. Learning to argue was the "safe route" for me to take in learning to stand up to defend what I knew to be the truth. Our interaction was loud, chaotic, stimulating, safe, most of the time, and fun. It was not peace-filled. It was passionate, emotional and sometimes, deeply psychologically upsetting, yet satisfying when all was said and done. It was love and hate, blood and guts, war and peace and it motivated me to imagine new ways of being in the world.

As a young girl, I witnessed violent domestic violence by my Dad and was subjected to physical, emotional and psychological abuse from him. Filled with anger and a hatred of the injustice and abuse, I understood, at a young age, deep inside myself, that Dad had been subjected to worse when he was young -- and that he was only "acting out" what he knew to remedy what he perceived as wrong. He sometimes lost control of his temper. I forgave him because he simply didn't know any better.

Silently, and alone, I began to build ideas about how to change Dad and how to change justice in the world. Although, I never was successful in changing Dad, I have been somewhat successful in raising consciousness about domestic violence by working for changes within the political and justice systems in behalf of women and children in the world. This was done by holding fast to ideals, thinking about what must be done to change things, hard political work and working to elect candidates who would pass laws to correct social injustices.

I learned to think for my self by reading and becoming educated. Education was my steed to personal freedom. Ignorance is not bliss. It is a prison that shackles the heart, mind and soul of the human being. I imagined a whole new life, one in which I could help shape a world based in peace, equality and social justice.

Using personal experiences and the teachings by Dad, I learned to verbalize and fight for my dreams. I learned to use the fire of anger as a catalyst to transform hatred into unconditional love. Passion, fired by deep feelings, is personal power. I learned how to empower myself by learning to sublimate deep feelings; by transforming hatred, a destructive energy force, into unconditional love as a constructive energy force. This was the key to unlocking the deep inner essential source of " authentic" self for self-empowerment. I learned these things through experience and education. Advanced learning taught me how to transform imaginative ideas into realities using politics and working within cultural institutions.

Along the way, I learned that imagination is also the mother of reality! Albert Einstein once said, "Imagination is more important than knowledge." Imagination will be the key to building healthy empires of the future. The visions we hold in our imagination today will be the realities of the future.

There is a need for the courage to make moral choices, based upon inner vision that is manifested into actions -- actions that reflect the values of honesty, integrity and a quality of life that goes beyond self interest. We must live "future focused" for the common good of humanity. This requires being true to one's self in one's personal economic and social life, no matter the culture or nationality into which we are born.

It is necessary that all peoples form a "global culture": a network of like-minded people who share the vision of peace, equality and personal liberation for self expression. This means that all people must stand up and speak up with compassionate communication. We must create a place where differences can be dialogued in a peaceful manner.

Respect for others is the basis of the "golden rule." Most religions have a similar code of conduct for civil interaction. Self-expression, as long as it does not impinge on the rights of others, is an inalienable right of human beings. We all need to work together to imagine a new beginning for civilization. Our resolution needs to be clear, so a global culture network can manifest the dream and transform ideals suitable for humanities evolution into a reality. This is necessary if humanity is to withstand the fires of the old dragons, those who are husked in outdated cultural traditions and obsolete dogmatic belief systems, often couched in religious dogma and political structures.

The wings of future time are presently being unfurled before the eyes of our civilization. This is an exquisitely rich time in the history of humanity. It is a profound time when cultural creative peoples are being called to envision life for those to be born into the new epoch. Our civilization stands upon a threshold of a new beginning! Humankind has endured past eras of war. Most of us know this is <u>not the way</u> for humanity to proceed. It is of the utmost importance that individuals break from past beliefs and create new imaginings based in peace.

It is important to begin by developing INNER peace, peace within oneself. It is not an external process, but an internal one. Peace is much harder than war. It takes more effort to do inner work and moral courage greater than that of a lion. The inner work is a Herculean labor, one that requires the fortitude of being able to stand the greatest tests of personal character. Personal honor and character will be tested by the fires of hellish events. The strong will stand tall and upright in the moment, realizing that the appearance of doom is only an illusionary moment in the greater expanse of the new era.

This is the age of yielding to soft power. Empires are first built in the mind, using imagination, long before the material event has manifested. Imagination, abstract thought, non-concrete thinking, intuition and instinctive reaction, learning to respond to instincts, are new skills that are necessary as <u>personal responses</u>. It is essential to cultivate them and encourage them in our young.

The new millennium was the beginning of a new era. Our inner impulses are guides to a positive future. Following dogmatic edicts and maintaining the status quo of a burnt-out culture will lead humanity into stagnation. Furthermore, these patterns could lead to descending patterns of existence that could endanger human life on planet earth. The danger in the new culture being born is binding new ideas to soon into laws and codes of behavior. The new civilization is being born and can only thrive by a living breathing society that is willing to risk following new impulses. Humanity has always expanded and developed a better quality of life when it unfolded the embryonic stage in expressions of art and cultural interactions in new ways.

Today's political system reveals politicians who spew rhetoric about education, but who cut budgets for art, music and creativity. The only funds appropriated are for education which trains the minds of our young with concepts of working for others and to fill existing jobs. There is little encouragement for the inventor, the innovator, the artist, to be found in modern day educational and economic systems. This is not news to many! We must show courage and move beyond our limits, think outside that proverbial box we all know so well. How do we do it? That is the question that must be answered by you and me in our everyday life decisions. How do we conduct ourselves in daily decisions? How do we to create small insignificant events that will manifest into great changes in future society? How do we build those elusive imaginative empires in the mind that will manifest a new culture that is beneficial to all peoples of the world?

Alvin Toffler said, " the only thing that is certain is change itself." How is this relevant to our time you may be asking? It is evident in today's culture that students do not learn in the same way that they did in the past. Research shows they are not reading for pleasure as much as they did in the past. Most young people of today are going to movies, watching television, using Internet, or playing video games. All of today's forms of information take place through repeated images coming one upon another until an image is impressed, that is, imprinted, on the learner's brain. Repetitive images are intended to motivate, to ensnare the viewer, in an emotional grab for veiled consumerism. A hidden agenda, non-transparent, corporate bottom line drives much of what viewers perceive to be educational or even entertainment.

The point is that much of what passes for "educational products" has the underlying motive and intent: profit. It is not about the vibration that drives the souls of people who are engaged in authentic self expression, which in turn drives the well-being of life on earth! Repression of society's soul forces, the natural vibrations of the age, can rupture a civilization's natural progression towards what is meant to be the natural order of evolution necessary to sustain the progression and ultimately the survival of civilization.

Every human being has latent wisdom that is driven by their internal unique spirit. This internal process than becomes the backbone of one's psychological and emotional make-up; which in turn manifests into physical acts of self expression. When the political processes of governments repress these impulses, society's impulses are manipulated and often turn violent over time. Wars are the outcome of government manipulation of the culture or society's natural impulses.

Peace filled societies are built upon freedom of personal authentic self expression. Too often, religious zealots grab the energy found in civilizations that are in transition. Political repression is a form of manipulation of the individual's spiritual inner fire. During paradigm shifts of great magnitude, masses of people, made up of individuals, are bestowed fiery spiritual energies. New religions are built upon these fiery, and extremely powerful, unique spiritual energies meant to catalyze the old civilization into the new epoch.

Humanity is a living organism, constantly evolving into a new form. As the form changes, many people become tremendous anxious, especially those who are most comfortable in status quo modes of lifestyle. Hopefully, leaders will bend like a blade of sedge grass in a rushing river, with the impulse of the times. It is better to follow the inner path of faith and bend gently into the unknown. New arts and sciences are being born at this time. Innovation based in new technologies becomes the wise path for the new civilization to build upon. The new currency is based upon new ideas and new forms of communication.

Wasting time and energy, trying to turn back the hands of time, is the fool's game. Once the genie is out of the bottle, you cannot put it back inside because it is the essence that is the power and not the form. Commerce and business is made up of interaction of people. Business can be a noble pursuit done with integrity and transparency, values expressed by people. The new code of honor must be, "Do the right thing," in the pursuit of economic activities as consumers and producers of goods and services.

Education becomes the link that will lead to sustainable changes in all aspects of life. If one is to develop self expression then one needs a conceptual framework and vocabulary suitable to identify events and express personal experiences. People need to develop the ability to use descriptive narrative language to express internal feelings and external events. Essential to building meaningful lives is the ability to discriminate between isolate and conjunct experiences and to be able to express this through language. Education is making what is unconscious, now conscious, by developing the ability to communicate by listening, speaking, reading and writing about intrapersonal and interpersonal relationships.

Drama and live theater performances aid in providing a place for self expression. In today's world this kind of education is often expensive and goes unfunded, due to cutbacks necessary to fund wars that take humanity farther backwards. Programs to develop artistic self expression are often viewed as wasteful, and so are not available to large sectors of youth in society. Yet I have found authentic self expression in live theater, music and the arts! There is no aliveness in repetitive, redundant reading of content material that is irrelevant to the student's life. This form of education leads the student to rebel against true learning. Reading material must be relevant; something in the material must be connected to the student's prior knowledge to provide a pathway, to meaning in the student's personal life. Language is culture. It is how we express thoughts and ideas. Language too, is shifting. The Internet and mass media are bringing world cultures closer together. Language has carried ideas from past cultures through diachronic periods of civilizations history.

What better activity can one provide the world than to imagine a Global Culture Network into existence? I seek to provide a means of self expression through this Network so people can communicate with one another across cultures. We live in an interdependent world, one where we are all connected to each other --- via networks that are invisible but real just the same! I have learned that I cannot flourish alone. My happiness and well-being is connected to interaction with others, especially, connections with uncountable others that are not visible in cyberspace, but who are real human beings.

I work toward building the new empire, the new civilization, by letting the empires of my imagination be engines to create new ideas. The new does not require production of "widgets," that are, material things. Building a Global Culture Network requires empathy, compassion, honesty, respect and time spent imagining ways to educate others in everyday life activities focused toward peaceful co-existence in a sustainable environment. It is a simple task really, one which only requires love in the heart and mindful interaction with others in everyday life.

I work to empower those who share the dream and wish to manifest the dream into a reality, birthing a new civilization, built one person at a time, into a Global Culture Network, all with shared visions toward creating a better quality of life for all living things. I and millions of others, who share this worldview, are members of a new civilization being born at this time. We value dignity for human life, respect nature and we work toward building a sustainable environment and to actualize peace for humankind around the world. Our work begins at <u>home</u> by developing inner peace and developing our basic interpersonal communication skills, then we begin to envision and manifest it in the <u>world</u>.

****

Loretta Scott was born in eastern Kansas, a farmer's daughter and eldest sister to five brothers. She learned land conservation and to work hard, be honest and to prevail against all odds in this rough-hewn family. She married early, which brought the gift of travel, a son and a divorce by the age of 23. Living in southern California, she became politically active. As a member of the Women's Auxiliary to the Typographical Union, she learned to work for labor legislation and political candidates by campaigning. Ms. Scott earned a Bachelor of Science Degree in Business Administration/ International Finance and a Secondary Teaching Credential in Business Education. Widowed on the first day of her teaching career at age 39, she taught Business Education for nine years. She has a loving daughter, son and grandson.

At age 49, Loretta received the spiritual gift of healing. She learned many ways to use this miraculous gift. Her work includes consciousness-raising activities in peace-making, raising the status of women and children by eradicating domestic violence, and building a sustainable environment in the rainforests of Brazil and the Pacific Coast wetlands. Loretta was very active in bi-cultural Mexico/U.S. Border dialogue about land use and international art exchanges. In 1997, she founded the non-profit organization Global Culture Network. She now resides in Colorado, where she completed a Master's degree in Education, specializing in English as a Second Language (ESL). Loretta can be reached via LScott29@aol.com

Books, Hot Dogs and Sharing in Vietnam:

The Global Village Foundation

by Le Ly Hayslip

Director, The Global Village Foundation,

Escondido, CA

****

What is a 'portable Library'? The Global Village Foundation (GVF) staff and volunteer team discussed for days whether they should bring American hot dogs and BBQ to the district of Que Son, Vietnam for lunch after our workshop on bringing "Portable Libraries" to Vietnamese villages. The staff wanted hot dogs to celebrate and launch our project! We were trying to work out how to serve such a lunch to the entire group of 1000 people attending their 2008 training workshop in Vietnam. The looming question by our team of volunteers was "Can this be done?"

Since the war ended in 1975, the relationship between two nations US and Vietnam has become very close. Since 1996, American companies have poured into Vietnam to invest in a wide array of businesses in cities: however, no one thought of cooking the American favorite, hot dogs, for Vietnamese! We were going to host almost 500 educators and 500 students in Que Son District. The planning began on Saturday evening, Feb. 23, 2008. After dinner, as the Global Village Foundation founder, I gladly met with our international volunteers team met at the lovely Vuong Trau ("Betel Nut") Family Resort in Hoi An, to plan long into the night the execution of our day-long workshops on spreading libraries in Vietnam, and discuss how we would feed the throngs of attendees.

Volunteer members flew in from many countries to join me and my staff in Hoi An. Once everyone arrived, I welcomed guests and prepared our work team for the next six long working days. There were a total of 13 volunteers from 5 countries: Thailand, Sweden, Japan, USA, and Canada, who worked together to make the training workshop a great success!

Our volunteers are truly that; volunteers! In order for them to come and be a part of this important and fun workshop, serving the poorest and most remote villages of central Vietnam, each team member pays his or her own airfare, hotel and food costs. This was the Global Village Foundation's third annual "Portable Mobile Library training Workshop" in Vietnam since 2005, yet no one had expected 1,000 to participate by 2008!

Some of the team members have been involved with GVF workshops in the past but most were first time volunteers, not knowing what to expect or what the outcome would be. However, as always, I am truly committed to this "peace work", having fun and getting the task completed. After team members were initially introduced, they had a brief five days to make all of the necessary "Portable Library" workshop preparations. Being a close knit working group, this was not a problem. The only problem arose from the issue of the American Hot Dog. "Where would we buy hot dogs?" "How were they going to be cooked?" "Who would cook them?" And most importantly "Was this the right thing to do, even if we could figure out all the logistics of feeding 1,000 people over the next five days?"

All volunteers voted in favor of serving hot dogs for lunch to all of the 1,000 participants at the workshop. However, the Vietnamese staffs were terrified, perhaps fearing the unknown. They did not understand, never having heard the word "HOT DOG", and certainly never tasting one! They were very much against the idea from the beginning and suggested giving out envelopes of money for lunch instead. They were out-voted though, since none of the volunteers were in favor of providing lunch money. Finally, after a great deal of discussion, every one agreed to try it out. The lunch and snacks menu was set to include American Hot Dogs, cookies, fruit, Tang orange juice, and milk. The team agreed to a two day trial; if we failed we would try something else for the remaining two days.

Sunday, Feb. 24   The van returned from Metro market (a huge wholesale store in Vietnam, like Costco) with a large van full of goodies and hot dogs. Success! After the first two days with American Hot Dogs for everybody, and one BBQ dinner for VIP's in the village, the hot dogs were a hit -- and the cooks all deserved praise and a pat on the back!

The American hot dogs were only part of the formula for success. We also trained the Vietnamese educators, teachers, superintendents, Province and Vietnamese government officials and children alike how to cook and serve large numbers of people in an orderly fashion. Each day, over 250 people were taught to stand in line and wait for their turn!

We turned the culture around by serving children first and adults second. After receiving food and drink, we instructed them on where to eat quietly and nicely, and on using the trash bags which we had set up in the school yards. We showed them the proper use and disposal of paper cups, napkins and snack wrappers, thus keeping the school grounds clean. We taught all our Vietnamese participants an important environmental lesson -- hoping that the learning would transfer to keeping their cities, villages and streets clean, like their neighbors in other countries. Our teamwork was very successful since we feel that we trained not only "classroom"-style reading books and telling stories, but also lessons to be used outside the classroom.

Each morning began early. Everything was set up by 7:30am: our registration table was all ready for Jackie and Alan to sign people in. Hung was our invaluable Global Village Foundation MC. First on the list for the opening ceremonies were the charming children's musical performances. These were followed by a short speech from the founder, Le Ly Hayslip, and then a long speech from Mr. Le Tu of the Vietnam Department of Education and Training. By 8:30am our "Portable Library" workshops were ready to begin; our volunteers raring to go!

First on the agenda were Kathleen Hamilton, her assistant Elaine Head and their translator Lan Tran, teaching English and training the teachers on how to use the Project Learning model to enrich the learning of reading in the classroom. At the same time Ms. Wachimat (Oil) and Ann Peterson worked with the students outside. Their teaching ranged from painting to drawing to creative games to being allowed to read books from our portable mobile libraries. Story tellers and others played out what they read and learned.

Jackie and Alan got ready for the 10 o'clock break for over 250 children and adults. At break time, Le Ly worked with Kathleen and Elaine to line up the children nicely. Lan and Ann helped Jackie, Alan, Bruce and Joel served the milk and healthy snacks to children, and juice and cookies to adults. It all went smoothly in an orderly fashion, while the teaching volunteers caught a quick 15 minute break. Le Ly, Hung and Vinh spent their time at various stations assisting wherever help was needed and made sure that we stuck to the schedule. We also relied on the food team to rent a stove and equipment to cook and serve the hot dogs. Crowd control was a challenge, with so many hungry villagers eyeing our supplies and delicious food. It broke our hearts to say "no", but our carefully worked budget allowed only enough food for the workshop participants...

After the 15 minute break, Oil worked with the teachers in the classroom while Kat and Elaine worked with the children outside. Oil shared her funny face, talented brain and humorous personality having a good time with children and adults. She makes them laugh hard and have lots of fun while learning valuable lessons and teaching techniques. Kat helped to bring out the creative side in both students and teachers using the Project Based Learning teaching method which is popular in North America; basically a way of making students and teachers think beyond what they read or copy off of the board.   By working with a team to research, critique, summarizing and illustrate the stories which they have read, our Vietnamese teams of adults and children became hungry for the books we were bringing!   Both sessions emphasized that <u>learning and teaching can be FUN</u> when stimulating creativity and imagination.

Lan and Ann both are Vietnamese but have lived in the US for a long time. Their translating was excellent. Alan and Jackie both grew up in California with Vietnamese mothers. They did a wonderful job of helping bridge the gap between the cultures in so many ways.

At lunch time Joel, Alan and Bruce, the hot dog team, got their chance to show off their talents. Bruce was in charge of cooking the hog dogs. Joel put the hot dogs into the buns. Jackie and Alan put the catsup and chili sauce in. Ann and Lan prepared the drinks. Le Ly and Kat handed out the hot dogs and fruit. Oil and Elaine helped the children and teachers stand in line and made sure everybody had enough food and drink. The team worked together efficiently, lending their strengths and energy wherever needed. We became the tight knit family that teams do when facing huge challenges, knowing that we were all committed to the cause and our planning was paying off! We were accomplishing our goals of bringing education and fun to the people of Que Son District... it was the best!

After all of the teachers and helpers were back in the classrooms, our hot dog team was in charge of clean up. They demonstrated to the children how to have fun cleaning up the trash and putting pots and pans away. The food team then had a 30 minute break before starting on the afternoon tea and cake break. Le Ly, Hung and Vinh with their microphones explained step by step in friendly Vietnamese our expectations for orderliness and kindness to others. Despite the newness of such orderliness and their obvious hunger, we think all 1,000 participants enjoyed the reassurance that our system offered and that everyone was taken care of.

After the afternoon break, the students joined our team volunteers for fun; art, song and dance. Meanwhile, the GVF staff spoke to the adults about how to deliver and handle portable library boxes at each school. We showed them how our portables rotate from school A to B to C to D and back to school A over a 2 year period. The four boxes cumulatively contain over 1000 to 1200 books. Each box has various types of books appropriate for different grade school levels. We had trained the teachers, principals and librarians how to use and "enliven" the books, bringing the stories to life! Now we taught them how to properly care for the books so that their students could enjoy them over and over again.

We also showed them how to set up a signing out system so that the children could get a book out whenever they wanted to. We discussed who would be responsible for transporting the books to and from schools in their district, as well as the time-frames for the necessary moves. Most enjoyable was watching how each school teacher tried to bring our Portable Mobile Library back to their school the very day of the workshop. To them it was just like a dream come true for their students and schools to have that many books at once. They strapped the books immediately onto their motor bikes so that they could begin the exciting adventure and exploration of the written word! Meanwhile, during the children's entertainment and lively adults Portable Libraries lesson, our cooking team packed things back into the vans and prepared to say good-bye to the school. Our evenings were spent preparing for the next day.

Before we left, and after each day of hard work, our team members would give out gifts to students who came to the class. The gifts were from Lan and her husband Kent, and Kat and her husband Dave, as rewards for the best and top students. Special thanks go out to our benefactors for their dedication and love for these children who <u>are</u> the future of Vietnam! We hope that because of our work, that future will be a little brighter.

This year's training was a big success! We improved the basic model for our delivery, by including strong lessons about environmental awareness and the ease with which large projects can be executed with proper planning, order and sharing information. We cannot bring the villages "out" of Vietnam but we can bring examples *to them*. The enthusiasm and energy of our team was very catching, and we are convinced that little by little, one step and one school at a time, change will happen and these villagers will find their place in the modern world.

By the end of our four extensive workshop days, in four main schools, we served 1,852 hot dogs. We distributed 48 portable mobile library boxes, with over 11,000 different kinds of books. As gifts to the children we gave out 2255 new notebooks and 440 pens from Lan and her husband, 500 Frisbees, 300 pins and 200 bracelets from Kat and her husband, Dave! More than 1,000 pairs of eyes (and hearts) were opened in Que Son.. Our Vietnamese staff has also learned about accepting new ideas, such as the hot dog! Everyone learned that working as a team to serve for humanity and entertain can be fun and that hard work is also fun especially when shared with family and friends.

After two days off over the weekend we were off on another project, this time to the leprosy village in Lien Chieu, Danang. After a long boat ride, we reached the isolated village, home to about 290 people. About 50 people in this population have active leprosy; another 45-50 cases have been arrested, but the victims often suffer the loss of sight and/or limbs.

Kind donations were received from a number of our team. Bruce and Elaine donated $500. Joel, Lan and Ann each put in $100. These funds were used to purchase 105 blankets, cotton and antiseptics -- which we distributed with the help of the village chief to each family. In addition, we delivered 75 hand knit bandages, made by a circle of women across the USA and Canada. These lovingly made bandages are 100% cotton, breathable and washable. The male nurse who serves this community had never seen these bandages and was very interested to see how they would stand up compared to the flimsy commercially made tropical bandages that he has been using. Thanks to Kat for bringing the bandages over from Canada. The school children were delighted with the supplies that we left for their spartan classrooms and they too were delighted Oil's magic balloons! This was a new project for GVF and the teams were all very moved by the experience.

Without funding, of course, we cannot further the Portable Libraries Project. This project, which brings books to life for village children, was adapted from a model from Thailand. The Thai National Dept. of Education has used this model for children's reading and development since 1979, and is now being used all over Asia. The results are well documented. We feel that the village children in Vietnam deserve this opportunity to learn and grow and become world citizens. The Vietnamese Dept of Education and Training, having seen the limited but astonishing success of GVF's library project in Central Vietnam, are now seeking our help. They are convinced by the training that they have witnessed -- and by seeing the delight of the children and teachers at having the resources to learn – they can replicate this model. To take advantage of this unique window of opportunity, having gained the support of the Ministries of Education and Training, we need funds to buy books, build portable library boxes, and pay for transportation to deliver these to schools, to buy training supplies and equipment. Our volunteer team is committed to making a difference and is once again willing to donate their services.

****

The Global Village Foundation was established in 1999 by Le Ly Hayslip, a Vietnamese-American who grew up in a poor village in central Vietnam during the Vietnam War. Her life story has been *the inspiration for several internationally published articles, books and films. She is the author of two autobiographical bestsellers, **When Heaven and Earth Changed Places** and **Child of War, Woman of Peace**, which were adapted into the 1994 film **Heaven and Earth**, directed by Oliver Stone and released by Warner Brothers Films (available in DVD at www.Amazon.com)*

In 1986, Hayslip returned to Vietnam after a 16-year absence and was stunned by the devastation, poverty and illnesses left by the U.S./Vietnam War. Seeing an opportunity to make a difference, she founded the East Meets West Foundation and became a bridge builder, by providing aid to rebuild her motherland and helping to open the dialogue between the U.S. and Vietnam. The positive progress of healing has been remarkable. Having accomplished her initial mission, Hayslip founded the GVF to empower others.

*A new documentary, "**From War to Peace and Beyond**", was recently produced for the 2006 Bridge of Peace Awards as a pilot for a longer film on Ms. Le Ly Hayslip and the history of GVF, focusing upon Le Ly's work in Vietnam, see www.globalvillagefoundation.org*

Remembering Norman Cousins: Activist for World Peace

by Bill Wickersham

Adjunct Professor of Peace Studies

University of Missouri–Columbia, MO

****

Norman Cousins was a writer, editor, citizen diplomat, health educator, and enduring optimist. He was also my friend for almost 25 years. Norman was born in Union Hill, New Jersey on June 24, 1915, and graduated from Columbia University Teachers College in 1933. His writing career began with brief assignments with the New York Evening Post and with Current History (a world affairs monthly).

In 1942, at the age of 27, he became editor of the Saturday Review of Literature (later simply titled Saturday Review), which, at the time, was a small literary magazine with a limited readership. Under his guidance, the magazine became a well-known, respected publication with a circulation of over 600,000. Throughout his life, he devoted his energies to the search for solutions of humanity's most pressing problems: the denial of human rights, environmental degradation, global poverty, the threat of nuclear holocaust, and the perpetual condition of international anarchy, evidenced by on-going wars and deadly conflicts between the nations of the world. As editor of the Saturday Review, he addressed those problems for almost 40 years. He was author of 27 books, hundreds of essays and countless editorials. From the day the atomic bomb was dropped on Hiroshima, Norman worked relentlessly to focus world attention on the full meaning of the nuclear age. In the same month of the bombing, he wrote an editorial which analyzed the bomb's effect on humanity and titled it "Modern Man is Obsolete". The piece gained instant, nationwide attention. A shortened version was printed as an advertisement in the New York Herald Tribune, and a host of other papers throughout the U.S. also ran the ad at their own expense or by other means of funding. Requests for copies numbered in the thousands. Letters came from people of all walks of life, including members of the Executive Branch and the U.S. Supreme Court, industrialists, scientists, clergy, educators, librarians, and many others. Shortly thereafter, Viking Press published an expanded book version of the editorial, and titled it Modern Man is Obsolete.

As a result of his instant acclaim, Norman Cousins became a leading proponent of the view that true peace and security for the people of planet earth depended on the lawful control of force, rather than the unregulated, tribalistic pursuit of peace by way of military destruction. He soon became prominently identified with the movement for a sane nuclear policy and vigorously argued from platforms throughout the world for world law under a greatly strengthened United Nations.

In 1953, following widespread travels in Europe and Asia, Norman increased his efforts for a strengthened United Nations and for a world order based on law rather than unfettered nationalism. In his 1953 book Who Speaks for Man?, he called for a new philosophy of education: "The new education must be less concerned with sophistication than compassion. It must recognize the hazards of tribalism. It must teach man the most difficult lesson of all – to look at someone anywhere in the world and be able to see the image of himself. The old emphasis upon superficial differences that separates peoples must give way to education for citizenship in the human community".

Throughout the 1950's, Norman wrote and spoke against atmospheric testing of nuclear weapons by the U.S. and U.S.S.R. In 1957, using his own financial resources, he co-founded the National Committee for a Sane Nuclear Policy (SANE). In the early 1960's, at the request of John F. Kennedy, he made trips to the Vatican and the Kremlin to explore the possibilities for a Soviet-American nuclear test ban treaty. When a limited test ban treaty was ratified in 1963, President Kennedy publicly thanked Norman for his assistance, and Pope John XXIII awarded him his personal medallion. Later, Norman provided key leadership for a program of citizen action and lobbying on behalf of the creation of the U.S. Arms Control and Disarmament Agency, which was eventually approved by the U.S. Congress. He received the Eleanor Roosevelt Peace Award in 1963 and the United Nations Peace Medal in 1971.

During the 1970's, Norman was an outspoken critic of America's role in Vietnam; he continued his criticism of the U.S./U.S.S.R. arms race, and always supported a stronger United Nations. In addressing the issue of super-patriotic nationalism, he wrote: "The essential lesson most people still resist is that they are members of one species. It is this that we all share – the emergence of a common destiny and the beginning of the perception, however misty, that something beyond the nation will have to be brought into being if the human race is to have any meaning".

In May 1970, Norman and a group of prominent world figures met at the United Nations to address the following questions:

1. What are the main problems that will confront the world and the United Nations in the next decade?

2. What strengthening changes are necessary in the United Nations in order to meet these problems?

3. How can these strengthening changes be made?

4. How can public support be developed for these purposes throughout the world?

The meeting, known as the Conference on Human Survival, was chaired by former Canadian Prime Minister and Nobel Peace Prize winner Lester Pearson. Attendees also included former U.N. Secretary General U Thant and participating consultants from fourteen nations representing every corner of the earth. A transcript of the conference proceedings stated: "...*It is essential to achieve the widest possible understanding of the role of the United Nations as an instrument for maintaining peace. Unquestionably, world public opinion can be developed and activated....And how the United Nations can interact effectively with the private sector... calls for scrutiny by the best minds in the world.*"

In an attempt to gain attention to that mission, and to focus world public opinion on the problems of human survival, Norman Cousins penned a widely distributed "Human Manifesto", which was signed by conferees of the Conference on Human Survival and a group of other well known public figures. The Manifesto states:

Human life on our planet is in jeopardy.

It is in jeopardy from war that could pulverize the human habitat. It is in jeopardy from preparations for war that destroy or diminish the prospects of decent existence.

It is in jeopardy because the air is being fouled and the waters and soil are being poisoned.

It is in jeopardy because of the uncontrolled increase in population.

If these dangers are to be removed and if human development is to be assured, we the peoples of this planet must accept obligations to each other and to the generations of human beings to come.

We have the obligation to free our world of war by creating an enduring basis for world-wide peace.

We have the obligation to safeguard the delicate balances of the natural environment and to develop the world's resources for the human good.

We have the obligation to place the human interest and human sovereignty above national sovereignty.

We have the obligation to make human rights the primary concern of society.

We have the obligation to create a world order in which man neither has to kill nor be killed.

In order to carry out these obligations, we the people of this world assert our primary allegiance to each other in the family of man. We declare our individual citizenship in the world community and our support for a United Nations capable of governing our planet in the common human interest.

This world belongs to the people who inhabit it. We have the right to change it, shape it, nurture it.

Life in the universe is unimaginably rare. It must be protected, respected, cherished.

We pledge our energies and resources of spirit to the preservation of the human habitat and to the infinite possibilities of human betterment in our time.

Norman's intent, and that of the signatories of the "Human Manifesto", was to use that document to increase the awareness of men and women everywhere to the overall planetary crisis involving the war system, population pressures, resource depletion and environmental destruction.

Shortly after the issuance of the "Human Manifesto", Norman and U Thant were named Honorary Co-Chairmen of a new educational effort called the "Planetary Citizenship Campaign", which established its offices in Ottawa, Canada. The primary goal of the campaign, which was aimed at the people of every country on earth, was succinctly described in the following statement by U Thant: *"We need to develop a second allegiance… first of all to our own state, and secondly, we need to have allegiance to the international community represented by this great organization."* (UN)

The basic idea of the planetary citizenship campaign was to initiate a program of world order activism, which would effectively place U Thant's "second allegiance" idea on the human agenda, and make human survival a primary goal of education for all the world's faith communities, civic organizations, school, colleges, and other audiences. In keeping with that goal, Norman developed a "Pledge of Planetary Citizenship" to be used by the campaign as a consciousness raising tool in a variety of formal and informal educational settings. The Pledge stated the following:

"I recognize my membership in the human community.

I recognize my allegiance to mankind while I re-affirm my allegiance to my own family, community, state, province or nation.

As a member of the planetary family of man, the good of the World Community is my first concern.

Therefore:

I will work to end divisions and wars among men;

I will work for realization of human rights – civil and political, economic, social and cultural – for all people;

I will work to bring the actions of nations into conformity with the needs of the world community;

I will work for the strengthening and improvement of the United Nations;
- *to give the United Nations the authority to act on behalf of the common will of mankind;*
- *to curb the excesses of nations;*

and, to meet the common global dangers and needs of the family of man."

Over time, the "Human Manifesto" and "Pledge of Planetary Citizenship" proved to be very useful consciousness raising, educational tools. They were used by parents, teachers, ministers, professors and leaders of non-governmental organizations to gain public awareness of the aforementioned, interdependent global problems which continue to require systematic analysis and ongoing, holistic treatment.

Sometime in late August or early September, 1970, the world Federalists U.S.A. (WFUSA) organization held its national assembly at the Waldorf Astoria Hotel in New York City. WFUSA, previously known as the United World Federalists (UWF) was a nationwide non-governmental organization whose motto was: "World Peace Through World Law With Justice". Norman Cousins was one of UWF's founding members, and served in several leadership positions, including that of president. He was also present at UWF's first meeting in Ashville, North Carolina in 1947.

As was often the case, Norman was one of the main speakers at the WFUSA Assembly. His topic that day focused on the dangers of the nuclear arms race between the U.S. and the U.S.S.R. During the course of his talk, he discussed various aspects of the U.S. Air Force's Minuteman intercontinental ballistic missiles, which were deployed throughout several mid-western and western states including: Missouri, Kansas, Nebraska, Colorado, Wyoming, Montana, North Dakota and South Dakota. As he continued, he gave a description of the missiles' deployment configuration and some aspects of their operational systems. As he did so, he looked down from the podium to the third row of the audience and spoke directly to me, saying something like the following: "Bill, you live in the midst of these hydrogen bombs, you have studied the problem, why don't you come up and tell us about the situation in Missouri?" Although I was a bit surprised, I was not totally taken aback. Since I'd first met Norman in 1965, he had been aware of my personal activism in opposition to the hydrogen bombs, which has been positioned near my home in Columbia, Missouri. I had also given him a copy of my 1969 study titled "Rethinking the Unthinkable" which described the missile deployments.

In response to Norman's invitation, I did move to the podium and picked up where he had left off. I described the 150 U.S. Air Force missiles that were located in 14 west-central Missouri counties. I noted that control of those missiles was directed by the base commander of the 351st Strategic Missile Wing at Whiteman Air Force Base, 65 miles east of Kansas City in Knob Knoster, Missouri. I explained that each missile located near a cornfield, high school, and interstate or state highway, or some other site, contained a warhead with 50 times the potential destructive power of the A-bombs dropped on Hiroshima and Nagasaki. And, because the missiles, which represented 15 percent of all deliverable Minuteman war-heads were located in Missouri, our area was unquestionably a prime-target for Soviet ICBM's which were on hair-trigger alert. Thus, it was possible for Missouri missiles to be launched near towns like Boonville, Sedalia, or Higginsville, reach the Soviet Union in about 30 minutes and kill millions of men, women and children. In like manner, the Soviet Rocket Corps could launch its ICBM's at the Whiteman Complex, the result of which would be a hole called mid-Missouri.

I concluded my presentation with information I had obtained from interviews with a young Air Force Captain named Rick Beal. Rick had indicated that the Minuteman missiles had no destruct mechanisms that could destroy the "birds" if they were launched accidentally or in an "illegal" manner. He also told me that he and three other launch officers could "illegally" launch 50 missiles with no higher orders from anyone (later research proved both statements to be absolutely true).

Following my extension of Norman's presentation, he and former U.S. Senator Joseph S. Clark, President of WFUSA, huddled in the back of the room. Later that day they both approached me with a job offer. The World Federalists U.S.A. board of directors had given them directions to hire a new field director and they wanted to know if I would take the job. Given the fact that I had recently been fired from the University of Missouri's School of Social and Community Services for anti-war and anti-nuclear activities, I jumped at the chance to be the World Federalist's new field director. This was the beginning of my deeper involvement with WFUSA and a precursor to my eventual hiring as Executive Director of the newly named World Federalist Association in 1981. I was actually offered the Executive Director's position in August of 1971, but due to personal family obligations I was unable to assume the position. In 1973, I moved to Iowa City, Iowa to work as College Program Coordinator of the University of Iowa's Center for World Order Studies, which was housed in the University's College of Law. In that position I did curriculum consulting and program planning with some 20 colleges and universities throughout Iowa, and with students, faculty and administrators to discuss Norman Cousins' "Human Manifesto" and "Pledge of Planetary Citizenship" using those documents as guidelines for the development of new undergraduate courses in peace and world order studies.

In 1975, I moved to Carbondale, Illinois and took a position as Visiting Associate Professor of Community Development at Southern Illinois University, and continued to use Norman's materials as texts for community dialogues and curriculum development on behalf of human survival and planetary citizenship. At that time, I was also asked to serve as chair of the World Federalist U.S.A. National Council, a position which enabled me to maintain regular contact with Norman Cousins.

On April 17, 1976, Norman published an edition of the <u>Saturday Review</u> titled "The Nightmare That Won't Go Away". In the introduction he stated, "Hardly anyone talks anymore about nuclear stockpiles. Yet, Like it or not, the nuclear threat is still alive, ugly, more menacing than ever." In an editorial, he went on to say:

Next to President Gerald Ford and Leonid Brezhnev, the most powerful man in the world is not Mao Tse-tung or the head of any government. The third most powerful man in the world in a commander of a Trident submarine.

A single (U.S.) Trident submarine today carries more destructive force than all the military establishments of Great Britain, Italy, Spain, Brazil, Argentina, West Germany, Japan, the Philippines, India, and Pakistan put together.

…A Trident has both the advantages and the disadvantages of being an autonomous war machine. The men who operate it are in a position, theoretically at least, to make their own decisions about the total power at their command. Suppose one of them decides out of what he believes to be a higher patriotism, to activate a thermonuclear bomb.

…We can be certain that every test for stability and reliability has been applied in the selection of Trident officers. But, psychologists cannot guarantee that any individual will not be seized at some point by a totally irrational idea or by an aberration. All we know for sure is that the Trident officers have in their hands more power than had been accumulated by human beings in recorded history up through 1945."

Norman's editorial on Trident operations was one of the early pieces, which seriously questioned the reliability of missile launch controls on U.S. and Soviet submarines. His foresight triggered other research, including some of my own, which was to have valuable payoff in bringing the ongoing threat of nuclear war to public attention.

In 1976, Norman wrote another article title "Anatomy of an Illness", which was published in the New England Journal of Medicine. In 1979, it was expanded into a best-selling book with the same name. In the book he described his own experience with a life threatening, crippling collagen disease, and how he used high doses of Vitamin C, positive emotions, and daily doses of belly laughter to overcome the disorder. In his writing, he generalized his own experience and observations by concluding that "the life force may be the least understood on earth" and that human potential is not locked into fixed limitations. Anatomy of an Illness triggered a wide response by medical students, physicians, and health educators throughout the United States. This response ultimately led to his appointment as Adjunct Professor of Medical Humanities at the UCLA School of Medicine, where he later raised substantial sums of money to found the UCLA Program in Psychoneuro-immunology.

In 1980, Norman was also serving as President of the World Federalist Association (WFA), whose headquarters were located in the Washington, D.C. area. In the fall of 1980, Norman and the WFA board of directors contacted me with an offer that I serve as the organization's executive director. I accepted the offer and worked very closely with Norman on WFA business from January 1981 until April of 1985. And, while he lived in Beverly Hills and worked in Los Angeles, he and I maintained regular contact via phone and periodic coast-to-coast visits.

During my four-year plus professional relationship with Norman, we worked on both long term as well as short-term goals. For us, world federalism saw peace as more than the absence of war and preparation for war. It was definitely, not simply, the period between deadly international conflicts. It was the presence of justice, order, law and government. In other words, we supported education for institutional change to provide for the regular, orderly resolution of international conflicts, and for international cooperation in the common interest. This vision would ultimately result in the creation of a constitutionally limited, federal world government, empowered to rule by law, and enacted by democratic procedures, which would ensure the wishes of the majority of Earth's inhabitants. This vision, including education for planetary citizenship, was the centerpiece of the WFA program. We also addressed a series of related world order concerns including nuclear disarmament, The Law of the Sea, world environmental protections, and other issues that were in line with WFA's larger goal of "World Peace Through World Law with Justice". In addition, we sponsored a "Caravan for Human Survival", which traveled to 80 U.S. colleges and universities to promote the widely supported "freeze" on U.S. and U.S.S.R. nuclear weapons development and deployment.

I left the World Federalist Association in April of 1985 to take a position with the U.S. Customs Service, and later with the U.S. Office of Personnel Management. However, as before, I was able to maintain contact with Norman until his death in 1991. Needless to say, his passing was difficult for me. The world had lost one of it truly outstanding peacemakers.

Celebrations of the Life of Norman Cousins were held in New York, Washington, D.C., and Los Angeles. Plans for the April 26, 1991 Washington celebration held at the Washington National Cathedral, were developed by WFA's Executive Director, Walter Hoffman, and other Washington area World Federalists. The ceremony was in keeping with a 1988 "letter of Request" that Norman had written in anticipation of his departure from the Planet he loved too much:

"I would hope that any memorial service held for me will be liberated from the solemnity that has never sat well for me. I am suggesting an ambience that is compatible with my belief that no tragedy or sadness is to be attached to a life fully and joyously lived."

One of the outstanding features of the service was the reading of "The Family of Man" prayer written and delivered on Sunday, May 2, 1943, by Norman Cousins before a congregation of all faiths at Norwalk, Connecticut, on the occasion of the observance of a "Day of Compassion for Jews victimized by Nazi persecution":

"God of all nations and God of all men, give us the wisdom to perceive the mutuality of mankind; open our minds and hearts to the truth which can tell us that the only race on earth is the race of the living; help us to join together in nobility and in respect of the people of all lands and of all colors in a family of humanity. In this our life on earth, help us to make of it a time of work, of peace, of progress. Give us the understanding by which we may know good from evil, and the courage and the strength to fortify the one and to destroy the other. Give us the perception to see the vastness of your handiwork, to see in the surrounding infinity one Design and one Reason that will give us one Belief. Give us the awareness by which we may learn as one man the dignity and reality of a common faith nursed by knowledge instead of ignorance, by

integrity instead of deceit, by hope instead of fear. Give us, O God, the higher intelligence to tell us that the earth we stand on is common ground, and give us the oneness of purpose and vision to build on that ground a home of eternal freedom."

Another highlight of the service was a responsive reading version of Norman's "Celebration of Life" credo. Walter Hoffmann served as Reader and the audience as respondents, as follows:

Reader: *These are the articles of my faith: I am a single cell in a body of three billion cells. The body is humankind.*

Response: I glory in the individuality of self, but my individuality does not separate me from my universal self, the oneness of man.

Reader: *My memory is personal and finite, but my substance is boundless and infinite.*

Response: The portion of that substance that is mine was not devised; it was renewed. So long as the human bloodstream lives, I have life. Of this does my immortality consist.

Reader: *I am not oppressed by, nor do I shrink before, the apparent boundaries in life or the lack of boundaries in the cosmos.*

Response: I cannot affirm God if I fail to affirm man. If I deny the oneness of man, I deny the oneness of God. Therefore, I affirm both. Without a belief in human unity, I am hungry and incomplete.

Reader: *Human unity is the fulfillment of diversity. It is the harmony of opposites. It is a many stranded texture, with color and depth.*

Response: The sense of human unity makes possible a reverence for life.

Reader: *Reverence for life is more than solicitude or sensitivity for life. It is a sense of the whole, a capacity for inspired response, a respect for the intricate universe of individual life. It is the supreme awareness of awareness itself.*

Response: I am a single cell. My needs are individual, but they are not unique.

Reader: *I am interlocked with other human beings in the consequences of our thoughts, feeling, actions.*

Response: Together, we share the quest for a society of the whole equal to our needs, a society in which we neither have to kill, nor be killed, a society congenial to the full exercise of the creative intelligence, a society in which justice has a life of it own.

Reader: *Singly and together, we can live without dread and without helplessness.*

Response: We are single cells in a body of three billion cells. The body is humankind.

Towards the end of the ceremony, it was my privilege to sing two songs, "A Song of Peace (words by Lloyd Stone, music from Jean Sibelius' "Finlandia"), and "Federation of the World" (words by Alfred Tennyson, music from Beethoven's Ninth Symphony). I sang the first verse of each song and the audience joined in singing each of the second verses.

The celebration closed with prayers by the Washington National Cathedral's Canon Michael Hamilton, and we left the Cathedral inspired to continue Norman Cousins' quest for peace, justice and human survival in a livable world.

****

Bill Wickersham, Ed.D., is Adjunct Professor of Peace Studies, University of Missouri-Columbia: bwickers@centurytel.net He served as College Program Coordinator of the Center for World Order Studies at the University of Iowa College of Law (1973-75) and Executive Director of the World Federalist Association (1981-85). He was a 2001 recipient of the Gandhi-King-Peace Award, presented at the Martin Luther King, Jr. International Chapel, Morehouse College.

A Peace Odyssey:

Adventures of a Guyanese Woman who Witnessed Freedom Movements in Africa

By Cleopatra Sinkamba Islar

World Bank, Washington, D.C.

****

"Where do you come from?" I hear every day. "That accent, where is it from?" I have been asked these two questions on numerous occasions since leaving my home in Guyana, a lovely nation to the northeast of Brazil, in 1974. I started this journey as a young and adventurous woman in pursuit of a career path. I knew that there was a world out there that I wanted to explore but I did not know how I was going to get there. I had no resources, human nor financial, that would make this even a remote possibility. Nevertheless, as I subsequently learned, miracles do happen and the key was to be able to discern them.

After graduating from high school, I chose to attend a Secretarial College as this was the fast track to a "good civil service job". Upon completion of my training, I landed a job with the government's Ministry of Education and this opened unbelievable doors for me. As a stenographer, I learned that my skill was very much needed in various parts of the developing world. At 19 years old, I was offered the opportunity to work in Lusaka, Zambia as a stenographer. I knew that this would be a stepping-stone to what I always wanted – to know life beyond my country's borders. Although I felt uneasy about the distance that I had to travel away from home, I realized that this was an opportunity of a lifetime and despite any uneasiness, it was clear that this was the path I had to follow in order to achieve my goal.

I had read very little about life in Zambia and really did not know much about Africa as a whole. Most of what I remembered was what I learned in school about the slave trade and the route from Africa to the West Indies. The short time I had to prepare for my trip did not allow me to do extensive research which, unlike today's Internet world, had to be done at the local library.   On my trip to Zambia, I traveled with thirty-one other stenographers but I was one of the youngest in the group. The stark reality of what I had embarked on did not hit me until I arrived in London, the half-way stop to Zambia.   I had lived in the *tropics* all of my life and never experienced the effects of cold temperatures!   This was most uncomfortable. I did not have appropriate clothing for this type of weather, home was far away, I could not speak to my family, the hotel room was very cold and I could hardly sleep. This was not what I expected leaving home would be like. I soon succumbed to a flood of tears. I wanted to return to the comfort of my home. Fortunately, my stay in London lasted only two days and by the third day, I was once again looking forward to life in a new environment.

What a culture shock! I found the Zambians to be a calm, peace-loving people. Despite the stories I had heard about the natives of some African countries, Zambia was different from anything I had envisioned. Although English is the official language, most people spoke the local languages in the daily course of conversation. Nyanja is the most popular language spoken in Lusaka, followed by Bemba, Tonga and a host of other dialects. My English sounded like a foreign language to the Zambians. I often heard, "Where are you from?" "What language do you speak?" I insisted that I spoke English but I would often see that bewildered look on their faces. It then dawned on me that it was my accent that was making it difficult for the Zambians to understand what I was saying. I learned to speak very slowly, pronouncing each syllable and word clearly and before long, I was able to communicate better with the locals.

The experience of a different culture and a new environment was very exciting. However, as I drew closer to the end of my contractual obligations, I realized that stenography was quickly becoming a skill of the past and it was imperative that I sought means of advancing my education. With much enthusiasm, I started the university application process by contacting universities in England. To my surprise, I was accepted by all the universities I applied to. However, due to a series of events, it became clear that this was not the path I was supposed to take at that time.

During the course of my employment in Zambia, I met a young lawyer whose ambition was to further his studies overseas. With focus and determination, he won a scholarship to attend graduate school at the University of Toronto, Canada. I was now faced with a dilemma. Should I go to England to study after my contract ended or should I go to Canada and get married? My heart won and at the end of my contractual obligations in Zambia, I traveled to Canada and got married in Toronto in 1976. Our first daughter was born in 1977 in Toronto. Three weeks after her birth, we returned to Zambia after the completion of my husband's studies in Canada. Within four years, our family grew to five – my husband and I, our daughter and our two sons. Life in Zambia as a married woman was certainly different as I was now preoccupied with raising a family. However, I soon became anxious to get back to work so I settled for part-time employment.

In 1980, while working with Anglo American Corporation in Lusaka, I was presented with the opportunity to visit the company's head office in South Africa. South Africa was a country torn by the apartheid system during this period and although I understood, in theory, what apartheid meant, I was still surprised to see the system in action. Johannesburg looked like New York or any other huge western city. I was surprised by the seemingly advanced infrastructure of this city compared to Lusaka. Yet, there was a dark, sad side to all that appeared bright and beautiful. I saw the signs everywhere that spelled "segregation". The buses, restaurants, and a host of public places were all segregated. It was then that I realized the importance of the freedom movement. I understood the struggle.

Meanwhile, Zambia's neighbor, formerly Northern Rhodesia, was in the last phase of their struggle for independence. The "freedom fighters" were given refuge in Zambia by the Zambian government and this caused the Rhodesian army to launch attacks on Zambia in an effort to dismantle the movement. I remember being at home and hearing a loud explosion which shook the foundation of my home. I later learned that the Rhodesians had planted a bomb at the home of Joshua Nkomo, one of the leaders of the "freedom movement" but he had managed to escape without injury. Despite the attacks, the movement gained momentum until the country obtained independence. Zimbabwe was born on April 18, 1980. It is no doubt that this achievement fueled the freedom movement in South Africa.

In 1981, I returned to South Africa. It is amazing the difference a year made. On this trip, I noticed that some of the segregation signs had been removed. There was less segregation and I could see that more changes were imminent. In the years that followed I witnessed the complete collapse of apartheid and the birth of "Freedom Day" on April 27, 1994. This was the day when the first democratic election was held in South Africa when all adults could vote irrespective of their race.

In 1985, my husband accepted the position of legal counsel with the African Development Bank in Abidjan, Côte d'Ivoire. This was another opportunity for me to experience a new culture and learn a new language - French. Unlike Lusaka, Abidjan was not as easy to adjust to. The French influence was most apparent in the service sectors and Anglophones had a more difficult time adjusting. The transition was a challenge but we soon settled into our new environment. This level of comfort was, unfortunately, short-lived. In 1988, I lost my husband in a beach accident which totally changed the direction of my family's future.

Standing at the crossroads of my life, I was now faced with the challenge of making decisions on my own. My husband strongly believed in a solid education for our children. He was a great role model and a perfect example of the advantages of pursuing higher education. I knew that life in Côte d'Ivoire would be extremely difficult for me as a single parent so I made the decision to move on as soon as I saw the opportunity to do so. The opportunity to move never showed up so I made a conscious decision to seek the opportunity by giving myself a deadline to leave Côte d'Ivoire. Looking back, I am thankful that I left when I did. Two months after I left Côte d'Ivoire, serious civil unrest broke out and until today, Côte d'Ivoire is still plagued by chaos and uncertainty.

Moving to America in 1989 was a positive decision that was made easier when I was offered employment with the World Bank Group. However, I soon discovered that life in America can be very overwhelming and exciting for newcomers. There are many distractions and attractions -- and I quickly realized that I had to keep my children focused and encouraged in order for them to maintain the goals and family values my husband and I had instilled in them.

The only way I felt that I could accomplish this was by going back to school with them. By doing this, I was able to challenge my children to keep up with me or do better. I managed to stay on the Dean's List for three of my four-year undergraduate studies at University of Maryland, University College, and proceeded to successful completion of graduate studies shortly afterwards. This alone has been a motivating factor for my children. Today, my children have all earned degrees in higher education from Manchester, Newcastle and Buckingham universities in the U.K. My daughter, in particular, has followed in the footsteps of her father, completing graduate studies in international law.

Life in America has grown more interesting with each passing year. I have become entrenched in American culture through marriage to an American, born and raised in Washington, DC. Our experiences in life have been extremely different but we both realize that communication opens doors to great relationships, regardless of culture. We have learned from each other's culture while still maintaining our individual values. We have also discovered that our core values are similar and that certainly makes it easier to agree on many important issues.

Today, I feel that I have accomplished most of the goals I had set for myself at the beginning of this odyssey, thirty-two years ago. The experiences I have had by virtue of the first bold step I took in 1974, venturing into the unknown, have yielded remarkable dividends. Although I lost a loved one and many friends along the way, I have also made many new friends and embraced new cultures in every place I have lived. As I look at my children, I realize that they too look at life as an odyssey. They all live in Europe and have begun to make trails into different lands, experiencing and embracing new cultures along the way.

I am often asked where I plan to retire. Having left my home since 1974 at such a young age, I have lost contact with most of my friends. Many of them have also moved away to other countries. The obvious answer would be to retire in America since I have spent almost seventeen years here. I hesitate, however, to confirm that assumption since I am not sure that I have come to the end of my odyssey. I have visited all but one continent and my goal is to travel to a country in Asia in the not too distant future.

All of these experiences have molded my character and given me a broader view of life. The most important lesson that I have learned thus far is that *we are all here to undertake a "journey."* It may be long or short but the decisions that we make along the way will determine where we end up. Moreover, striving to be an <u>instrument of peace</u> is essential as we take that life journey.

కకకకక

Cleo Islar now lives in Maryland. She has continuously made strides to become more involved in activities that foster better communication and understanding within her new environment of the metro Washington D.C. area. She has held the position of Vice President of the University of Maryland Alumni Association (International Management Chapter) and Vice President, Education, of the Word Bankers Toastmasters Club. She works at the World Bank and is involved in many international development projects worldwide, and can be reached at cislar@hotmail.com.

My Life in Iraq: Before and After

by *Hana'a A. Al-kaabi*

Denver, Colorado

****

First of all I would like to talk a little bit about my country, my culture, and my people…and describe my own personal path towards peace.

Baghdad

I was born and grew up in Baghdad, the capital of my country, Iraq. In addition to Baghdad, Iraq has 17 states. Baghdad is a small state in size compared with other states, but has 8 million people. Baghdad is a densely populated area made up of several adjoining cities. It is divided into 2 parts: old Baghdad where there are old buildings and stores, small houses and narrow streets. The other part is new Baghdad where there are big fancy buildings, big stores and major streets.

My family lives in new Baghdad, in an area called Al Amyria. Our house was not that big. It was 1000 square feet or 200 square meters. Our family has a small yard that is 50 square meters. My mother likes gardening, so we once had many flowers and trees in our yard.

Daily Life & Education

Kids play soccer and other games in the streets in modern Iraq. Women usually go to the market in the morning. After they are done shopping, they start to fix lunch and supper. Kids leave for school early every morning, Sunday through Friday, according to the Muslim calendar. The education in my country is free from preschool through college. Are you surprised?

Both boys and girls have the opportunity to get an education. In the big cities families encourage their children to continue their higher education, but in rural areas families want their sons to help them with farm work. Usually the school starts in September and continues through until June. Then we have summer break for almost three months.

Geography and Climate

My country is the size of California. The population was more than 26 million people. There is a big geographical variety in Iraq -- we have mountains in the north, desert in the west, and marshy areas in the south and east. We have very hot summers, and normally our weather is dry and hot in summer, and cold and dry in winter. It only snows in the north part of Iraq.

Clothes and culture

Most Iraqi women wear head scarves, called a *Al-hejab*. Young women usually wear bright colors, but old women wear black, brown or navy. All women wear either pants or a skirt. Both are acceptable! Women are assertive in my country. They work in government and business offices, hospitals and stores. They own and drive their private cars.

Neighborhoods

In some areas of Baghdad, people are friendly and treat the neighbors like family. They share good and bad times. In higher class areas, people live separate lives and don't care much about their neighbors. In my neighborhood, some people are friendly, but they are also curious about private things. We had a very curious next door neighbor. She always wanted to know what we were doing!

Food

The most common Iraqi food is called Dolma, a mixture of rice, beef or lamb and vegetables wrapped in grape leaves. It's really delicious and I love it. Food is related to our various Muslim holidays, especially the religious ones.

Customs

Iraq has a diverse population. The two largest ethnic groups are Arabs and Kurds. They both have different customs in many aspects of life. For example, the customs are different in marriage, in religious holidays, and in clothes and food. Small communities like Christians, Jews, Baha'is, Mandaeans and Yezidus have their own customs, too.

We have two feasts in the year, the minor and the major feast. The minor feast is three days after the Muslim fasting month (which is called Ramadhan). Men usually go to the mosque to say the feast prayer. Women stay at home to bake pastries similar to American cookies. People start to visit each other and exchange gifts. Additionally, they go to parks and recreation centers.

After the annual pilgrimage to Mecca called *Hajj,* a major feast begins that lasts for four days. The first day people slaughter sheep and calves and visit cemeteries where their ancestors are buried. In other days of the feast, people visit each other and do the same things as the minor feast. We also celebrate special months of year. People cook a huge amount of food and share their food with neighbors and relatives. People in my country also celebrate the New Year in the same way as western people.

Marriage

Most Iraqis get married in a traditional way. The young man who wants to get married will give his *mother* permission to choose his bride. A few people get married after they fall in love with each other. Sometimes marriages occur within families. In Iraq, it is legal to marry a first cousin.

Before the wedding, the couple should have some parties, like an engagement party, the marriage registration in the court party and a party before the wedding day. Finally, they have the wedding party. All these parties take place at the bride's house except the wedding party. It is held at the groom's house. Some families prefer to have the wedding party in a hotel. The bride usually wears a beautiful white wedding dress, and the groom wears a suit. There are no wedding organizers. The groom's family takes care of everything. In most wedding ceremonies people serve food like rice with meat, meat broth and a drink made of yoghurt. At the fancy wedding ceremonies they serve cake with coke or juice, and some pastries or snacks.

Most couples move into the groom's parent's house. They usually have one room which contains some new wooden furniture like the bed, the dresser, clothes cabinet, rugs, TV, air conditioner, etc. More than one couple may live at the same house. For example, there are thirty people living in the same house in our neighborhood.

Family

The average family size is five to ten people. Nowadays, couples don't want a big family. They try to have two to three kids and that is all. Small families are important because parents want to raise them well. Most Iraqis own their own houses. The house size depends up on the financial ability of the people. Poor people have small and humble houses, but rich people have big and beautiful houses. In Baghdad, there are special sectors of the city just for rich people. This is not fair at all. I don't like this division of the people's social class level. Any way, I've never been in most Iraq states so my knowledge is limited.

My Peace Story

My name is Hana'a and this is my story…

Many years ago, I was very happy girl. I had a nice grandmother and she spoiled me. I used to have many toys, nice clothes, jewelry, and happiness. My grandfather got sick and died, and my grandmother was so upset. After that she also got sick and died a few months after his death. While she was dying, I felt that my life was going to change. At that moment, death started to play its rule with me.

My parents decided to move to another city within Baghdad. Then the economic condition of my family became bad. Even though my family suffered bad living conditions, I continued my higher education and became a veterinarian. I worked as a technician in my University, I liked my job and I was very happy. I became independent. I shared my income with my family, and I helped my older brother in his marriage.

However, I wasn't that happy. I wanted to marry an educated young man. It was my big dream. I refused many offers of marriage by men who I thought were not of a quality high enough for me, until I met "him". He was studying his Master's degree in pathology. He was also a technician but in another state in Iraq. I admired him very much, but I didn't think that he would ask me to marry him because he was rich and from a very famous family. I was a simple young lady from a modest family.

By an accident, (if there are such accidents) a woman friend who worked with me as a technician was his friend too! One day she asked me if I would "agree to meet him". I did agree to meet him because he told her that he wanted to marry me. It was a big surprised to me! A few days later, I met him and he told me of his desire to marry me.

Two months later, we got married. My mother insisted that the wedding ceremony take place in his state because she realized it was his wish. I agreed. The wedding party was huge. His father invited many important people. I was thrilled. After the wedding I spent four days at his parent's house. It wasn't comfortable for me. We were still on our honeymoon, when he decided that we would go back to Baghdad, where our new home was to be established. But we didn't get to our beautiful new home.

Instead, a terrible car accident changed our plan. We hit an improvised electronic devise (IED). In one single instant, my life was changed forever. He died one hour later and I became a paraplegic. Without the use of my legs, life changed.

After staying seven months in the rehab hospital in Baghdad, I moved into my parent's house. In the meantime, my professor Dr. Majid Nassir was in contact with Dr. Paula Cowen, an American veterinarian who works in USDA (United States Department of Agriculture). Dr. Nassir had been emailing her. He had an ongoing and historical contact record with her for two years regarding a young veterinarian in the Surgery Department. As a result of that departmental communication, Dr. Cowen learned about me and my situation.

She made it possible for me to come to the United States, with the help of Hope Cassidy, director of Northern Colorado Therapy Center in Greeley, Colorado. I spent three months in the rehab center. I received the gift of physical and occupational therapy.

It was a huge cultural shift for me to live in another country and to leave my home. However, an Iraqi lady came with me as a companion: she is my Professor's wife. She is an educated woman and she had lived in Australia for six years while her husband was studying for his Ph.D. Therefore, her English was pretty good. She is a very assertive woman, while I am shy and my English is weak. She helped me to make new friends. She wanted to help me meet nice people in my new life in America. At that time, I felt safe and surrounded by my new friends. Before I finished my rehab, my companion decided to return back home to Baghdad.

Life has its way! In fact, it wasn't easy for me to accept the fact that I was going to have to live in the United States alone even though I have new friends. I was in that "in between" the old life and new life stage of existence. It was, and sometimes still is, hard to believe all that has and is happening to me.

I had mentioned to Dr. Cowen that I wanted to pursue my study in food safety and to get a Master's degree from a University in the United States. Dr. Cowen helped me with everything that that dream entailed. She has empowered me in numerous ways that have given me the opportunity to start a new life. She takes care of me and gives me her love. She also supports me financially, so that I am able to attend the University. She is a great person. I am lucky to have her as a friend.

I am fortunate to have many friends in Greeley and in Fort Collins, CO who help me and take care of me too. Right now, I am studying at CSU (Colorado State University, Fort Collins, Colorado) in the Intensive English Program. I am looking forward to starting my graduate program in animal science in the fall of 2007. For the future, I have many dreams, but the most important dream for me is peace for my people in my country, and peace for all people in the world.

****

Hana'a Al-kaabi is 31 years old and actively involved in expanding her career via Graduate School studies in her new home of Colorado, where she is studying for her second Master's Degree. We are blessed to have her story in our Anthology. ~The Editors~

Writing Gandhi's Story:
THE MYTH AND MYSTIQUE OF THE MAHATMA
by Uma Majmudar

Dept. of Religious Studies, Emory University

Atlanta, Georgia

****

I have never seen Mahatma Gandhi, nor have I met him in person. I have only heard his voice on All India Radio in the mid-forties, a voice so feeble it was hardly audible. But what a magical effect it had on all its listeners—young and old, men, women and children! Bapu's (*Bapu*: father) was the voice that stirred souls, that inspired the people and spurred the whole nation to action—to launch the first bloodless revolution in history against the mighty British Empire that had ruled over India for 150 years.

When the Mahatma spoke, the Indians were awakened, and the British alarmed. Gandhi's voice had the same charisma and character of the man; it made the weak strong and it made the strong, softened by kindness. His voice had the power to move mountains, to make the lame walk, and to cause the tongue-tied to speak. Gandhi's was the clarion call that awakened the people of India to "do or die" for freedom—to win over the British by suffering for truth, for justice and for human dignity.

Many a poignant memory of my childhood flashes back on my mental screen. The first to come alive in my mind is the year 1942. The Indian independence movement was in full swing. The slogans of—"British quit India," "*Mahatma Gandhi ki jay*" (Hail to Mahatma Gandhi"), "*Jay Hind*" and "Gandhi is our Hero!" still keep ringing in my ears! Not only the slogans, but also the ongoing nonviolent protests and parades, the curfews and the Indian flag-holding students being shot down by English officers—all come alive from somewhere in the labyrinth of my mind. Those were the times in which, as Wordsworth described: "Bliss was it in that dawn to be alive, but to be young was very Heaven!"

My second flashback emerges from my pre-teen years. Like the dizzying raptures of falling in love for the first time, I still feel the thrill of that momentous moment in history—when at the stroke of midnight on August 15, 1947, India became "free at last." This time, however, I was not a witness, but a part of all the exhilarating celebrations.   I vividly remember how India, adorned like a young bride, looked stunningly beautiful that night, --a night that was impregnated with great expectations of a new dawn awakening for us and for our beloved country!   Close to midnight, I joined the teeming millions who milled around the *Bhadra Killa* (fort) in downtown Ahmedabad (the biggest industrial city of the Gujarat state in West India) to see the most dazzling display of lights on all the government buildings.   The people danced wildly in the streets as the sounds of *shahnai* sweetened the air; the temple bells chimed in harmony as the devotees chanted prayers in Sanskrit and offered coconuts, flowers and sweets to their deities. The decorated elephants and horses, the trucks, buses, cars and rickshaws—all vied with pedestrians to make their way through the needle-narrow streets, but nothing moved.   Traffic stood still.   The people, shoving and pushing one another, climbed up the treetops or telephone poles for a better view.   Some managed to go over to the rooftops of buildings or hung out from windows.   Small children, perched up on their parents' shoulders, had the best view of the lights, the parades and the fireworks.   Not an inch of space was unoccupied.

Only the father of the nation, Mahatma Gandhi himself, stayed away from all the Independence Day celebrations; for him it was a "Day of Mourning," because much against his will and efforts, what he called "the vivisection of his Motherland" or the "partition" took place. Upon Muhammad Ali Jinnah's insistence, a separate nation of Muslims was carved out of India; it was called Pakistan (*Pak*: pure and *stan*: place).

The third memory which still stabs my heart and would probably never heal, is that of Mahatma Gandhi's assassination on January 30, 1948—less than six months after India's independence.   I cannot forget that cold and dark, dreary winter evening when coming home from school, I heard my older brother sobbing his heart out.   I knew something terrible must have happened.   I knew in my heart someone must have died.   But who?   Even though afraid, I asked him what was wrong, and my heart sank as he continued sobbing like an orphaned baby. I ran inside to my Mom.   Grieving, yet in control, she told me that an extremist Hindu had shot and killed Gandhiji just prior to his evening prayer session in New Delhi.   The whole country was mourning like a widow that night, which seemed longer and darker than any other night in the history of India.

Sharp at eight o'clock that evening, like millions of other families in India, our family also huddled together to listen to the national radio broadcast by Jawaharlal Nehru, the first prime minister of independent India, speaking from New Delhi. With his heart breaking and voice failing, Nehru bid his last farewell and homage to his "Beloved Bapu"; the words coming straight from his heart have, ever since, gone down in history:

Friends and comrades, the light has gone out of our lives and there is darkness everywhere... The light has gone out, I said, and yet I was wrong. For the light that shone in this country was no ordinary light...For that light represented something more than the immediate present, it represented the living truth.... the eternal truths.... (Nehru 1948, 127)[i]

Today I am reviving my childhood and teen-age memories of Gandhi not only for the sake of nostalgia, but because they serve a specific purpose in both personal and impersonal ways. Personally, of course, these vignettes touch a deeper chord in my heart, because it is through them that I am connected to my past--to my "Indianness." Impersonally, however, and even more significantly, it is Gandhi's spirituality and integrity, the quality of his life and the ethical principles by which he lived and transformed his own and other lives, that have continued to influence me indirectly but positively throughout my life.

Fifty years stand in between then and now, and yet I am more aware now than ever before of my continuously growing and maturing interest in Gandhi and his profound influence on my thinking, my values and ideals, and my perception of self and God. I also realize today that my earlier interest in Gandhi, although sincere, was emotionally biased and intellectually limited; I had not yet developed a critical or reflective ability to delve deeper into the workings of Gandhi's mind and soul. What happened to fulfill my inner need to know Gandhi from the inside out? What served as a stimulus to rekindle my earlier memories but only to deepen and augment my understanding of the spiritual Gandhi?

Call it a coincidence or my *karma*, but almost fourteen years ago, unexpectedly; the stimulus came in the form of a course I took as a Doctorate student in the Graduate Institute of Liberal Arts of Emory University. In Fall 1987, James W. Fowler taught an Ethics course— "Wholeness, Evil and the Ethical," which introduced me to Erik Erikson's major works and to his two psycho biographies: *Young Man Luther* (1962), and *Gandhi's Truth* (1969). The latter touched me deeply, as the major historical drama of Gandhi's *satyagraha for* the textile millhands in 1918 was played in no other city but my own hometown "Ahmedabad." I was elated, uplifted, and motivated all the more to dig deeper into Gandhi.

Another golden opportunity came again in the summer of 1988. Professor Fowler taught another short, intensive course, this time on his own Structural Developmental Theory of "Stages of Faith" to which I was partially introduced from our discussions of Erikson and Gandhi in the previous class. It was this course that opened for me a wide vista of learning and exploring Gandhi. I was delighted for two reasons: first, to have found a fresh new angle, a comprehensive approach and an original method to investigate the "stages" of Gandhi's spiritual growth in light of Fowler's theory; and second, to my surprise, I also discovered during my doctorate research that in spite of countless biographies of Gandhi on his moral, political, social and religious thoughts, no comprehensive, structural developmental study had yet been undertaken of the "stages of Gandhi's faith" or the process of his spiritual growth. It was a moment of lightning—of knowing from within—that this was **the** subject for me to explore, to research and to write about Gandhi.

The selection of my book's title (published in 2005)—Gandhi's Pilgrimage of Faith: From Darkness to Light— reflects, in a way, my own scholarly, developmental journey of seeking and finding what I had been looking for, albeit unconsciously, all these years. This book is a culmination of everything I experienced, felt, heard, knew and studied about Gandhi, including those childhood reminiscences and my adolescent fascination for this extraordinary spiritual genius of our times and perhaps times to come. Above all, this is the ripened fruit of my years of researching and making meaning of Gandhi as a spiritual seeker after Truth.

The Mystique and the Myth of the Mahatma

"Out of my ashes a thousand Gandhis will rise," forebode Mahatma Gandhi in *Harijan* (16 January 1937). His words could not have proven more prophetic, although Gandhi never claimed to be a prophet or a saint. Out of one Gandhi who freed India from the foreign British bondage rose an American Gandhi (Martin Luther King, Jr.), who fought and died for the civil rights of his fellow African-Americans; a South African Gandhi (Nelson Mandela) and many more Gandhis, who silently carry on Gandhi's message of peace and nonviolence in their own countries and local communities. Like an Indian Banyan tree spreading its branches in all directions, Gandhi's message and his methods have spread far and wide, changing lives and changing the map of the globe.

Millions around the world revere Mahatma Gandhi, yet only a few know the man Mohandas Gandhi and the internal journey of his soul. What manner of man was he at the core? Which power nourished his soul and held together his complex and paradoxical personality? What was the secret of his universal appeal and influence?

Although the market today is flooded with books on Gandhi, none seems to focus on the soul and substance of the man, namely, his ever deepening and growing faith in God as Truth and his own internal self-developmental journey to Truth.

The charismatic Mahatma seems to have overshadowed the man, who remained a mystery to most people—not only to strangers, but even to his intimate friends. One of his disciples wondered, who was the "real Gandhi?" Like Taj Mahal, the multifaceted Mahatma looked different in different lights and at different times.

In addition to being a mystery, the Mahatma was also controversial. One who transformed the lives of so many people of dissimilar temperaments, backgrounds and talents, was also the one who exasperated the British; he shocked both—the orthodox Hindus and Muslims—by his unorthodox religiosity, and made the Maharajas squirm in their seats by his outspoken truths upon his return to India from South Africa.

Yet controversy only added to Gandhi's charisma. Not even his staunchest enemies could resist the spell of this man who did not fear death, nor was attracted to pleasures of the flesh or things material—wealth, power, position, prestige or honors; they could not but respect this man, who, though adamant on principles, harbored no ill-will or hatred toward anyone, but only love and forgiveness for all. Friends and foes alike admired Mahatma Gandhi's superior spiritual stature; yet, they knew not this ordinary yet extraordinary man of flesh and blood. The Mahatma was worshipped, but the man and what he stood for was forgotten; the real Gandhi lay concealed behind a veil of mystery and the cobwebs of myths began to grow around him.

Regarding the "myth-making" of the Mahatma, Jawaharlal Nehru wrote in his foreword to D.G. Tendulkar's biography of Gandhi (1951, vol. 1): "Even during his life innumerable stories and legends had grown around him," and he saw that "this legend will grow and take many shapes, sometimes with little truth in it."   Nehru, with his extraordinary ability to see through the myths surrounding Gandhi, observed:

Certain rare qualities which raise a man above the common herd and appear to make him as made of different clay. The long story of humanity.... is a story of the advance and growth of man and the spirit of man (ibid).

Referring to Gandhi's "rare qualities", even Albert Einstein, Gandhi's great contemporary, wondered: "if generations to come, it may be, will scarce believe that such a one as this ever in flesh and blood walked upon this earth!"

At the same time, one of the rare qualities of Gandhi was that he never claimed greatness or infallibility, but considered himself to be only "a simple individual liable to err like any other human being." Unlike others, Gandhi was humble enough not only to admit his "Himalayan blunders," but also had the courage to retrace his steps. He knew courage was costly; he also knew he was making himself vulnerable to enemies, embarrassing friends and inviting criticism of "being inconsistent." Yet, unruffled, he rebuffed in *Harijan* (23 April 1933): "I am not at all concerned with appearing to be consistent, my only commitment is to be consistent to Truth at any given moment." He implied thereby that "Truth" had never been a static point in his spiritual journey, but rather a dynamic, divine force activated by nonviolence or "the largest love." His faith in and commitment to Truth kept growing, deepening and expanding, as he too grew in wisdom and maturity.

Since Truth was the <u>sine qua non</u> of Gandhi's life, searching for his own true self-identity became a part of his ongoing search for Truth, which is why he called his Autobiography, <u>The Story of My Experiments with Truth</u> (1948).   Although he started out telling the story of his inward journey to Truth, he could not continue or finish it because of his constant mobility and incarceration during the Indian independence movement. Thus, "the story of the advance and growth of the man and the spirit of man," which Nehru mentioned, still remains untold despite countless biographies of Gandhi.

This "unfinished story of Gandhi's spiritual experiments" needs to be told the way Gandhi intended—in the spirit of scientific inquiry and with "Truth" as its objective.   With that intention, I have authored <u>Gandhi's Pilgrimage of Faith: From Darkness to Light</u> to conduct a systematic, developmental study of Gandhi's life and faith—his internal spiritual journey to

Truth. The book argues that first and foremost, Gandhi was a spiritual seeker after Truth, a man of prayer and vision, with a deep and abiding, ever-growing faith in God as Truth. As Carl Heath put it, "Gandhi is himself an incarnation of soul-force. Above all his political and social activity he remains always the man of the soul" (Radhakrishnan 1944, 99).

This book focuses on the inner developmental journey of Gandhi, "the man of the soul." It proposes that the power that empowered Gandhi's soul and sustained him through the darkest hours of his life—the thread that wove together the multiple dimensions of his complex personality and made him "whole"—was his unshakable faith in the ultimate triumph of Truth and in the innate Godliness of the human soul.

****

NOTES: Dr. Fowler, Charles Howard Candler Professor of Theology and Human Development at Emory University, received his doctorate from Harvard University and has taught previously at Harvard Divinity School and at Boston College. The Director of the "Center for Research in Faith and Moral Development," Fowler is well-known for his pioneering research in the field, and as an author of his major book "Stages of Faith" followed by many more (see the bibliography). Since 1994, he is also the Director of the "Center for Ethics and the Public Policy and the Professions" at Emory University.

A leading figure in the field of psychoanalysis and human development, Eric Erikson is the winner of both the Pulitzer prize and the National Book Award for his major psycho-biographies, Young Man Luther: A Study in Psychoanalysis and History (1958) and Gandhi's Truth: On the Origins of Militant Nonviolence (1969).

Also see Nehru, Jawaharlal, A Selection Arranged in the Order of Events from the Writings and Speeches of Jawaharlal Nehru (1948) and Nehru on Gandhi (1948) Nehru was Gandhi's political heir, confidant and the first Prime Minister of India after its Independence from the British in 1947. Full citations can be found in Uma Majmudar, Gandhi's Pilgrimage of Faith: From Darkness to Light (SUNY Press, 2005).

****

Dr. Uma Majmudar is a Lecturer on Religion in the Department of Religion, Emory University,

and dedicated her book to "all those interested in the spiritual journey from untruth to Truth,

darkness to Light, and death to Immortality." She may be reached at

umamajmudar@yahoo.com

CONCLUSION

Peace stories which inspire us are all around us. Thank you for reading our book, and we would like to encourage you, in the pages which conclude this volume, to draft your *own peace story*. As you travel and reflect upon your life, what stories would you like to hand down to future generations? Write these for your family and friends! Drink deeply from your own "peace well" and many others will be refreshed by your stories.

Namaste! Patricia Rife, Ph.D.

WEB SITES related to PEACE

Council for a Parliament of the World's Religions http://www.cpwr.org

Physicians for Social Responsibility www.psr.org

The Millennium World Peace Summit of Religious and Spiritual Leaders
http://www.millenniumpeacesummit.org

Peace Action www.peace-action.org

Religions for Peace: World Conference on Religion and Peace   http://www.wcrp.org

Global Dialogue http://global-dialogue.com/sites.htm

United Nations Development Programme (UNDP) www.undp.org

World Faiths Development Dialogue   http://www.wfdd.org.uk

The Interfaith Center of New York   http://interfaithcenter.org

Women's Learning Partnership   www.learningpartnership.org

Population Services International: Youth AIDS Program   www.psi.org

CARE www.care.org

International Interfaith Center   http://www.interfaith-center.org/oxford

NAFSA: Association of International Educators http://www.nafsa.org

World Congress of Faiths   http://www.worldfaiths.org

The Inter-Religious Federation for World Peace   http://www.irfwp.org

Gender Action   www.Genderaction.org

Family Care International   www.FamilyCareintl.org

North American Interfaith Network   http://www.nain.org/

The United Nations University for Peace   http://www.upeace.org/

Modi Foundation http://modifoundation.org/

RESULTS for Microfinancing: A Global NGO   www.results.org

The National Conference for Community and Justice
http://nccj.org

The Forum on Religion and Ecology   http://environment.harvard.edu/religion/

Inter-religious Dialogue in Indonesia
http://astro.temple.edu/~dialogue/indonesia1.html

Initiative of Change (a Conference Center and growing network)
Caux (Montreux), Switzerland
http://www.caux.ch

Opportunity International   www.opportunity.org

Save the Children www.savethechildren.org

"Let peace begin with me"

Let there be peace on Earth, and let it begin with me....

Your Peace Story Title: _____

Name: _____

We are interested in hearing from you! Please send us your story, no longer than 10 pages, in MS Word format, to BusinessCenterWritersExpress@yahoo.com

My Peace Story:

My Peace Story continued:

Peace, to me

is a cool, still lake

Peace to me

is a flower

Radiant, pure

Perfection within

Calming,

Hour by hour

Peace is stillness

Peace is joy

Remember this state

dear girl and boy

We can <u>cherish</u>

Our peace

from within and without

If we dar

Take a stand

To BRING

Peace about

Cherish your

Good times

Remember the sad

And learn from the peace

Times

That make you feel

glad